LIVING AFTER MIDNIGHT

LIVING AFTER MIDNIGHT

LEE K. ABBOTT

G. P. PUTNAM'S SONS
NEW YORK

The following stories have been published previously, some of them in considerably different form: "Getting Even," *The Southwest Review;* "Freedom, A Theory of," *The Gettysburg Review;* "Sweet Cheeks," *Harper's;* "How Love Is Lived in Paradise," *The Kenyon Review;* "The Who, The What and The Why," *Boulevard.*

"It'll Come to You"
Written by John Hiatt
© 1988 Lillybilly Publishing (BMI)/
Administered by Bug
All Rights Reserved / Used by Permission

G. P. Putnam's Sons
Publishers Since 1838
200 Madison Avenue
New York, NY 10016

Library of Congress Cataloging-in-Publication Data

Abbott, Lee K.
Living after midnight / Lee K. Abbott.
p.   cm.
ISBN 0-399-13656-8 (alk. paper)
I. Title.
PS3551.B262L5   1991   91-2915 CIP
813'.54—dc20

Printed in the United States of America
ı   1 2 3 4 5 6 7 8 9 10

This book is printed on acid-free paper.
∞

FOR
LEIF AND SUSAN
JESSE AND ERIC

CONTENTS

GETTING EVEN   11

FREEDOM, A THEORY OF   37

SWEET CHEEKS   59

HOW LOVE IS LIVED IN PARADISE   75

THE WHO, THE WHAT AND THE WHY   95

LIVING AFTER MIDNIGHT   111

DELIVER ME FROM DAYS OF OLD.

—CHUCK BERRY

GETTING EVEN

The ruckus started while I was on the phone to my fiancée, Mary Ellen Tillmon, attempting to explain why I was in the El Paso Airport Hilton Hotel instead of in her arms there in Denver.

"I got bumped," I told her. "Continental said they'd get me on tomorrow's flight. Promise."

"Oh, Walter," she said, "you just naturally find ways to foul up, don't you?"

That's when we heard it, the hooting and shrieking, and if I'd known then that out in the hall, that August 1968, was a kid named Alton Corbett—"Buttermilk" to those in our fraternity who knew him better—then there'd be no good versus evil to tell you about, and I'd be just another grown-up here in Deming, New Mexico, concerned only with the beef cattle I raise, the dues I owe the Mimbres Valley Country Club and the bad rings that cause my Jeep to go *chuck-chucka-chug.*

"Get up, you sons-of-bitches," he was hollering, running from one door to another, banging and kicking and stomping. "Watch what's going on!"

"Who you got in there with you?" Mary Ellen said. "You're in the bar, aren't you?"

There was screeching that was neither jet planes nor the

Clyde and Jim-Bob cowboy music from the lounge on the first floor.

"Wait a second," I told her, half scared. I had nearly three thousand dollars on me, down payment on a shipment of yearling shorthorns my daddy had sold to Del Norte Packing, a feedlot outfit.

"Out of bed, out of bed, out of bed" is what I heard when I eased my door open, and what I saw, flying at me an arm and a leg at a time, was a young person, hair like a haystack, wearing Beach Boys swimming trunks and hurling himself against every closed door on his way.

"Turn on your TVs," he was ordering, smacking a wall a few paces from my own. "They're beating the living shit out of us."

"Buttermilk?" I said, not loud enough to be heard. A Senior, he'd been the pledge chairman when I rushed Lambda Chi as a Freshman, and back then he'd looked like my mother's idea of a bank teller.

"What is it?" Mary Ellen said.

I had switched on the TV—to what the next day's papers would describe as the "overreaction" of the Chicago Police Department to the demonstrators, people more or less my own age, protesting at the Democratic party's national convention. "Ladies and gentlemen," an announcer was saying, "Ladies and gentlemen—"

"Walter, answer me," Mary Ellen was saying. "You still there?"

"Yes," I said. "I'm here," I said.

On the screen, people were being chased by Jeeps with barbed-wire barricades attached to their bumpers, and out in the hall, harsh and spooky and impossible as the images CBS was showing me, raged Buttermilk Corbett.

"I gotta go," I told Mary Ellen.

She was yapping about her own father, Harvey ("Hootie") Tillmon, and what he expected from a son-in-law, which concerned a character upright and stubborn as a tree stump, when I heard Alton Corbett calling a West Texas hotel guest a retrograde, neo-bullshit Fascist fuckface.

"Listen," I said, "I'll call you tomorrow."

"You don't get involved, Walter," she said. "You hear me?"

I had graduated from New Mexico State University in Las Cruces the previous May, but what I knew about Vietnam and foreign policy and LBJ or Hubert Horatio Humphrey and The Vietnam Day Committee was vastly inferior to what I knew about Natural Resources Economics, Agricultural Materials Processing Systems and Field Crop Breeding, the courses I'd taken so that I could inherit my father's ranch and thus be as carefree, raw-boned, tanned and well-regarded as he. That's what I was thinking about when Alton Corbett slapped my door—what crop-drying and soil conservation had to do with riot and turmoil and head-banging.

"I know you're in there," he was hollering, thudding at my door. "Channel four. It's happening, the revolution."

I'd been face to face with Alton exactly once: He'd stopped me outside Young House, the English building, snatched off my Derby Days hat, and told me to recite for him—backwards, for crying out loud—the Greek alphabet. "Now," he'd said, and that was all until, when I sputtered between omicron and tau, he shrugged and muttered, with more sympathy than malice, "Good God, what a geek."

Down the hall, in front of the room that turned out to be his, Alton was engaged in a dramatic finger-pointing and head-wagging conversation with a man built like an Amana refrigerator, while across from me a woman in a poofy cocktail dress red enough to glow in the dark was saying, "Get him, Billy Puckett. Punch him in the nose."

"See?" Alton hollered. "This is what it's all about."

Up and down the corridor, folks, like bystanders at a car wreck, were peering out their doors, abashed and aghast, why-mouthed or huh-faced, and maybe—I'm not sure—I had the idea to shoo them away, or turn this off like the TV Alton had ordered us to watch.

"What're you looking at?" Alton was saying. "I'm an impassioned man, that's what. You people are weasels."

You couldn't hear much from Billy, the big man, except a

kind of growling and, given the fury his size could be, the oddest, most inappropriate phrases, like cussing in church: "Pipe down, son. Put a lid on it."

Alton's head jerked up and down, hands waving. He shouted a sentence about brutality and injustice and what would come around if it went around. "Go ahead, clodhopper. See what happens."

"Aw, Jesus H. Christ," Billy was saying. "Why me?"

We'd come to a point where that hollering woman's boyfriend (I found out later that they'd known each other about five hours) had decided—with real reluctance, I believe—to coldcock my former frat brother.

"Son," Billy began, his fist up for everyone to see. This was less to hurt than to get Alton Corbett's much-divided attention. "Why don't you go back to your room now? You got everybody excited here."

"Go on, Billy," the woman shouted. "Mash that little bug. I hate them when they grin like that."

She had a cigarette going, her face as shiny as an eggplant, and I thought how nice it would be to see her catch fire and disappear in a cloud of smoke; and then my attention shifted to Alton Corbett and how his eyes, now fixed on mine, had filled up with light and recognition.

"What say, geek?"

Something hot shot through me at that instant, I swear, and my instinct was to throw up my own hands and wave all of them—Alton, Billy, the woman, that man in his baggy pj's and that lady in her pink bathrobe—into never-never land.

"What're we gonna do with this here proto-dipstick?" Alton said. "I recommend we give him kisses then turn him loose with a grin and a way to go."

Here it is, when I play these actions back in my mind, that what happened becomes less a movie than a slide show, each image sharp and surprising, violent as a nightstick: Sighing as if extremely tired, Billy punched; Alton Corbett collapsed; Billy said something intended to be the final word; Alton

Corbett took exception and, from his knees this time, toppled over in a heap; and then, with Billy trudging back to his girlfriend—"I'm sorry, folks," he was saying, "I'm normally real peaceful myself"—three El Paso policemen appeared, and Alton Corbett, a welt on his cheek and his lip already swollen, arranged himself on the carpet, crossed his legs at the ankle and folded his skinny arms across his chest as if for a nap.

"Hey, Walter," he called. "This is what's called passive resistance. We go limp and think about being communists."

"Yes," I had said on the phone. "I am here," I had said.

"You know that shithead?" This was Billy's girlfriend again, her face a puzzle of pride and contempt, and I saw in her then what I eventually saw in Mary Ellen Tillmon when, over the next six and a half years, I screwed up.

"Outrage, repression, lies," Alton was saying, less his inner-mosts than an *i*-before-*e*-except-after-*c* recitation. "Shame on you bozos. This is a bourgeoisie insult."

In the woman's room before the door slammed shut, Billy was slumped at the foot of his bed. Behind me, my TV was going, the shouts and screams from it tinny and too cowboys-and-Indians to be real; and down the hall, a cop holding each wrist and the third grabbing his wriggling legs, Alton Corbett was being dragged toward the exit.

"Hey, Walter," he said. "Are you gonna help me or what?"

Then it was over, everybody else back indoors, nothing to indicate who'd done what or why. I felt cold, I remember, and took in the interesting way goose bumps came to my arms then disappeared. I could hear my own breathing, not ragged or quick, and wondered what hour it was, what day.

Something happened to me that night, I have concluded. Something as dire as death—or marriage or childbirth or bank-ruptcy—is for others; but as these events took place—when I was twenty-one, smart only about what multiple-choice and fill-in-the-blanks can teach you, and stuffed with facts the value of which I couldn't have said in a million words—I didn't know what to think; or, having thought, what to do. Instead, feeling sneaky, I tiptoed to his door, pushed it aside and stepped in, my conscience, which I imagined in the Hibbs and Hannon cowboy hat and Tony Lama boots my father wore, saying, "Walter Junior, you dumb peckerwood."

Alton Corbett's room was the mess a whirlwind leaves behind. Plus it smelled like four dogs had been in there, stale and close and wet. The linen from the twin beds, mattresses shoved sidelong, was flung everywhere (I found a pillow in the bathtub), and the towels, soaked and knotted, were piled on a chair. This had been a place of panic and frenzy, as wrong as an umbrella blown inside out. What clothes he had—Levi's and socks and two button-down shirts like lawyers wear—were scattered on the floor, his Converse tennis shoes atop the TV, which was on but silent.

On the screen, crowds were running helter-skelter, as my cattle do when heat lightning strikes. A kid who looked like Wally Cleaver was dragging a sawhorse and pumping his fist, his mouth gulping air after air after air. In another scene, junk—ashtrays and trash cans and an easy chair—came hurtling down from the upper floors of a building that was itself a Hilton Hotel. The pictures kept coming, jagged and bouncy and tipped over. You heard not words, I was sure, but grunts and moans independent of thought, not from the brain but from other corners of the body.

Alton had a case of Coors beer in there, and I drank a can, the first mouthful tangy but still cold. Outside, it was quiet, eerily so, as if, were I to peek out the curtains, I would find myself upward toward heaven, my company the twinkly faraway stars children wish upon. "Alton Corbett," I said, not the last time I'd say his name to myself. I wondered how he'd gotten his foolish nickname and recalled that he lived in Raton in the north near Colorado. He could flat-out shine a shoe, I'd heard, and owned the first waterbed in the frat house. His pals were named Mink and Univac and Rubberman, and his car—I don't know why I remembered this—was a Chevrolet Monza Spyder, gold with wire rims; and then, at the moment I noticed his half-eaten room-service hamburger, next to his Longines wristwatch on the dresser, and observed a squad of blue-helmeted Chicago police charge willy-nilly into a line of boys and girls, I felt myself seize up inside, as if the engine of me had clicked and clanked and stalled, nothing in America to start me going again.

"Aw, Christ," I muttered, my words those Billy Puckett had used when he too realized he had unpleasant business to do.

Alton was being held at the Stanton Street precinct house, a cinder-block box that now is a Bob's Big Boy restaurant; the man I had to talk to sat at a counter in the booking room. Behind and above him hung video monitors showing what was going on in the cells: Alton was curled up on his cot, still barefooted but now in a too-small T-shirt.

"Been like that since we brought him in," the man said. "Did some singing for a while, then zonked out. Real polite."

I held up Alton's overnight bag.

"Could you see he gets this?" I asked. "Personal articles."

The man passed me a property sheet to fill out. *A comb,* I wrote down. *A Norelco electric razor.* I watched my hand on the page, noticed the pen I was using so badly. I was having trouble spelling, which I am usually expert at, and could not scribble my address down without getting the Star Route backwards. Overhead, like a ghost, Alton lay on his back, his dreams evidently agreeable enough to make him smile.

"How much is bail?" I said, and this time the sergeant showed me another clipboard of papers, an arrest card smudged with Alton's fingerprints, plus information regarding hair color and date of birth. He was a flyweight, I read. He had brown eyes. He had a vaccination, smallpox, on his upper left arm.

"Let's see what we got here," the man said. It was a list of misdemeanors that seemed little-related to what I'd seen hours before: disturbing the peace, public nuisance, interfering with something-or-other, assaulting an officer, fourth-degree vandalism, failure to this and that, giving false witness—

"What's that for?" I wondered.

The sergeant smiled. He had forearms like Popeye's and one tooth brown as saddle leather. "Claimed he was Fidel Castro."

Alton's had been the last room in the back of the frat house, over his door a hand-lettered sign: ABANDON ALL HOPE YE WHO ENTER HERE. It was Dante, he'd told everybody, a name laughable in my sophomore World Lit lecture for ideas of hell that didn't include sand and sun and wind, the natural elements we were familiar with.

"How much?" I asked, wondering why my head hurt.

"Almost two thousand. Which he forfeits if he doesn't show for court."

I was thinking of a course I'd aced, Principles of Animal Nutrition, and the joke-minded professor who'd taught it, then looked down to find my wallet in my hand. *What do you get when you cross a gorilla with a vulture?* we'd been asked once. *Who's buried in Grant's tomb?*

"You a relative?"

I shook my head. "Acquaintance."

This wasn't anything, I was telling myself. This was merely Walter Seivers Johnston, Jr., all six feet of him. This was but one person helping out another, much as strangers will do. This was only money and did not involve, like love or friendship, other things that can be given back and forth.

"You gotta sign," the sergeant said. "A receipt."

I made the *W* and *J* of me readable from across the room, and was almost out the door to the parking lot when the man asked if I was going to stay. "Be a half-hour," he said. "More paperwork."

Omega, I thought, suddenly as Greek as Aristotle. Psi. Chi. Phi.

"You can pick him up around back," the man said. "Gonna be real difficult to get a taxi."

"No," I said, and, a dozen giant steps later, I was gone.

* * *

Almost six years would pass before I would indirectly hear about Alton Corbett again, during which time mine was a life that proceeded fecklessly from A to whatever B was. I married Mary Ellen Tillmon in 1969 and lived four entirely blissful years as the ramrod for the Double H spread northeast of Colorado Springs. Every morning I showered in cold water, ate with a he-man's heartiness and hollered "how-do" to the outdoors before me. Then, in 1973, as my father was campaigning for the state senate in New Mexico, he had a heart attack and, according to my mother, after cursing himself and every derelict Democrat he knew, he died, which brought to the ranch me and Mary Ellen (then almost a mother herself to what is now the most helplessly beautiful girl in the Southwest). In the next year, notable in public affairs because of Patty Hearst and the resignation of President Nixon, my mother moved out to town, a tidy Victorian house on Iron Street (where she still resides and from which she calls me nearly every day to learn how her wealth is doing).

I liked this life, I am telling you; I was content doctoring spavin and founder and worms and wolf teeth in my wide-ranging livestock, and congratulated myself on knowing what grasses are edible, what not. I liked my foreman, a Jalisco wetback named Rojo, and my mostly good-humored roached-mane cutting horse, Skeeter; and there was much pleasure to be found, in our Julys and Augusts, in just floating naked in a stock tank, my brain as uncluttered and calm as the horizon, any notion of Alton Corbett as far from me as the moon is from Miami.

"I'm an old cowhand," I'd sing, my warbling weak in the wind, "from the Rio Grande."

I liked, too, sitting in my office, an outbuilding I'd converted, where I studied graphs of the stocks I owned, seeing how, in a pattern heartening to behold, my BioGen and PolyTch had gone mainly up and up and up. I had my *Wall Street Journal*, rousing shoot-'em-ups by Eric Ambler and the man who gave us James Bond, plus what reached me via the

Deming Headlight and *Sports Illustrated,* and conceived of relations among folks to be as straight and true as a surveyor's section line. Hell, I was even pleased to learn—from KTSM, the only TV channel my antenna could pick up in those days— that Billy Puckett, the man who'd whacked Alton Corbett, was a coach with the University of Texas–El Paso Miners. I was pleased with all close and not, until Mary Ellen, citing irreconcilable differences (which had to do, I think, with the seductions towns are and how shopping is at the malls in Albuquerque), moved out, taking our daughter, June Marie, with her—whereupon I went from stunned to baffled to very, very quiet.

And Alton Corbett entered my life again.

It was a small item really, six lines in the "Transitions" section of our alumni magazine—that page where we learn the bad luck liver cancer is or who married or what had become, say, of that chunky cheerleader who, on a dare, did the splits in Intro to Natural Philosophy. Alton Corbett, I read, was employed in Chicago, Illinois, as a financial analyst for Arthur Andersen & Company. He had married Bonnie Shaker, of Philadelphia, and they were living in Lake Forest (where, I have heard, the movie star Mr. T has a mansion).

"Well," I said, "isn't this a fine turn of events?"

I remember perusing that entry several times—the "married" and the "financial" and the "Chicago" parts—and then meandering into my kitchen to have a swallow of Jack Daniel's. I was not jumpy, or particularly smitten, as if I were no more connected to Alton than I was to the others on that page—that '71 graduate who now attended law school at UCLA, for example, or that woman who'd been appointed superintendent of the Belen Consolidated School District.

"Hang the Key on the Bunkhouse Door" was the song uppermost in my mind, by Wilf Carter.

Like an ordinarily nosy person, I had "Who" questions, and "What" and "How." I wanted to know, in detail, how he'd gone from radical (if that's what he'd ever been) to Republican, what breakfast was like in jail and even how it was to wear a coat and tie for the do's and don'ts in life. I could hear my house ticking and observed what plantlife I could see—brittle-brush and fireweed, monkey flower and beaver tail—and then, while I stood at my sink, my jelly glass empty, I thought to make that long drive to the El Corral bar in Deming and, for the first time since Mary Ellen departed, raise some pure-D, grade-A, washed-behind-the-ears Cain.

That was the night I met Jean Furgeson and fell enough in love to be her steady companion for the next four years.

"It was just one of those things," I sang, plopping onto the barstool next to her, "just one of those fabulous flings."

We'd known each other in high school, and she still looked as lively as she did in the Wildcat marching band she played trombone for—a woman whom the years had not robbed of her desire to toot, toot, toot.

"I know you, Slim?"

Hers was a suspicious face, to which, over the next few minutes, I aimed to bring a chuckle or a tee-hee-hee. Onstage Uncle Roy and his Red Creek Wranglers were providing a twangy background, a potent mixture of slide guitar and yodeling that came at you like a truckful of turkeys.

"Would you like to dance?" I asked.

Her eyes shifted to and fro, and it occurred to me how life-affirming it would be to breathe the mist or gel that made her hair so upswept and Spanish-like.

"Now, why would I want to do that?"

I managed a left-and-right with my rump, which showed I wouldn't be coarse on the dance floor, bowed as a humble servant might and at last opened my mouth to say I was filthy rich.

"Well, well," she remarked immediately, and sashayed into my arms. "This is my lucky day, isn't it?"

I want to tell you now, without meaning evil by the contrast, that Miss Jean Furgeson was as different from my former wife as gunfire is from gargling. What's more, she had virtues too—

not the cooking and sewing and small-talk kind—some of which I understood while we moseyed round and round, Uncle Roy crooning to us, and to the citizens who were our confederates that night, his hand-me-down sentiments about love and the losing of it.

"Bueno," I said, when she told me that after high school she'd gone to Hollywood, where, in a slasher movie titled *Hanging Ten,* she'd played a coed especially photogenic at blood-curdling. *"Bueno,"* I said, when she told me about the bungalow she rented on Olive Street and how, cross her heart, she enjoyed her cashier's job at Meachum Chevrolet-Toyota near the interstate. *"Bueno"* was my word to her sign, which was Scorpio, and to her secret ambition, interior design. *"Bueno,"* I said, us sliding back and forth, the balance of her well-fit for my arms, her lips the real-life equivalent of moon-June-swoon lines you can read for yourself in ancient poetry.

And then her brow knit, and her eyes took on the telltale glimmer that is Oh-my-goodness itself.

"Why, you're Walt Johnston!" she cried.

I was, I said. I truly was.

"Hell, nobody's seen you in a long time." She gripped me by the arms, like dry goods, twisting me this way and that, looking me over. "I heard you were in Montana—maybe Wyoming."

Well, I wasn't, I said. I truly was not.

"I like you semibald," she insisted, poking me in the roll that is my stomach, and, strange to say, I felt compelled to speak about my personal life—the hollow it had lately been, its sockets and hinges, the quakes and boom-boom-boom it sometimes was.

"I like your moustache too," she said, adding that I resembled Burt Reynolds, as large a compliment as it was a lie. "You look downright jaunty, Walter Johnston."

Here we stood, cheek to cheek, cowpokes and cowgirls spinning past us in a clip-clop that is one form of music too, and I said, from the deepest parts of me—the parts that had been too long lonely, and the parts, I ignorantly believed then, not linked to anything Alton Corbett meant to me—"Miss Jean, with all respect, why don't we go to your house and be sweet to each other?"

Minutes later, separated by a squeaky brass bed and as charming in our undies as we can be, she declared, "Walter, this is for pleasure only, see?" I was watching moonbeams pour off her body and thinking unmistakably glad thoughts about the world and what we're here for. "I've been married," she said, "to Buster Levisay, you remember him?" I did not: She could have been talking about a poinsettia. "Anyhow," she said, "I'm looking to kick up my heels for a time, just have some fun, okay?" I could grasp the wisdom in what she was saying and, in a paragraph, told her so.

"Good," she announced. "I knew you were a gentleman."

She stuck her hand out and it was no effort at all for me to lean forward to shake it.

"I'd like to do some kicking too," I said. "Maybe high as yours."

These are the years—before I heard directly from Alton Corbett—that whooshed by as swiftly as years can. For my birthday that April, my thirtieth, I hired a caterer from El Paso, over a hundred miles away, who erected a tent under which, for three noisy days and nights, cavorted and romped virtually everybody I knew in Deming. Even my mother drove out, escorted by our banker, Mr. Dillon Ripley. The Aggie Ramblers played for me, fast tunes and slow, and a thousand times I had to drink to my health or, like the ability to juggle, another piece of good fortune. We hunted jackrabbits at night and cooked up enough beef barbeque to feed most of Luna County. Miss Jean gave me golf clubs I had no innate talent to use (like a parasol to a penguin!) and made a speech about my best point, which was honesty, and my next-best point, which was—har-de-har-har—the singing voice of a chicken.

"Mr. Johnston," she said to me later, "you're not very serious, are you?"

We were watching Buddy Merkins, the manager of the Ramada Inn, do a handstand on a picnic table, and from the scrub beyond my tack room we heard Bob Pettigrew yell about nitpicking he wouldn't anymore put up with.

"What do you mean?" I asked.

"I mean, I'm trying to figure out what I've got myself into."

I considered her and me and what there was yet to know in the world, and I decided, I think now, to take what was then my usual way out.

"Miss Jean," I confessed, "I'm just a college-educated shit-kicker with a big bank account and an open mind."

In the next years, we bet the horse races at Sunland Park and tried snow skiing at Cloudcroft and twice drove over to Arizona to see the spring version of major league baseball in Tucson and Scottsdale (dutch treat, of course). I introduced her to my daughter and was, in turn, introduced to her ex-husband, Buster Levisay, a lineman for Southwestern Bell. We were together no more than three days a week and, as the Bible says we should, I endeavored to avoid the backward glance: She had her personal business, I mine. Still, I was happiest at sundown, extreme and too stark for any artist I know, when I stood on my patch of lawn, heedlessly whacking golf balls into the hinterlands—my swing a tragedy of flying elbows and unruly knees—while behind me, on the porch, Miss Jean Furgeson, mirthful as fireworks, blasted out Beatles songs on her gleaming King trombone.

Then, as we'd begun, we ended.

"Riley Meachum has asked me to marry him," she announced one day. "And I have accepted."

She'd driven up my dirt-and-gravel road, and from the moment her red pickup pulled off the Farm-to-Market highway over a half-mile north of my house, I'd felt a shift in me, slight but as definite as what tides make.

"Hey," I said, waving good-naturedly. "What're you hungry for?"

She was stopped near my front gate before it registered that the truck bed was full of boxes and, wobbling back and forth, the wicker rocker I'd given her.

"C'mon in," I hollered. The radio was going—yakety-yak about the Ayatollah, I think, and our embassy hostages—and I had nothing to fret about but fly rubs and the quality of steel T-posts.

"You stay right there for a second, okay?" she said. "I have to compose myself."

Here it was I had a thought, too scattershot to be complete yet, and the desert, from the parched hills that looked like bumps in the distance to the crooked, scrawny mesquite bushes nearby, appeared remote and inhospitable—too farfetched to be any place but a planet like Mars.

"I have your stuff," she said.

I could see that, I told her.

"I kept the coat, all right? Sentimental reasons."

She was referring to a fox stole, her Christmas gift, and I remembered the flip-flop my stomach did when she wore it at Sylvia and Marv Feldman's New Year's Eve party.

"You should keep it all," I called. "I'm a generous guy."

In those boxes, which one by one she unloaded by herself, were other presents and necessities it had given me genuine satisfaction to buy her: stoneware and matching crockery from Sweden, the *Encyclopaedia Britannica*, porcelain figurines she'd oohed over at the White House department store, a Mickey Mouse desk lamp, a Yamaha cassette player with buttons to satisfy every need related to the playing and recording of music, a portable RCA color TV so fancy it took me a Sunday to hook up—and now the whole of it, haphazardly piled and teetering, looked like, from pictures I've seen, what those pathetic dust-bowl Okies used to tote toward wherever it was they ran out of gas.

"Don't get up, Walter," she ordered.

I had made a step forward and so, good at following directions, backed up to squat on my porch. I had two wishes: for a cigarette, which I'd given up, and a bourbon, which I hadn't.

"I'll be done in a few minutes," she said.

A name had occurred to me, Alton Corbett; and, in ways central to the explanation that this story is, I felt only curiosity—not despair or fracture or anger—about what was to happen next or after that.

"You want something to drink?" I asked.

Riley Meachum, she said. Sober-minded Riley Polk Meachum. Who didn't pace at night. Or spill on himself. Or get crazy quiet. Riley Meachum, who was so chubby and wholesome it was impossible not to like him.

"This isn't strictly personal, Walter. I hope you see that. I got to be looking out for myself now, that's all."

I considered the far and near of my place—the tumbledown bunkhouse, the corrals there and there and there, one windmill yonder creaking round and round—and immediately I understood: there was a hole in me, she was saying, a fraction of me that was void as space itself. I was not a hundred percent anything, she said. Not lover or friend or daddy—not, leastways, like Riley Meachum, who was one hundred percent himself, which could be sad or gleeful or plain old humdrum, and consequently not unsettling whatsoever to be with.

"Bueno," I said, a word still meaningful between us.

My possessions were now tottering against the fence and she'd swung her truck around, its polished chrome the last of her I'd see.

"Maybe I could kiss you good-bye," I said.

She looked doubtful, then aglow with an insight.

"Let's shake hands," she said.

Up close, she did not appear riven or otherwise rent inside. This was the end, is all, and we had reached it.

"Maybe you ought to lose some weight, Walter."

A wind was whistling through the center of me, bitter as those in Alaska, and for a second I was saddened that she did not feel frozen too.

"Adiós, Miss Jean," I said, releasing her and standing aside so she could speed away.

Many, many months would pass before I'd hear from Alton
Corbett, but I did not—gossip to the contrary—become addled or crumble to pieces. I was being prepared for something,
I felt. I was waiting, alert like a sniper. In the meantime, dawn
to dusk, I was your common *i*-dotter and *t*-crosser. By day, I
herded cattle from one scrub-flecked range to another, their
mooing and hoarse bawling as sensible as any phrase from my
ranch-hands. I paid for hay, fifty-pound blocks of iodized salt
and the services of Dr. Weems, our vet; I rode fences and set
traps for coyote. In need of shirts or pants, I marched into
Anthony's department store on Zinc Street and afterwards
treated myself to chicken-fried steak at Del Cruz's Triangle
Drive-In. I talked on the phone to my mother, said "yes" and
"no" as appropriate, and comported myself like a citizen with
a serious private life.

"Alton Corbett," I said to myself. "Butter-goddam-milk."

By night, I played Nintendo Donkey Kong or watched movies like *Rambo* and anything featuring the Pink Panther. I
forsook alcohol entirely, even beer. I took up reading, finding
hours of delight in the crackpot vision of us offered by Sir
Walter Raleigh, as well as what opinions a Dallas author
named C. W. Smith had concerning good and bad. I was not
shattered, I say, nor in distress nor modernistically dark-
minded. Alton would phone, I felt. Or he would drive up my
road. He would have a respectable haircut, shaved at the neck.
And shined wing tips to see yourself in. He would be softer,
spongy in the belly the way we all are, and more mindful of
authority. He would have his kids, Marvin and Roylene; his
wife, Bonnie Shaker; his poodle dog, Fifi. He would tell me
exactly what he'd mumbled to Billy Puckett, the gent who'd
clobbered him, and how fistfighting felt. He'd tell me what
he'd been doing at the Hilton Hotel, specifically the circumstances that had sent him howling into the hallway. He would
have words for me—dozens and dozens and dozens—and afterwards the hole in me would be filled up and gone forever.

News of him reached me in March, while I was scrubbing

dishes and ruminating over such crossword clues as "lark or
light preceder" (three letters, across) and "saturate" (six letters,
down). I saw Cash Corrum, our mail carrier, park his Buick at
my box next to the highway, heard him honk to tell he was
done, and—saucepan there, coffee cup here—I did well to
ignore the clatter and jangle and rattle my feelings were.

"I'm an old cowhand," I sang, riding my Honda trail bike
over three cattle guards to a stop beside blacktop that ran east
and west into nothing.

I could smell rain, I remember, and noted the cloudwork
rumbling my way from California.

"Okay," I told myself, and opened my box to find what I
knew would be there.

In typeface fussy as that Miss Jean had bought to announce
her nuptials almost two years before, it was an envelope from
Hewey, Stone, Tyler & Dowes, "Investment Counselors" on
Montrose Street in Houston. An alarm had gone off in me,
wicked and whiny, and I wondered naturally how Alton had
gotten from Illinois to Texas. I thought about his wife, whom
I imagined to be as tall and red-headed as Dr. Kissinger's Jill
St. John, and the thousand-dollar smile she could turn on and
off. I'd visited Houston and found it to have not one downtown
but several, as though its people—those who needed counsel-
ing and not—were restive or too heat-soaked to make up their
minds.

Sitting by the roadway, my motorcycle making a putt-putt
that an hour of tuning can't reduce, I regarded the other mail
Cash Corrum had delivered: catalogues to thumb through
(Sears, Monkey Ward's, Horchow), bills to pay out of pocket-
money, a notice about who was appearing at the Thunderbird
Lounge, and a rolled-up poster that said Rob Pettigrew's
goods—his four-wheel-drive Ford, his portable troughs, his
ranching-related etceteras—were up for auction (courtesy of
Milton Wolf and Sons).

"Goddam," I muttered, the word from me that stood for,
in six letters across or down, misery and silliness and time.

It was a check, nubby as braille, plus a sheet of stationery on which interest had been calculated.

This is for your trouble was the first sentence.

A face bushwhacked me from memory—not Alton's, but Mary Ellen Tillmon's, my ex-wife's, and I heard again what she'd called me in divorce court. "Lunkhead," she'd said. "Foolhardy," she'd said. And "supercilious," an insult I'd had to buy a Webster's dictionary to check on.

At the bottom of the page was his signature, more a doctor-like scrawl than penmanship you'd recognize as heartfelt.

This isn't about him, I was thinking. This is about me.

We're even now was his second, his last, sentence.

Inside me, crude and thick, valves opened and closed.

Astride my motorcycle, I sought to concentrate very hard; and, if it helps, you can imagine Walter Seivers Johnston as an Alfalfa-like grade-schooler faced with a three-page math problem and a half-hour time limit.

Alton Corbett was even with me now, yes. But I was not even with myself.

Like a starved dog to a soupbone, I went to Billy Puckett—who had, I am happy to say, risen over the years from coach of the UTEP Miners' secondary to offensive coordinator and associate professor of physical education. The morning after I'd read Alton's letter, I filled my Jeep with gas and told my foreman, Rojo, that he was in charge. "This could take a day or two," I said. "Maybe longer." In a nearly singsong state of mind, I was joyous to see sunshine and inclined to honk "howdy" to those I-10 motorists who zipped past me in a hurry; and hours later, light-footed and what-have-you in spirit, I presented myself to Mr. Puckett's secretary, in his field house office, with the news that I was a reporter for the *Headlight* of Deming, New Mexico, eager to hear how his football team might fare the following fall.

"He's in a meeting," she said. "That man is a meeting fool."

I could believe that, I said.

"Would you like some coffee?" she asked. "We have Coke too."

"That's very considerate of you," I said, scooting up a chair to talk personal to her.

Elaine Brittle, mother of two boys (though now separated from their tomcatting father, Archie Lee), was just tickled as all get-out to be working for a man like Billy—who, by the by, preferred to be called that instead of his whole name, which was William M-for-Murphy Puckett II.

"Do tell?" I said, mine the other cheerful voice in that room. "That's just like him, I hear."

On the walls hung photographs of athletes past and present, the constant in each a smiling or serious-seeming Billy Puckett. Dressed in shorts or long pants, wearing a gimme cap or headphones, in hooded sweatshirt or orange pullover with UTEP stitched on the breast, he seemed as huge as I recalled, his a personality that boys and men alike wanted to stand next to, like a shade tree.

"You want some candy?" Mrs. Brittle asked me. It was a Valentine's gift, she said, from Billy, and the one I chewed into, though old, was itself as gooey as her point of view.

I was cool, my smile as disconnected from my inner organs as shit is from Shinola. Billy was another work of wonder to me, like magic to a kid. He had a wife, Maureen, and three children, the oldest of whom, Lilly, was a sophomore music education major and as show-biz on the piano as Van Cliburn. He had a house in the north valley and a membership at the Coronado Country Club, El Paso's sagebrush Beverly Hills. He was Baptist—"though not the rednecky kind," Elaine whispered—and a Rotarian, not to mention a man who could read, well, Henry David Thoreau and tell you what was cockeyed about selfishness. "You ought to see that man fish," Elaine Brittle confided. "He'll drop a line in a sewer, I swear."

I was collected, an ice cube inside, and mentally removed enough from myself to be in the other corner of the room, plotting; and by the time he walked in, as large in life as he was in time, and we were formally introduced, I knew his boot size, his allergies to the milk family of foods, and what year he'd recieved his master's degree from Lousiana State University.

"We're gonna be miserable this season," he laughed, my hand thoroughly buried in his. "I got athletes out there with only one leg, or blind."

He had aged, yes, but not as remarkably as some I knew from back then; he had a face like a cupcake, plus the fine, square-cut hair you can find on a shoebrush.

"How's Harley Edwards?" he asked, referring to the editor I'd claimed to work for; and then, in Billy Puckett's office, him camped behind his desk and me in a chair next to a window that opened onto several basketball courts a couple of stories below, a look came to his eye—a glint as important, I think, as my own—and he said, "I know you, don't I?"

His was an office spacious enough to wrestle in, and I struggled to put in order all thoughts unique to my mission here.

"Names, I'm no good with," he said. "Where I know you from, son?"

So I told him—about Alton, about the Hilton, about that night and all that had descended from it, about the sour-minded shrew he was with—

"Rita Bates," he said, his mood a bottom condition entirely, as though she was a mistake he wasn't yet through paying for. "I wasn't married then, you understand? It was a matter of oat-sowing. A matter of bad judgment."

"Me too," I said. "I was engaged."

He had put his feet up on the desk and was, with the deliberation of a traffic judge, studying what the ceiling could tell him. The air-conditioning had switched on, a frigid blast on my face, and I was waiting for some pops from my chest, something to say the cords in there had finally snapped.

"So what can I do for you?" he asked, which made it my turn to look up and down for inspiration.

"If it's all the same," I began, finding breathing easier than expected, "I'd like to slug you one."

We shared a moment then, fraught and time-filled, pointed

as a nail: his feet slipped slowly to the floor, his chair groaned, his fingers went tat-tat-tat on his blotter, and there were, in the eye-to-eye we had, about ten thousand things to think about.

"Friend," he said, "your leg is shaking."

I grabbed my calf and, soon enough, brought my limb under control.

"This is important to you, I guess."

I admitted that, given the givens I was stuck with, it was.

"Holy moly," he said, not for a second speaking about God or righteous living. "Holy damn moly," he said about eight more times, and I could see his mind, as betrayed by his eyebrows and pursed lips, confront my proposal and race around it at a dozen speeds. He was bemused and taken aback and perplexed, as if I'd suggested he push a pile of peanuts across the room with his nose. I had learned from Elaine Brittle, his secretary, that he'd majored in sociology and that once he'd bench-pressed nearly four hundred pounds, and now these facts were as plain in the tilt of his head as the facts of how he slept at night and what he hollered in defeat.

"Lordy," he said, "I hate politics, don't you?"

I hastened to agree with him.

He had stood now, his shirttails tucked in, and moved his Rolodex to a spot by his phone, which was by his pencil holder, which was by his stopwatch. You could tell that, however peculiar, a decision had been reached.

"Is here okay?" he asked.

Modestly, I assured him it was.

"Hellfire," he laughed, "it's been ages since I had anything lunatic to talk about at the dinner table."

Alton Corbett wasn't with me when I hauled myself up: he was as meaningless to me as most science or what suffices for entertainment in darkest Africa. Instead, I was arguing with my knees, which seemed rusted stiff, and was tempted to apologize for the tight trousers I was wearing.

"You ever been in a fight before?" Coach Puckett said. "I mean, one with blood in it?"

I had not, so, patient as a preacher, he showed me how to make a fist, thumb outside the fingers.

"Thank you, sir," I said.

I felt like a player of his—or a former waterboy, say—who had, unaccountably but profoundly, lost his obvious way in the world.

"Call me Billy," he said.

He arranged himself then, hands on his hips, his chin thrust out palooka-style, eyes wide as if this were the Memorial Day pie toss, and I took a step back to wind up. There was only one more question to ask and, without hemming or hawing, I mustered the courage to ask it.

"You wouldn't want to get on your knees, would you?"

He tsk-tsked a bit, looking inexpressibly sad. "They're all busted up, plus there's my dignity, you know."

I knew, indeed, and stepped back again to gather myself from the million places I'd been.

"Ready?" he said.

And, for the first time in a slew of years, I was.

FREEDOM,

A THEORY OF

I.

The story my father told—before he abandoned my mother and me, before he reappeared years and years later to beat the stuffings out of me—concerned his sister Shirley, who, at seven years old in 1927, burst out of the ladies' room on the third level of the old steamship *Seeandbee*, a five-hundred-foot all-steel side-wheeler from the Cleveland & Buffalo Transit Company, went through the railing ("Stumbled," my father insisted), and pitched overboard.

"Presumed drowned," he always said. "Body never recovered. Four days of dragging, searching."

I began hearing this story, I am told, only months after my birth in 1947; truth to say, there was not a time before he walked out on us—drove, actually—in September of 1956 when I can't remember hearing it, or some detail, week in, week out. I heard about the condition of Lake Erie ("Few waves," my father said, "excellent visibility, water temperature moderate"); what celebrities were on board (Johnny Risko, the heavyweight who'd fought Gene Tunney, and his manager, Dapper Danny Dunn); the men with whom his own father, the Judge, was that night playing poker in one starboard parlor (Shondor Birns, a gangster from the Ten-Eleven Club; WJAY personality Red Manning; musician Pee Wee Jackson from the

Smiling Dog Saloon; and W. Burr Gongwer, eventually
Cuyahoga County's Democratic party boss). I heard what band
was playing (Shaw Sissle from the Trianon Ballroom); what was
eaten by those gentlemen (the deli trays, Schmidt's beer, several bottles of bootleg Canadian whiskey); and what, other
than va-va-va-voom, could be said about certain hootchie-
kootchie sorts.

"The details," my father used to remark. "I just can't get
over the details. Stupid, huh?"

I wondered, a kid decades removed from the event itself,
what all this had to do with me; for there were thousands of
times, hearing him tramp up the stairs in our house in Shaker
Heights to wish me sweet dreams, when I knew, and dreaded,
that he was bringing me something new, or newly discovered,
about Shirley. Her favorite ice cream (toffee vanilla). How
expertly she tap-danced. That her middle name was Nemea—
which is a valley in ancient Argolis.

More than once, buried under the covers, I curled myself up
to look like sleep, and said, "My name is Carter Hopkins
Garner. I like blue. I like Y. A. Tittle. God is great. Five times
six is thirty."

He was obsessed, yes, though "haunted" is, I think, a better
word. You could see him—at the dinner table, say, standing to
carve a roast, bone-handled knife clutched, his vest unbut-
toned; he'd clear his throat, perhaps to make an observation
about the gravy boat or the flatware, then pause, eyes narrow-
ing, his head suddenly tilted, as though he'd heard, faint but
clear, her voice, any of the help-words she might have hollered
in panic in the water. Or, bent over a putt at the Canterbury
Golf Club, me to one side holding his bag, he'd pull himself
upright, a hand thrust up to hush the rest of his foursome, and
empty his face of everything except a single horrible thought—
the way he looked, in fact, the day he drove past me in his
Dodge, mechanically waving bye-bye to me, to my mother, to
autumn itself; to a world that had, one cloudless night in the
twenties, wobbled out of its precious and perfect groove.

* * *

I never really took note of my father as a creature independent of his Shirley-stories until, the afternoon he left us, I walked home from Geoffrey "Jeep" Freeman's house, where I had been playing, and found my mother, composed as a movie star, reclining on the divan in the sun-room, radio playing, smoking a Viceroy cigarette as though, any minute now, a brass band, its oompah-pah deafening enough to be impressive in New York City, might march through our front door to whisk her away.

"What is it you'd like for dinner, Carter?" She was looking yonder, beyond the flagstone patio, to the oaks that are the rough for the eighth fairway at the Shaker Country Club. "Marie has rib eye, I believe. That would be lovely, wouldn't it?"

I could hear Marie, our cook, in the kitchen, pans banging.

"Could I," I wondered, "have cereal?"

She looked at me then, straight on, the way my wife, Allison, looks at me when what is to be heard must be absorbed one significant syllable at a time.

"He's not coming back, you know."

I was nine years old, wearing a Santone Manner surcoat, my hands out of my pockets as I'd been taught, and I believed that Mother—a Smith College graduate, a woman who'd met Consuelo Roosevelt and could tell you what to do with bagworms—never looked more beautiful than she did the moment I said, too grown up for the hour, "I know."

"He isn't a bad man, Carter. Not bad at all."

I understood that too, and said so, few other sounds in the world as important as those peculiar to me and her.

"If you're thinking," she said, "that I know where he's going, then you're mistaken."

"Yes," I said, very much not wanting ever to be mistaken.

"Nor does Marie," she said. "Or Mr. Abel."

I thought of Abel, our gardener, and how fussy he could be about dirt I was not welcome to dig in.

"Is this a tragedy, Mother?"

She took her time then, a wonderful amount of time as big and sun-filled as the room itself, and came round to my question in at least seven or eight visible ways, her chin going up and sideways, a gold earring dangling, blinking as if I'd asked how far Neptune was from this very spot.

"It's a setback, darling. A serious inconvenience."

That was how we talked in that household: "inculcate," "deliberate," "insouciant"—a highfalutin language to describe the few we were and what we did.

"We shan't speak of this again, Carter."

She wanted agreement and, ignoring the rattle in me, I gave agreement to her.

"The Judge will look after us."

I said "yes, ma'am," a phrase I wasn't absolutely connected to, and thought to leave—for where, I had no idea—when she stood, as though a bell had clanged, and gave a sigh so theatrical it could have come from Deborah Kerr in *Tea and Sympathy*, one movie in Metrocolor we'd seen. "Give us a kiss, mister."

Cheek to cheek we stood, her bent and me on tiptoe, me thinking about the Judge and his moustache and his wall-wiggling way of going ha-ha-ha—before I realized she had more to say and would not let me go until she said it.

"Don't hate him, Carter. Promise?"

She smelled like lilacs and cigarettes and gin.

"I won't, Mother."

She squeezed me a little and I was no longer a boy talking like a grown-up or able to know much more than my name and street address.

"The Garner family does not hate," she said. "Ever."

She was wrong about that—as she was wrong about Elvis Presley ("Who ever heard of a song about, gracious, a hound dog?") and Bishop Fulton Sheen ("To me he looks like a rodent"); as she would, before her brain cracked, be wrong about Fidel Castro and what to do with *Lady Chatterley's Lover.* In fact, I began to hate my father—to feel for him all the contrary and cowardly thoughts the word suggests—less than a week later when I found myself in his second-floor study.

"What is all this?" I said.

I had been standing behind his desk, observing his clutter, one hundred percent fascinated by a book, *Decedents' Estates & Trusts* (The Foundation Press), and watching phrases like "inter vivos" and "per curiam" rise up from his well-scribbled yellow tablet. He had been struggling with a case that required him to know "Nontestamentary Acts" and "Death Without Issue," as well as what had been decided in *Root v. Arnold* and *Spencer v. Childs,* and now, wherever he was—in Outer Mongolia, in Timbuktu—he was no longer an attorney for Andrew Squire or obliged to speak about "Rules Restricting Creation of Remainders to Heirs."

I touched nothing. Not his files on the floor like oversize playing cards. Not his Crosley TV. Not his Julius La Rosa and Perez Prado records on the desk chair. "Breathe," I told myself, and did, taking in a room that smelled like Vitalis hair tonic and the Old Forester he liked.

"Father," I said, a word it was possible to utter without heart or anything else essential.

Across the room, in his closet, hung his three-button center-vent Hart Schaffner & Marx suitcoats, his Dobbs hat, his ties from the Haband Tie Company of Paterson, New Jersey. "Details," I may have said. "I can't get over the details." He wore shoes from the Massagic Company and Kara-Lon sweaters and used Scuff-Kote shoe polish from Esquire. As still as a sentinel, I studied his room, saw a hair on his blotter, observed that he'd made a note—in handwriting as formal and forward as the way he sat in a chair—about a Montclair hardtop coupe in persimmon and classic white.

He was not here and yet I could sense him, imagine him completely from the X and Y and Z he'd left behind. Two incidents came to mind. In one, a year earlier, he was standing deep in the backyard, by the arbor, with Abel. There had been a discussion about weeds—or compost, or pruning—and so, me at Father's side, under our umbrella while Abel stood an arm's length away, water streaming off his hat, my father cleared his throat. A question had occurred to him, something vital, and, still staring at the squishy ground, he said, "Abel, do you believe in life after death?"

Abel's head turned slowly, as if on a screw. In his eyes were amazement and wariness, one then the other.

"I believe in just rewards," he said. "I don't have a clear picture of heaven."

My father, still concentrating on the earth, nodded, and I remember watching Abel swallow—he had an enormous Adam's apple—scratch lazily at his ear and turn his head so that they, not exactly shoulder to shoulder, were again focusing on whatever problem they'd discovered at their feet.

"From now on, Abel," my father said, "call me Willy."

I was hearing something, I thought, something new and special, and I watched Abel, whose surname was a Polish jaw-breaker with too many *c*'s and *y*'s, hear it too.

"Good, Mr. Willy," Abel said. "Heaven, Mr. Willy."

"Everybody calls me William. Or Bill. But I like Willy. It implies—what?—brio maybe."

The second incident that occurred to me the day that I began to hate my father also involved Abel: we were playing checkers in the dining room, my father and I, and Abel came in, hat literally in hand, to complain about the climbing roses behind the garage.

"Mr. Willy," he began, "no good. No good for nothing, those roses."

My father jumped several of my checkers, said, "King me," and then flung himself into a paragraph six or seven minutes long about, Lord, "use" and "meaning" and "authenticity," his the sort of sentences I remembered from summer camp—dense and flopped-back on themselves, singsongy and always barbed at the end. He began slowly, fingers stabbing the air, until, just before he ran down and the light came back to Abel's eyes, my father was yattering headlong, not out of control but excited, as if the only sense worth having was sense you discovered by going loopy and inside out and topsy-turvy.

"I am talking about reconciling desire to responsibility," my father said.

Abel agreed, quietly.

"I am talking about urges which we have, and their denial. Say this with me, Abel. Say—"

It took Abel another twenty minutes to get out of that room, words like "evidentiary" and "testator" zooming at him, and me, like wasps. I remembered this, I say, that afternoon I stood in his office, my mother having told me not to hate him, and I swear I didn't until I recalled that, speaking of "mettle" and "modesty" and "rage," my father had plucked from his jacket pocket his Ace comb and, still hollering about time and what can be lost or won by it, had begun fussily and furiously combing his hair.

"Freedom," he had shouted that afternoon, "A Theory of."

Days had passed, days and days and days: He had driven away, Mother had spoken to me, I had come to his study, and suddenly, as able to do this as I was to give my height or the color of my own hair, I went out his door (which is now my own and behind which I figure out who's owed what), shut it carefully and said, "I do hate you."

Jeep Freeman, my best friend, noticed my father first. Jeep, who now knows what highs and lows there are in real estate to brag about, plus the fortune you can make from them, had just caught the football I'd thrown, made a wiggle-waggle on the model of Alan "The Horse" Ameche of the Baltimore Colts, squeaked when I tackled him and thumped backwards with the words, "Isn't that your father?"

Down the way, past several yards of what "greensward" was

probably invented to describe, my father was painstakingly
backing out his Dodge, his every movement, like burlesque, an
exaggeration of what gets taught in driver's education: adjusting the mirrors, rear and side; scooting his seat back; locking
his door; engaging this, releasing that; hands at ten and two,
as erect behind the wheel as Higbee's store window manne-
quin.

"Where's he going?" Jeep wondered.

We were standing, nine-year-olds with grass stains on our
knees and little else to be entertained by, and for the life of
me—a cliché I use deliberately, with respect for the sentiment
it originally expressed—I couldn't figure out what my father
was doing at home. It was three-thirty, and he was supposed
to be downtown, at Ninth and Superior Avenue, his a life—like
my own now—of putting wealth into words, of puzzling out
how to pass on the lowboy and the pewter and the mutual
funds to Cousin Mabel, to a dog named Fifi, to the Wicked
Witch of the West.

"You want something to drink?" Jeep asked. "I'm thirsty."

I had taken two giant steps toward the street my father was
in the middle of, and it is more true than less that Jeep Freeman, thirsty best friend, had disappeared from me; he would
reappear for me only after my father was well up the road,
when I could snatch my football away and say for him, school-
mate and buddy, to mind his own damn business and to leave
me alone and to go wherever it was fat boys like him went when
they weren't being pests or know-it-all busybodies.

Instead, I was watching my father and his car rolling toward
me—odd to say—a piece at a time: hubcap, grill, hood ornament, windshield, headlamp, Dobbs hat, hand, eyes, door handle, light and shadow and silence the size of winter. As distant
from myself as I sometimes get when I drink too much, I
approached the curb. There was a crack to stand on, a leaf.
There was a spot near the street, I knew, for me to occupy, an
X on the earth I can still see from my study window.

"One-alligator," I mumbled, aiming to count high as need

be, until I would be yammering numbers it takes several breaths to complete. I had put the trees out of mind. And the grass and the clouds, the big houses there and there and there. And then my father, sitting high as a pasha, pulled abreast, head turned a fraction my way, his hand ticking back and forth like a metronome.

Good-bye, that gesture was saying. *Good luck.*

I was full of question marks—huhs and whats and whys.

To and fro went his hand, manicured and long-fingered, more suited for piano-playing than pencil-pushing: *So long, kiddo.*

Yes, I thought. *No.*

He was thinking of Shirley, I guessed. Of deck rails to slip over, of edges to tumble from, of corners to step around, and of darkness, like death, to vanish into.

"Wait," I said, my first word aloud.

But he was already past me, indifferent as stone, attending to what lay in front of him and away, and I had only me to wonder about and one thousand thoughts to fumble through before I could face Jeep Freeman and say where he could go with his Erector Set and Lincoln Logs and likewise cheap view of life.

II.

Correct: I became as obsessed with my father and his disappearance as he had been with his sister and hers; and over the years I told that story as often as he'd told his. The next fall, in Mrs. Sweeney's fourth-grade class at Hawken, the prep school that raised me up and made me a spelling champ, I made it the subject of an essay, "Where My Father Went," an essay surely as whichaway and inside out as this story but filled with lingo like "scoundrel" and "blackguard" and "scalawag," words as mean as I could make them. Later, at the Upper Campus, I afflicted him with scabies and lesions, likened him to a viper, made him a drunk or bully who'd cheat at bridge. I cast him (yes: "cast," whose proper use you can look up in John Milton) as far from me and my mother and our house as I could, given how little I knew of the big world: along the Narbada, among thieves and cutthroats; in Nara, among yellow barbarians; in the Lesser Sunda Islands, among lepers and animals happy only in the dark and the wet.

Still, there was a part of me—is there a bone for this idea, or a tissue?—that thought he might return, and so, on important occasions (graduation, my birthday, Christmas), I kept expecting him—still slender, I thought, still as smooth as a beau brummel—to step again into my life. The Fourth of July after my sophomore year at Duke, for example, I felt sure he was close—on the next block, maybe, on Public Square down-town, on Fairmount Boulevard. I couldn't sit, nor go a step without turning. I picked at my fingers, read the paper haphaz-ardly, brushed my teeth again and again. In the backyard, my mother, wearing a straw hat the size of a parasol, sat in a chaise, reading, next to her a highball (that's what she called it). It was afternoon, bright as a postcard; the radio was saying what was up with Muhammad Ali and what folks my own age were doing in Haight-Ashbury; Jeep Freeman, still my best friend, was waiting for me to pick him up so we could go to the stadium to see the Indians play the Tigers; and I, watchful and nervous and stupid, was standing on my front porch, listening to the neighborhood go about its holiday.

Okay, I told myself. Okay.

Up the street, far enough away to be possible, a car had turned my direction. It was a Dodge. A Ford. A Cadillac. Yes, I said. Of course. I managed a step toward the sidewalk, now miles and miles away. That car was green. It was red. It was persimmon and classic white. And I was moving, the heart of me going click-click-click. It wasn't Father, in fact, but the part of me that hated him didn't know that. A thought came—having to do, I believe, with fear. And another—this as black-minded as any from a storybook villain. "Yes," I said, this with hiss enough to be meaningful. "Come on," I said. I had my fists up—not for the last time, it would turn out—and was jumpy the way the frightened are. And then the car swerved into a drive a few up from my own. Out climbed a woman and three children, in swimsuits and towels, noise reaching me that was neither important nor dire; and immediately I was grateful no one was nearby to see me, trembling, rig myself together one ragged piece at a time.

I last expected him in 1974, the year of the oil embargo, the year Hank Aaron clobbered the home run that gave him one more than Babe Ruth. I was a lawyer by then—"Say 'attor-ney,'" my mother always insisted. "Lawyers are what crooks have"—for Jones Day, a firm too big to do anything but make money. The occasion was the death of Judge Garner, my grandfather, my father's father, who is buried in Lakeview Cemetery with President Garfield as well as three or four stingy Rockefellers. It wasn't a wake we were having at our house as much as it was, well, a cocktail party, entertainment provided by old Freddie Webster from Val's in the Alley, a nightclub the Judge was a cutup at, and WGAR disc jockey Harry Pildner, who had eyebrows bushy enough for Congress. Everybody was there—old-timers mostly, from the *Buckeye Press* and the defunct *Cleveland World,* papers the Judge had written for when he was known as Mad Manny Garner, when he played the tenor sax and was secretary for the American Federation of Musicians, Local No. 4.

"Isn't it marvelous?" Mother kept saying, cornering me every hour or so to read a telegram from this muck-a-muck or that, urging me to introduce myself to Mrs. Dorothea Beal of Gates Mills or to D. P. Sells, Jr., of Medusa Cement. "The Judge would have loved this," she said. "Hoopla, you know. He dearly loved hurly-burly."

Yes, the Judge would have loved the celebration. There were women with heavy perfume and men in green suits, not to mention ruder sorts who called me "Bub" and laughed with their mouths full; there was high-stakes chitchat, more than one fistfight in the garden, an awning that collapsed, a redhead named Reva Something-or-other who showed us her garter belt and sang in French, a Victor Borge look-alike who tried to sell me a Vermont Christmas-tree farm, three tubs of crushed ice—and it was no work at all to imagine the Judge in the dining room, surprisingly nimble for the roly-poly he was, doing the Cleveland Chicken, a dance with too much elbow and knee for the unpracticed, his head shiny as a light bulb. And then somewhere in here—after the streetlights flickered on but before Meech Sims toppled into the liver pâté—the air went funny and cold.

"What's wrong, Carter?" It was Allison, my girlfriend then,

my wife now. She was wearing a hat my mother had pressed on her, a cockeyed contraption with feathers, of which, so the joke went, there were only a dozen in Ohio.

"He's here," I said.

She was seeing what I was, I think: Elmer Smits telling an Apache story; Libby Wellington tugging at her girdle; Otis P. Miller doing an imitation of the bishop of Pittsburgh in an inner tube.

"He's not here, Carter. He's not anywhere."

I was trying to move, telling my legs to move, intending to go room by room by room.

"Stop it," Allison said, gripping me at the bicep. "You'll embarrass your mother."

I yanked myself free. My mother was in the library. My mother was with her lady friends—Alice Tipton, Dottie and Marion Levisay, Margaret Harding's snooty sister. She was laughing. She was guzzling vodka. She was singing a verse from "The Courtship of Yongy-Bonghy-Bo," stuck on the verse where "the early pumpkins blow." She needn't know what I was doing. She needn't.

"Wait here," I told Allison.

I was a fool, she said. An ignoramus.

I believe I put my finger to my lips, scrunched my face up tight—evil à la Vincent Price or other matinee ghoul.

"Shhhhh," I whispered. "Don't move."

In the pantry I found Shelby Humes, a cousin by marriage, a sissy I meant to shove sidelong with a shoulder. *"Pardonnez-moi,"* he said, wiping his Manhattan off his shirtfront. "Aren't we a rough customer." My father was here, I was convinced. He was in the sun-room with the Lewellyn twins, or in the kitchen peering into the refrigerator. In the backyard by the peonies, or in the front leaning like a boulevardier against the willow. He stood in the light. In the shadows. By the foyer. Next to the deacon's bench in the center hall. He was on the tree lawn, perfecting his wedge shot; in the garage, banging on a steam pipe.

"Are you satisfied?" Allison asked when I passed her a second time. She looked collapsed, thoroughly defeated by my craziness. With an ache I wondered how it was that she, a blonde *cum laude* economics major who could cuss you out in German and hit a volleyball as fiercely as any we send to the Olympics nowadays, had found herself with me.

"Please," I said, not certain what to be asking for. "Just give me a minute here, okay?"

Again I was gone, racing up the stairs, heading for the study—once his, now mine.

At the door, I tucked my shirt in, smoothed my hair. I had carted all his stuff—his papers, his handsome clothes and pricey toilet articles—to the basement years before, after I'd moved home; and so I wondered, light-headed and antsy, what he could be looking at in there. I had clutter, yes, mounds of it. I was not as persnickety as he. So what could he make of my books, the trash I get lost in, like *I, the Jury* and the artful typing more than one professor had patted me on the back for knowing? That shrieking yakety-yak by Faulkner, say. Or what drippy insight Wordsworth had about tintinnabulation. I imagined my father, suspicious as a cop, studying the ticky-tack on my walls: a picture from a catalogue of a trout that would, if you snapped your fingers at its mouth, wag its tail; a business card from the Medical Mission Sisters of, quote, Our Lady of the Highway, unquote; the complete lyrics to "Louie Louie," supposedly the dirtiest song in America.

"Father," I said.

I was not going in. There was no reason to. Instead, I was taking in the character of my hall, the gloom it was, and shabby. Down a few doors, past my own room, was my mother's, the bedroom—now that Mother is in a nursing home—that Allison and I share. The floor near me was stained, white spots like bleach on the hardwood; the carpet runner, once festive-seeming, its print intricate and tidy as long-lost needlework, seemed threadbare and dusty. The wallpaper had peeled in spots from the wainscoting, itself scratched, its walnut panel inlays wobbly and cracked in places. Plaster was loose, you could see that, and three bulbs were out in the chandelier at the far end, and instantly, to the hand of me that let go of the doorknob and to the legs of me that backed up unsteadily, as if the whole place were rocking wildly in a storm, it made more sense to be somewhere, anywhere else—downstairs, for instance, by the living room fireplace, hearing Baron Henley tell us for the zillionth time how a gentleman shines his shoes.

"You're right," I said to Allison much later. I was drunk then, all of real life draining with a gurgle into a hole between my feet.

"I know," she said, patting my head.

I was a boy again—ill-behaved, ashamed, very sleepy. I had an idea, one as serious as money or death.

"Allison." Her name came out with too many *l*'s and not enough breath to be beautiful. "You will marry me, won't you?"

There were two of her, then three, each blurry at the edge, wobbling round and round like cars in a Ferris wheel.

"We'll see, Carter," they were saying to the left and right of me. "We shall see."

These are the facts as I learned them from my father the afternoon, only a few years ago, he reappeared to beat me up: In Calumet City, Illinois, he'd led a labor strike at the Globe Iron Works; had given a lecture at the Harvard Club in Newburgh Heights; had worked for the Pfaff Company in Los Angeles, for the El Dorado Golf Club in Arkansas, the Surf Club of Miami. He'd met the *Chicago Tribune* cartoonist John T. McCutcheon and, at the Porcupine Club, the novelist J. P. Marquand. He'd danced the cha-cha with Clare Boothe Luce, toasted the Broadway opening of *Repent in Haste.* He'd toured the carrier *Tarawa* at Norfolk, taught one semester at The Winsor School, had his appendix removed at the Anna

Jacques Hospital in Newburyport, given orders for a month to the staff of *Cosmopolitan,* ridden in a golfmobile manufactured by the Ford Motor Company. He had had dreams of going to Bangkok, to Cairo, of visiting Pandit Nehru, of staying at the Savoy in London. He'd been drunk with men named Cabot and Denny, women named Adelaide and Pearl. He'd fixed a typewriter, blown a bugle, peddled kitchen cutlery. He'd sailed a yacht named *Stormie Seas,* saddled a quarter horse named Thomas Harrow, lassoed an ostrich.

"I have cavorted and raised Cain and mingled like a savage," he announced that afternoon. "What in hell, boy, have you done?"

We saw him at Eaton Road where it crosses the Shaker Country Club golf course between the eleventh green and the twelfth tee, a figure as out of place in 1980 as Sinbad the sailor.

"Who's that?" Jeep Freeman asked, the two of us men of leisure and would-be robber barons.

"Don't know," I said. "Don't care."

I was in my element here, I say. I was married, the father of twin girls, thrifty enough to vacation three times a year, knowledgeable about wraparound bonds and what gets reported in *Gourmet* magazine, able to tell Mozart from Mahler, and slick enough to get in and out of every soiree in the United States. Plus, that day I was blasting the ball like Jack Nicklaus.

"It's your honor," Jeep said, as sour-mouthed as it is possible to look when you have lipped out a thirty-dollar three-foot gimmee.

I was happy—pleased with the bees, the birds, the clouds tumbling my way from the west.

"Life is easy," I said. "Watch this."

Here it was that I noticed the man—not my father yet—standing to one side of us, his a suit you might find on a Hollywood has-been: wide lapels, cut too full through the chest, necktie like a dinner napkin.

"Pardon me," he said, addressing Jeep Freeman. "Would you excuse us for a second?"

Jeep looked confused, perplexed, his face doing all the things
I like it for—opening, closing, wrinkling, grinning. Then he
shrugged, said sure, what the hell. He'd just go in the woods
there, he said. Take a leak. Maybe pray a little. Maybe shoot
himself.

"Thank you," the man said, and for a minute we watched
Jeep haul himself over a hill, his a green-and-yellow ensemble
flickering now and then through the trees. "Fine young man,
that Jeep Freeman."

Something hardened in me, my loose insides settling with a
clatter in the flat, hard bottom of me. I was cold, I believe, the
winds from a million directions, the world part water, part
whoosh. I had recognized him.

"You," I said.

He winked, still a sly man. "Me."

I would like to report that something dramatic happened
immediately, a set-to as slapdash and colorful and heedless as
that in prime time, but, except for a truck honking and dog
barking, there was nothing to concentrate on but the production—fussy as any biddy you might know—William H. Garner, Esq., made of stripping himself to his shirtsleeves.

"Do you know boxing?" he asked.

Instantly, I became a youngster answering a grown-up: "Yes,
sir."

He had folded his jacket over a bench, pulled out a tiny
notebook.

"I understand you've had ugly things to say about me," he
said, flipping pages. He'd kept track, he said. Of all I'd said—
the ugly things, the cruel, the unwarranted. I didn't know, he
said. I hadn't the vaguest idea. I was as unthinking as a stump.
He had contacts, associates, companions, with wonderful
memories.

"How'd you find me?" I wanted a cigarette, business to do
with my hands and mouth. "I mean, how'd you know I'd be
here?"

He'd called my secretary. He'd called Allison, claimed to be
a client. He'd even talked to Beth Ann, Jeep's wife.

"Nice woman," he said, "if a bit bubbly for my taste. Tedious, you know. Too much gosh and golly."

In the trees, Jeep was singing, a yodel-like enterprise with too much nose, being the clown he's famous for at parties, and half of me—that part now tired and slack-kneed—wanted to be in there with him messing up lines from the Rolling Stones.

"What I propose is this," my father began. "A punch-up, a settling of old scores."

Was he thinking of Shirley again? Or of what, stupidly, she and her death stood for? I didn't know. I just remembered the times he'd come to my room or besieged me in the backyard— not with discoveries, I think now, but with illustrations of how tenuous it was, our life. How we are knocked together and tipped headlong by luck, good and bad. How, mostly, it is chaos we learn from. How broken-off and hit-or-miss living life is. How cramped and split we are inside.

"I go first?" I said.

"Then I go," he said. "Let's try to do this with honor, Carter, shall we?"

Something was being settled here, as decided as are wars and games.

"We don't have to do this," I said.

"Oh, but we do."

I could say I took an inventory of myself at this point—the in and out I am, the up and down—but I did not. Instead I was looking at my hands, pleased at how soft they were. I was not a fighter. I was not violent. I was not angry. These are the things, I contend, that I was not.

"I don't hate you anymore," I said.

"Of course you don't," he said.

He had his legs flexed, and was as white-haired as Santa Claus but too skinny to sock in the jaw.

"We'll have a drink afterwards," he said. "Some civilized palaver."

That was a good idea, I thought, and said so, strangely proud of myself.

"You'll be going away again?" I asked, relieved to hear him

say yes, alas, he had engagements, appointments, faraway places to be.

"Anytime you're ready," he declared.

I put down my golf club, oddly aware of how expensive it was. The sky was like poster paint, primary and impossible. I could hear a bird and traffic, not sure what to make of either. Yes, I thought. Yes. I hung on to myself, the rips and ruins and jags I was. And then, at the moment Jeep Freeman stumbled out of the woods whistling, I flew forward with a fist.

SWEET CHEEKS

In the end, all she had was, well, the whatnots: doodads as odd and silly and, to use her daddy's phrase, downright unnecessary as tits on a teacup, whatchamacallits useless and excessive enough to offend a soul as merry and rich as Old King Cole. To her, it was "stuff," no more sensible to have than was a bikini at the North damn Pole. But afterwards—after he'd moved to Dallas, and July had turned into November, and there was scarcely an A, B or C about him she did not dream of—she found herself unable to junk any of it: which, as she told the plenty in Las Cruces who listened, was the problem, wasn't it?

She'd met him, the lawyer, at the Southside Johnny concert at the Pan Am Center at NMSU, and later, when they knew each other by first name and she could see he wasn't just a spiffed-up cowboy with spit for brains, he took her to El Patio, a bar in Old Mesilla, and, what with his talk about, quote, wrongful employer discharge and antitrust, unquote (plus an entire chorus of "It's Not Unusual" he could hum the Tom Jones of), he succeeded in more or less sweeping her right off her too-damn-big feet.

At first he didn't spend the night. He'd call her at the bank, Frank Papen's ten-story eyesore on Main Street across from the

Loretto Shopping Center, and say how about the greyhound races in Juárez. Or dinner at the Coronado Country Club in El Paso. Or let's go up to Picacho Hills and play ourselves some golf. And she'd go, him the sort who watched his language and used his turn signals and was at pains to say excuse me every time he went to the gents'. They'd bet the dogs, or eat high on the hog, or play nine holes of the most agitated golf in the desert, then he'd drive to her house on Calle del Sol, the three-bedroom piece of cardboard her old man had bought her after she graduated from ENMU in Portales. They'd sit around watching Letterman or Arsenio and whatever shoot-'em-up TNT had on cable, maybe do a little reefer she kept in her nightstand, trade shots or just drink straight from the bottle, then they'd make love, as shy and solicitous and eager-beaver as what the word "naughty" tells us. But he never stayed over. You'd hear him in the A.M., clattering in the bathroom, or getting into his pants, humming sha-la-la's from the Beatles half of history, and next he'd be at her ear, saying, Good night, Cheeks. Or Babycakes. Or Sweet Chips. Crapola that there ought to be a law against using with an honest-to-goodness grown-up.

By Halloween, the stuff had started coming in. The Turd-riffics first, no kidding. Miniature soccer and football players made out of, get this, sanitized horse manure. Whoa, she said. What the devil. But he raised his finger to his lips, storybook and sweet-as-you-please: shhhhh. Next arrived the leather ash-tray. After that a plaster-of-Paris frog in polka-dot panties and brassiere. An argyle sock to fit King Kong. The USS *Constitution* in a bottle. EX LIBRIS bookplates. Then, yup, books: *The Redneck Way of Knowledge,* which was blank, and a pound of Nostradamus gobbledygook that should have been. A Beefeater gin refrigerator magnet. Sea monkeys. Ash from Mount St. Helens. Alvin and the Chipmunks reciting *Hamlet,* that section about being and not. What on earth, she said. What the heck. And each time, his face lit by that smile the white-collar teach the blue- in Disneyland, he'd say it was for fun.

Gags to cheer everybody up. Laughter, medicine, all that jazz.

A week later he'd told her he loved her. Gosh: all those words, and without the singsong that gooey is. And she, caught off guard by the sixty-pound concrete candlestick sitting at her feet, asked him, please, pretty-please, to repeat himself. He got down on one knee, à la Valentino, clasped his hands across his chest, his an expression that shot right to the core of her. No kidding, he said. Around them—on the floor, against the walls, chockablock on the shelves he'd nailed up one weekend—were six months of UPS and parcel post: a game of Twister, a crackpot's idea of the Eiffel Tower in toothpicks, a Bayer aspirin the size of a chafing dish, every color Pez candy in the universe, a papier mâché Roman Colosseum, and here came those words again—and again and again, as remarkable as a blizzard in Panama. Wait, she told herself, and tried to. Wait. But she got only to three-Mississippi before she yanked him up by the necktie, her heart thudding in her throat, saying that, Gosh Almighty, she loved him too.

She really really did.

Still the stuff came—each the each special is. A wrought-iron Liberace. Three "Money Back Guaranteed" pennies from heaven. A state-of-Alabama-approved electric chair (batteries not included), an old-timey hatbox that said DO NOT OPEN: CURSE IN EFFECT, and an ooh-la-la nightgown that in block letters warned moms and dads everywhere to KEEP OUT OF REACH OF CHILDREN—itself an hour's worth of ha-ha-ha. And she supposed the stuff would be coming still if, of course, he hadn't told her in July that he'd taken a new job. In Texas.

She was sitting and he wasn't; then he was and she'd found the other dozens of places in the room to lean against. She felt like a juggler, tossing an apple—or a chain saw—beyond her limit: an absurd image. It was an opportunity, he said. The chance of a you-know-what. Dewey & Howes was the yamma-yamma-yamma: after a moment she didn't know what he was saying, only that, eyes fixed to the left of him or to the right or on what was reported to be a certified hairball from a

certified Montana polled Hereford, she was saying yes, the
do-or-die parts of her insides cracking or instantaneously drying
up. Yes, she did understand. Yes, they would stay in touch. Yes,
this was rotten luck. Yes, no reason this had to change anything. There was, after all, Trailways and American Airlines
and her own Buick LeSabre. Yes, yes, yes—a hiss that, for all
the difference it made, you could have heard in Zululand.

They made love that night, their last. They mumbled "ex-
çuse me" a lot. And "pardon me." And damn near tried to
keep their give-and-take free of any chitchat that had an *L* or
an *O* or a *V* or an *E*—trying, it seemed already, to reach each
other across time and distance, plus whatever other dimensions
heartache could be measured by. As before, he got up early,
and, courtesy of a Ronald Reagan night-light, he tiptoed
around the bedroom, pulling on his loafers, tucking his shirt in,
zipping his trousers. A minute later he stood in the bathroom,
combing the hair he was proud of, brushing his teeth, gargling,
and making the other sounds it was not possible to ignore—
those ten or ten million notes the Rolling Stones had once
upon a time used to assert that things were bad and might not
get better. Then, appearing like a ghost beside her, he bent to
her ear, the smell of him as hopeful and promising as the
money she was around day after day after day.

"Good night, Oodles," he said.

The first man after that was a polo player from that Hurd
rich-boy bunch up the Hondo Valley near Ruidoso, a so-and-so
as subtle in courtship as a thunderclap. Next was an Aggie
assistant basketball coach, Irk Something Something: on the
dance floor of the Roadrunner Lounge and to the *wah-wah* of
Uncle Roy and the Red Creek Wranglers, he didn't even make
it to the bridge of "Loving on Back Streets" before he was
whispering sweet blah-blah-blahs about Helen of Troy and
Cleopatra, anybody from any age with the right chromosomes.
So, while she waited for the tabs and slots of herself to fit
together correctly, there wasn't anybody.

Away from work, she felt lost. She didn't stop at, say, My Brother's Place. No Cork 'n' Bottle. One time she went into Ikard's Furniture across the street, but without him—the lawyer—it wasn't the same. She didn't know, for example, what the dickens could be done with a settee. So she went home. Watched Sam Donaldson pick on some under secretary of whatever. She made it about a third into *The Name of the Rose*, always quitting where what's-his-name, you know, found about the thousandth croaked monk. Jeepers, what a life, ratty and cockeyed and dull. She watched ESPN, the International Barefoot Skiing Championships, then switched the channel to yell the questions at the boneheads on Jeopardy. Sure, she and the lawyer talked, fairly often at first. He called her—what?— Sweetums or Honey Bunch, bragged about the Simon Legrees he'd saved a dozen good guys from, asked when she was coming for a visit. Six Flags, he said. The Texas Schoolbook Depository.

That was his word, "visit," as if she were one of his Lambda Chi brothers, as if he weren't the only person she'd ever, ever, ever wrenched herself inside out for. He didn't mean to be cruel, she knew, but there it was anyway—miles and miles of dirt and weeds and a big blank sky between what was and what most assuredly was not. It was a form of fate, she decided, forces as manifest as the Elvis Presley piggy bank on her bureau. Sometimes the bear this, sometimes the bear that— wasn't that how love went? Yin for an hour, yang for two. No, she assured him, she wasn't mad. No, not upset. No, not at all. And suddenly he was gone, in regard to love nothing to listen to except the crackle and buzz that hanging up sounds like.

One day she tried to get rid of his stuff, the goodies. In the kitchen, she sought to imagine the world without sixty percent of the doohickeys piled on her dinette table. Without the clamshell lamp. Without Christ on a Crutch. Without that glow-in-the-dark Thumbelina or Tinkerbell some Taiwanese Wong Ho had snazzed up with a Scarlett O'Hara hoopskirt and a rhinestone wand. From the utility room she dragged out a box, but, after coming oh-so-close to just plopping into it whatever she grabbed first, she thought *what the hell* and started wrapping each piece in newspaper—the dribble glass, the New Guinea witch doctor's shrunken head—as if, like in the poem, so much depended on the relation of one object to another, and that to yet another, until all objects—this plastic piece of lunacy and that—were related exactly as, well, fate had intended.

An hour whooshed by. Down the street, the ice cream truck was playing its chimes, "Popeye the Sailor Man." An Uncle Sam know-it-all had come on NPR to say who was losing in Latvia, Estonia, among poor Baltic bastards everywhere. Another voice, this also sleepy and full of private schooling, repeated gossip about—who?—Johannes Brahms maybe. Christ. She poured a drink, Johnnie Walker, poked at a ham-salad sandwich, then she found herself, chin on her hand, wondering what the dickens she was going to do. She had a box. It was full. Now what? From the phone book she scribbled down the numbers of the DAV, the Salvation Army, the Military Order of the Purple Heart, and she was only two digits from a tax deductible donation when she realized, as much with her heart as with her head, that by the weekend she could be telling a do-gooder named Tito or Floyd that what he had lugged to his truck was a genuine imitation-body-part chess set: toes, ears, eyeballs—the works. A token of affection.

That Friday she went out with the service manager for Lackey Chevrolet-Toyota. It was November, time not to be damaged anymore. Grow up, she scolded the self in the mirror. Pull the shoulders back. Put on a happy face. They drove to the Double Eagle, where she ate, she had to admit, like a pig. Gulf shrimp the size of a fat man's fingers. Chicken stuffed, rolled, dipped and every other cooking verb from France. In the lounge, knee-to-knee in chairs so low you needed help to climb out, they had cocktails: a bourbon for him, for her a green thing with a paper parasol. He was her age, twenty-eight, and divorced but not nearly ruined from it. He was a Libra to her Cancer—the two of them, they agreed, as suitably matched as any with houses and cusps and sun-sign mumbo jumbo.

At her doorstep, she thought to invite him in—God, she did not want to call it a nightcap—but she wondered how to explain the, you know, stuff. The coasters from Triassic-period limestone. The shopping bag of Wacky Wall Walkers. The *s-t-u-* double-*f.* It was late, he said. Big day tomorrow, Saturday, he had to go. She started counting again—one-Mississippi, two—numbers enough to say or do anything that could be said or done in her condition. She imagined she was already in bed alone, staring at the two-person sombrero on the wall. She remembered the dreams she'd had—the weird they were, and the cold—the way they seemed to afflict a look-alike named Mary Jo. He'd call in the morning, he said. Okay? She considered his eyes, which weren't a whit like the lawyer's; and his hands-on-hips way of keeping his tummy in. Why not, she said. That would be terrific. And then, the second after she jiggled her key in the lock, he kissed her as she hadn't been kissed since high school, lips too mashed to be anything but meaningful.

She tried to love him after this. Boy, did she. At the bank, a mortgage application from a Greene or a Mendoza spread on the desk like gigantic playing cards, she'd think of the ways her service manager was good to her. He liked slow-dancing—the Conversation, the Quarter-Waltz—and even knew "the alibi," a ballroom trick for getting out of a corner. He could boil Italian, he said, a joke. Raised a Baptist, he didn't know what he was now (here his hands flew all over the place, like crazed birds), but he believed in something, if only the whole being greater than the sum of its widespread parts. He'd played football for the Aggies, but, not altogether engaged by the biology and American lit and Tuesday-Thursday sociology he sat through, he quit. He knew about flowers: zinnias, azaleas— the herb family. When he was going to be late, he called. He didn't nag her about smoking, and, best of all, that first night he actually entered her house, the night they slept together, he didn't utter one evil thing about the knickknacks she was the full-time mistress of. "Neat" was what he exclaimed. He couldn't believe it. Wow. He picked up the itty-bitty Hong Kong rickshaw, studied it as thoroughly as painstakingly pointless handiwork can be studied. Will you look at this, he said. He touched the Popsicle-stick birdcage, the .44 Magnum cigarette lighter, the Texas jackalope. Wow.

It was clear, she thought, that he loved her—that his, too, was a world tilted and loose and loud—and she wished she could see inside him (as she could see inside her anatomically correct man doll) and thus find out what his organs were doing. His thumping heart. Those pink, wet wrinkles of the brain. She took his hand, could smell on it the work he did, and steered him toward the bedroom. She would learn something, she hoped, and when they were undressed, his outfit more neatly hung than hers, she did.

The lawyer, she began. Her service manager was holding her—his name was Bobby and he was blond, even his movie-star moustache—and here she was, hers the tone best used for "true" and "false" in school, telling about a guy, the lawyer, who'd filled her up and set her spinning and given her eight becauses for every event, good or bad, under high heaven. She described a trip to White Sands—the national monument, not the missile range—and how the sun worked in that flat, wasted world, and what common animals the clouds were, plus who said what when, and why time went bang-bang-bang. She told him about the afternoon the lawyer shampooed her hair, the nerves he'd struck. Her service manager was holding her—his name, yes, was Robert Ray Dunbar and he could sew a coat button, he supposed, and spoke enough Mayfield High *español* to be understood in jail—and here she was, harebrained as any mad scientist she'd heard of, talking about, as it has been talked about to her, asset-based financing, as well as which Japanese sedan to buy and why. She told him about window-shopping with the lawyer, in particular oohing over a bed big as a wrestling mat, and how scared or dumbstruck he'd been, as if humbled by what could be accomplished in that faraway corner or this. He hailed from Nebraska, she said. A Cornhusker. His parents were Ellen and Russell. He'd had a mutt named Moe, after the Stooge. He threw right-handed, hated Brussels

sprouts, read Leon Uris and anything *Time* magazine said was
funny. Salsa made his nose run. In eighth-grade shop he'd
planed a mahogany table, kissed his first girl the night Jimmy
Carter campaigned in Omaha—what else?

She was shaking. She had taken everything out, she believed,
hook by hasp by hinge by nail, and now she was herself a
million-zillion thingamajigs, each vital and tiny and dumb, and
she guessed she had only four-three-two minutes to find them
there and there and there and so make herself whole again.
What, she said. What? Her service manager held her—his
name, Lordy, was Bobby, like a kid, a charter member of the
Vic Tanny Health Club on the bypass—and here she was,
watching her arms tremble and ordering herself, for crying out
loud, to pay attention: there was much in life to know and
maybe life enough to know it. It's all right, he was whispering.
Truly.

Then, not with all his might, he squeezed her, this decent
Bobby person, and she grew curious to learn what he might say,
or do, if he discovered that beneath him now, wriggling and
moaning "ah-ah-ah," was not her at all but only the bone and
hair and flesh of a fool using her name.

Each day, she thought, became a wall between herself and the
lawyer. Each day a wall. She tried new food—Thai and Jew-
ish—and this too became part of a wall. So did the clothes she
bought: the too expensive espadrilles, a blouse a red she'd never
seen before, underwear as wicked as she could stand without
snickering. The wall, she told herself. She subscribed to *Southwest Art* and, more foolish business, to *The Sporting News*,
aiming to lose herself in the mysteries unique to batting aver-
ages and Remington Indians on the warpath. She and Bobby
went to the community theater at the old State movie house
on the downtown mall, what had once been as bleak and
windswept and jerkwater a main street as any she could conceive of, and, sitting in the front row, she willed herself into

that September-remember world of *The Fantasticks* or into what woe-is-me drama eight bucks had bought. Another day. Another wall.

One weekend—was it already May?—they went to Albuquerque, driving almost without saying a word, nature racing past at sixty, sometimes seventy, miles per hour, Bobby's pickup as quiet as a capsule in deepest space. He had something to tell her, he announced when they reached the Holiday Inn. She didn't have to listen, he said, but he was going to speak his mind anyway. She regarded herself and this place. There were no windup toys, no herky-jerky contraptions that chattered and squeaked and went snap-crackle-pop. There was a bed, not seriously meant to live with, and a too-high table and a too-hard chair and a Motorola color TV, plus carpet that must've been the ugly brown easing cleaning is—but no felt cloth duck appliqué flyswatter. No coffee mug with elephants on it having sex. No four-leaf clover hunting hat for Bullwinkle the moose.

Instantly, she knew what Bobby was hemming and hawing about, the exact words he'd use, what the entire unfair, stupid, me-me-me sentence would be. Even if he took a half-hour, even if he stood on his head (which he could), it would start with "I" and end a billion years later with "you." Don't, she said. He snatched up her suitcase, set it down, moved it twice more, then told her "fine," his expression sideways and not simple as one-plus-one anymore, and then—bless him—he said anew what a grand old time they'd have that night.

In July she took her vacation, which, except for a weekend at her daddy's cotton farm outside of Portales, she spent at home. In the afternoons, content with himself and everything else under the sun, Bobby came over, usually with a six-pack of Bud Light, once with a bottle of Cuervo Gold they quit before the bottom of. Bobby fixed the grease trap in the kitchen sink. He barbequed, his secret sauce with one part Skippy peanut butter. They went roller-skating, did the hokey-pokey with nearly one hundred other folks thrilled to be falling

down. Oh, it was summer, the valley hot as those drugstore joke
postcards' scenes of hell, the sky too far up to be real or blue.
She lay on her stomach in the backyard, her pillow a Scrooge
McDuck beach towel, her bathing suit the one she hadn't worn
since college. Bobby, she said. Two giant steps away, he was
on his knees, painting an Adirondack chair he'd thought might
be cheap to send away for, and immediately she didn't know
why she'd called his name or what, if anything, might blurt out
of her. He was wearing Bike athletic shorts, splotched the
green from the bucket at his feet. Bobby, she said, at last sure
what was going to be said next. She had been thinking about
the heat—the dry, close, mean kind this world was—and now
his head came up, cocked, his hair so blond you wondered how
he got here to planet Earth. Yes, he said. Not "yeah," not
"huh," not "what": yes. So, given what was what, who who,
she wondered the only thing she could: Are you happy?

He looked—wasn't this goofy?—high and low, as if he'd lost
his wallet, and said at last, as she knew he would, sure—an
answer that came with a smile, and a shrug. What about you?
A neighbor dog was barking, Rex, somewhere a door slammed
too hard, and way off Mikey-Mikey-Mikey was being hollered
for. Yes, she said. I guess I am. And in a second, the center
of her still as night, she actually was. Happy. She had a thought,
too fast to catch up to; then another, this the one to hold. In
her bathroom, above the toothbrush holder, was a Siamese cat
clock, its ticktocks eyes that blinked each second. So was she
happy? On her dresser sat a wooden hobnailed-boot pencil
holder. So was she? In her guest lavatory hung Esperanto
wallpaper. Yes, she was. Still on her stomach, she watched
Bobby painting—swish, swish, swish. Here was a man who
couldn't whistle, who loved Fernando Valenzuela and every
other Los Angeles Dodger, who was allergic to mustard. Here
he was. Eyes closed now, she was concentrating, a picture in
her mind of gizmos tightened and arranged and sorted and
swept clean away, of a room empty as the horizon, of surfaces
shined and sterile and hard; of herself, strong and honest as a

nickel, letting go of at least a year of stored-up laughter. And then the vision was gone—poof—and she had not jumped up squealing to give this man the hug of his very own life.

July. September. Thanksgiving. Happy New Year. This is how her year went—in chunks, in spasms. She'd roll over in bed and a month would be gone. She'd stub her toe and look up to see Lincoln's birthday on the calendar. One night she kissed Bobby, and March, its raw wind and sometime frost, disappeared. April became an afternoon, May a day with no junk mail, June a doorbell going dong-dong-ding. Soon it was July, and she knew, every cell and tissue and blessed thump-thump-thump of her knew, that he'd call. The lawyer. She arranged to be home as often as possible. She had a project, she told Robert Ray Dunbar, busy work from the bank. A merger, she told him. Don't worry, she said. She needed a month, that was all. Everything was fine between them, she insisted. She used her daddy's word: hunky-dory. He seemed doubtful, scratched his cheek, looked near and far for help: You sure? She smiled, smooched him as a mother might: Of course, what was not to be sure of? You could see his brain work, the clever gears and cogs of it. I'm getting a speedboat, he said. They'd go water-skiing at Elephant Butte, okay?

After he'd driven away, after he'd honked to say bye-bye, she shut the door to wait. He wouldn't call tonight. The lawyer. Her phone was a Coke can, but it wouldn't ring. Not tonight. She just flat-out knew. It wouldn't ring until between him there and her here, as between the moon and Mars, there was noth-ing, not even an idea. So, patiently and deliberately, she began taking down the walls. Those many, many days. That western novel she'd chuckled to the rootin'-tootin' end of. That kit to knit with. That color of hair she now had. A bottle of crème de menthe had to go out, as did a spider plant. Her Volkswagen wristwatch had to be set, her Tiny Alice tea service polished.

Oh, he'd call, bet your bottom dollar. And the conversation, sigh-filled and helter-skelter with whys and wherefores, would rattle on for hours. I love you, he'd say, words never said before anywhere, anytime, words meant to stand for everything you could make or wish for. I miss you, he'd declare, and she would feel in him the holes and hollows she felt in herself. The backwards time ran, the topsy-turvy. Again he'd say it. Again. The food of it, the warmth. The phone, its innards composed of wires and solder and miracles. A breath from her, deep as deep goes. Hello, she'd say.

"Honey pie," he'd start, "is that you?"

HOW LOVE IS LIVED IN PARADISE

Though I am still called Bubba by some I do and do not like, my real name is Cecil Fitzgerald Toomer, and this adventure that's happened to me starts with the idea, no doubt loony to ordinary citizens in the big world, that what I know about love comes not from falling in it once, but from watching, years and years ago now, nearly one thousand yards of Super-8 movie in the cinder-block film room at the University of New Mexico and seeing something in football that, by the end of it, had me quietly, well, weeping over the 265 pounds I was.

This was 1970, a year that seems like "yore" to the private sentimentalist I am, and I was in my second year as the line-backer coach for the Lobos. I'd graduated three years before, played a season and a half with the St. Louis football Cardinals as a late-round draft choice, blew up one knee, then its partner, and spent a summer wondering what would become of me, until my old head coach, Mr. Emery Ewing, called up and asked how I'd like to work for him—which meant finding and thereafter teaching huge American youngsters to be semi-bloodthirsty and entirely reckless. I could have the linebackers, he said, and be as fierce with them as Baytagh was with his Tartars. He was always fond of me, he said, considered me prime this-and-that, claimed I possessed a first-rate mind—the flattery of which I was happy to agree with. "You think about it, Bubba," he said, his voice perhaps the tenth human thing I'd heard since the previous May. "You're a born teacher, boy. I can see you now—kicking tail, rousing passions, the works." Coach Ewing had a colonel's shaved head and an unlucky man's violent temper, and he was enough like my own father, who was dead then and probably mayor of the harps-and-honey afterlife he believed in, that I said yes too loud and drove eighteen miles to tell a girl I'd haphazardly courted that we ought to get married.

That August I stood around in the sunlight and yelled at muscular teenagers. "Hit that sumbitch," I'd holler. "That pissant is insulting you, son." They were named Ickey and Tongue and Herkie—nearly a hundred who thought nothing of mud and hurly-burly as the medium to be distinguished in. They'd squat, heave, make mostly chest-derived noise, and afterwards hie themselves to me for more high-decibel instruction. When they were good, I'd snatch up a bullhorn and say so to all of downwind Albuquerque; when they were not, as they often were, I'd invent belittling names for their male parts, plus urge them, then and forever, to contemplate their miserable inadequacies.

Once the season started though, I hit the road, recruiting high schoolers in those portions of Texas that Coach Ewing had given me. I tossed my bags in my Fairlane, said *adiós* to my wife, Stacy Jean, and spent the next four of every seven days driving Interstate-this and FM-that, knocking on the depressingly flimsy doors of folks who lived in Marble Falls—or De Leon or Jacksboro or Devine—any town, one horse or more, that had a kid playing football and dreaming he was a Cleveland Brown or a Ram from L.A. I preferred these boys to be big and quick, with eyes that didn't roll much, and I'd sit in their living rooms, or at their coach's house, and tell them what I and the University of New Mexico might offer—which was meals, books and tuition waivers. Lordy, these were exceptional moments: Mudflap or Ricky T. or the Prince of Frigging Dark-

ness sitting across from me, Ma and Pa Darkness gussied up
as if for a job interview, and me saying how goddamned grand
it was to be bushy-tailed and strong and unafraid of headlong
contact.

Yet it wasn't football I was talking about, really; it was
having a way in the world: somewhere to go and the means to
go there. I was talking, as Coach Ewing and my father had
once talked to me, about a point of view, sensible and righteous, to have; and how, as interested folks, we admired the
self-reliance that Thoreau wrote of, plus what is underlined in
such volumes as *The Pathfinder* and *Huckleberry Finn.* In
living rooms in Crockett and Woodville and Baytown, anywhere plastic pads and Riddell headgear were common, I'd tell
about weight rooms and adequate housing and the eggheaded
tutors who could make Goonch or Elvis or Tattley know, and
care about, Geoffrey Chaucer and, say, thermal transfer and
what the kings and queens of England meant to freedom.
Letters of commitment in hand, I'd talk about—my voice
scratchy and cracking from the effort—how physical prowess,
the business of jumping high or running far, was just a chance
to know the world by throwing your body at it; that what
Jimmy Jeff or Poot or Del Ray might sweat on the gridiron was
given in fair exchange for the delight it is to know the achieve-
ments of Hannibal and Hammurabi and Mr. Thomas Stearns
Eliot, plus conflicting views of us as hollow men or reeds that
cerebrate. That old flimflam, I'd say, of a football player being
dumb was just plain wrong. A noseguard, I'd insist, was a
psychology major with stump-size thighs, a Lambda Chi minus
the body fat. "A linebacker," I declared once, "is a scholar who
learns his Trotsky on the scrimmage field." Football, yes, was
meaning too, just swifter and largely ignorant of please-and-
thank-you.

Then there was the film, the miles and miles of it I studied
when I was not driving one flatland or another. Shut up in the
film room, deaf to the chatter of the antique Bell & Howell
projector, I looked for those who were fleet or passably nimble-

witted, studying—in slow motion or backwards sometimes—a Tiger or a Rocket or a Red Raider who had girth and but one violent notion on his mind. I'd receive a half-dozen cans a week, usually with a note attached from the high school coach: *Look at Morris*, it might read. *He's pure-D remarkable. He wants nothing more than to whack the wigglies out of everybody on your schedule.* They had personalities, these boys from the hinterlands. Despite grainy film stock and no sound, they revealed themselves as bewitched, eccentric, often inspired sportsmen. Rained or hailed on, slogging in mud or red dust, they said, as one's actions can, that they, in this heap or that, were vain or Republican or downright evil. R. C. "Gumball" Weed might be a lunatic with only six yellow teeth and the engaging disposition of a catfish, but he recognized a misdirection when one was tried and you could see the umbrage he suffered from it. Tall and short, black and white, thick through the middle or bottom-heavy like bowling pins, they were what you and I are—a percentage wicked and childishly joyful when triumph calls.

Such was the boy, indeed, I was watching the night, years and years gone, when I ended up alone blubbering. A left outside linebacker for the Flowers, Texas, ISD Rebels, Boyce Fowler had speed that seemed inconceivable to the porky sort he was. He possessed great feet, which is coaching argot for the tiptoe that is necessary among twisting and toppling bodies, not to mention sufficient strength through the chest to pitch aside those dim-witted enough to take him on straight ahead and manlike. You needed to be sly with him, I thought once. You needed to trap-block, leg-whip when the back judge was blowing his nose. You needed to call him "Queerbait" or puke in his earhole—anything to make him leave you alone and go back to the wet waste he'd oozed from.

I don't remember when I stopped watching him, only that at some point a sound burst from me—what the word "agog" suggests—and I put down a ham sandwich perhaps I'd taken one bite from. This wasn't a large moment, I tell you, no bells or "aha" of surprise—just a moment when I heard from, as we now and then do, that vigilant creature inside of us whose job it is, when we can't, to look behind and above and afar. While the film rewound, I approached the window, eyed the way the Sandia Mountains were raised and how, north of us, the light at dusk had turned almost wintery and thoroughly depressing. For the last half-hour, I had been watching not the virtually Marine-like Boyce Fowler and the savage services he performed; rather, I'd been watching—or that creature in the heart of me was watching—a youngster from the other team, a runty black wingback about the age then of my own son now. Eventually, I discovered his name, Purvis Watkins, and came to know how he wanted his steak cooked and what Motown records he sang along to best, but in 1970 he was mere arms and legs, a whirl my Boyce Fowler collided with fifteen, twenty, twenty-five times one dry Friday in November umpteen umpteens ago. I was drawn to this Watkins kid not because he was so good, though good he was, but because, in ways romantics understand, he had chosen this night to be a hero, to lead his much overmatched, poorly outfitted team against the big and the pretty and the rich. It was the melodrama I was captivated by, a modern equivalent of the big-little set-to that was David and Goliath.

More than once, after I started the film anew, I found myself abandoning the high perch my disinterest was supposed to be—the one from which I was supposed to say, as scientists and the really wise do, this is this, that that; more than once I put aside analysis and dispassion to slip instead straight into the silent, black-and-white world Purvis L. Watkins, Cougar Senior and piece of work, was being excellent in. Folks, I flat-out identified with that sport-mad juvenile, dashed where he dashed, hopped when he did. I scooted hither with him, and thither, felt hostile flesh flatten me; and when he saw stars, as he did a couple of times, I saw them too—twinkling and liquid, not at all where they ought to be in high heaven.

Through the first and second quarters, when his Cougars

were being crunched and made laughable to the five hundred farmland Texans who'd gathered to watch, I trudged with him to the huddle and regarded most sympathetically the beleaguered faces of his, and my, teammates. I wasn't film-watching any longer; I was there, on a chewed-up playing field in Borger, Texas, eyeballing my skinned knuckles, picking clots of turf out of my facemask, and muttering to myself, as Purvis Louis Watkins was muttering to himself, "What's going to become of us here?" A measure was being taken that had to do with the misconceived notions of distinction and honor and personal worth. A standard was at work here, a goofy code he'd absorbed from Marvel comic books or what grown men habitually yammer in locker rooms. A line was being drawn, as in epics lines are drawn and drawn again, and Purvis Watkins, not to mention the parts of him that were me, was saying that it—all the things in him and me and us that lines stand for and that are the butt of mean-spirited Hollywood humor—would not be crossed or violated. Purvis L. Watkins, I say to you, hauled himself back to the huddle after one disastrous play, and I knew, from his bobbing head and what finger-pointing signifies, that he was saying, "Boys, this shit's got to stop."

And, come the second half, it did. Stopped cold. Those Cougar boys, what eleven kinds of motley are, returned from halftime with only victory on their minds. They hit, they ran, they blocked, they tackled, and presently it became clear— even to the talented felon Boyce Fowler—that this wasn't sport alone: it was evidence of what we aspire to without vanity or pettiness. Clearly, this was beauty, which is composed of all you love and cannot survive without, and time after time I found myself rocking back in my chair to holler the wildest words I knew about the bliss that warmed me. I pounded the table I leaned against and the wall that also kept me upright. I cried "Shit-fire!" and "Hot damn!" and other things that are mostly the ooh and aah of our best nature, and then all that remained was my fist in the air, pumping like a piston, and the throaty strangled sound my joy was. There would come a moment, soon enough and terrible, when I would be absolutely goddamned hobbled by the void left behind when this joy vanished, but for twenty minutes yet, I got to climb up, as Purvis was doing, those mountains Coach Ewing said challenges were; and up there, jubilant and not at all mindful of what tragedy teaches us, I said, "Well, ain't this something?"

I hooted, I hollered, and twice, swept up as in verse the radiant are, I laughed—from the deepest nooks of me, without regard for where my spit was going. Purvis scored. Dived over a feeble free safety and scored. Purvis threw a block, using everything but his toenails, and let another score. And there occurred that dancing now popular on every gridiron in America: what shameless grind the hips do when you are alone and mirthful—part humping and part hootchie-koo, the effect of it purely gratifying to the half of you that doesn't think.

I ran the film in slow motion; I wanted to see—and scribble down maybe—how his parts worked, what could be made language about the bones and muscle and wind he was. It was the creature in him, and me, I was attending to—the thing that in flight looks smooth and intent and imperturbable. The meat of us that turns toward light and sound and shrinks from an unfriendly touch. "Yes, indeed," I remarked several times. "All right and amen."

Later that night, over the big man's meal of pot roast and carrots my wife had cooked, I tried to explain what had happened. I described how I sat there, more in the action than out, while Purvis led his people. I mentioned the scores, which grew closer and closer. I mentioned how those home fans—every Sadie and Edna Mae and Bucky-boy of them!—had suddenly gone church-quiet and wholly respectful, and how the light lay in that ticky-tacky stadium. I used the word "grace" to say the noises we eek when we see meaning moving this way and that. Stacy Jean was herself gracious during these minutes, encouraging and tolerant of my mumblings. She fetched me more Coors beer and sat across from me and did not go ha-ha-ha when I described how Purvis, for what would have been the tying touchdown, went flying for eight yards. I thought he had scored and was halfway out of my chair, a war whoop coming to me, before I realized that he'd fumbled; and in that moment—and the many moments afterwards, I told Stacy Jean—I broke, as Purvis L. Watkins never did, into a dozen widespread pieces. I could see it all: the ball there, Purvis yonder, that Fowler boy leaping in ecstasy. I could see what had befallen him, and me. We had done everything: been smart, been courageous, been hopeful; and then there we were, on our knees, not slumped yet, staring in the direction we had come from so heroically. We—he in his time, me in mine— were dumbfounded: the object we loved and prized, a fifteen-dollar shape of leather and string and heavy thread that said who we were in the world and what could be done, was way gone and we were only stupid again, a thousand miles from the lights of wonderland.

He was cold, I think; I know I suddenly was. He was not sad yet, nor to my knowledge did he ever become sad. He was simply astonished that life had turned out this way. But if he was not sad, I, his distant confederate, was. I was thinking again, is what. I was being the history major I once was. I was recollecting the A's I had and the dates I was graduated for repeating. Compare, I may have told myself. Contrast. But the brain in me—those folded pink tissues that could say this was only football after all—had just stopped sending what it conveys to the thing in us that is monkey or lizard or slop we eons ago crawled from. I couldn't move. I had hands that weighed twenty pounds and would not close when I begged them to. I had a heart that went thump-thump and breathing that sounded far away and labored. And then I heard it, which is the pronoun for the me I was. It was crying, folks. It—with its flat tummy and its sportsman's crewcut and its twice-broken nose and its weight-lifter's chest—was sobbing, silently but steadily. For itself and not. For Purvis and not. It wanted help, I tried to tell Stacy Jean. It wanted knowledge. It wanted to know, for example, why time couldn't be turned back and suspended at the moment Purvis L. Watkins and his faraway fan were shining and smart and true.

That year Purvis L. Watkins went off to East Carolina State University, and I went forward too—a man with a job, two babies, a wife who looked tasty in expensive South Seas swimwear, and a worldview thought to be generous and informed. Yes: forward. And, I hold, generally upward, which is one metaphor I learned for those improvements we endeavor to make in ourselves and the world we crisscross. I am in a looking-back humor now, a state of mind that wonders how we come to this intersection of the here-and-now and not another. First, it is 1972 and your narrator resides in Ames, Iowa, the recruiting coordinator for the Iowa State Cyclones. He is happy, he believes, and learning to cook meals like Rôti au Vol, Légumes Garnis; he is losing a little hair, watching his weight go and learning how it is to live with snow and four months of falling temperatures. Then it is 1976, and he is in Fayetteville, Arkansas, one defensive coach for the Razorbacks, and he is watching his wife, blonde as straw, walk toward him in a bias-cut Patou tea gown he has ordered from I. Magnin of California. It is another year, and he is doubled-up with worry about government and the secret, dangerous deeds done to preserve it. His oldest boy, Bobby, has braces, and then he does not. His youngest, Samuel, breaks his arm, then it is healed. Next it is 1981 and Bubba Toomer lives in Dallas, recruiting for Southern Methodist University. He is drinking too much and not drinking at all. He is smart, then not. A TV watcher and not. A book reader and not. A Democrat and not. Looking back, I wonder who this Bubba Fitzgerald Toomer was. Is that his crooked smile? Is that his opinion about party etiquette and how anger is definitively expressed? And then it is 1986, and he is in Albuquerque again, the defensive coordinator, and, Lordy, Coach Toomer is in love.

As we are told in that old song that birds must sing, so was

I meant, I think, to fall in love. It was in my nature, I believe. Maybe it was my nature itself, the huffing and puffing and going to and fro I am, the blue eyes I have and the way (not becoming) that my arms hang and swing too far like a march. Corny it might be, but I may have fallen in love with Mary Louise Tipton the instant she entered my office to announce that though she was a tutor, a PhD in literature, she had only the most meager respect for the teaching that coaches did. It was a corrupt and demeaning undertaking, this football thing. One class, an underkind, that served another. It was stupid as recreation and retrograde as ideology—words, which, as they came from what is a beautiful mouth, seemed alien as chatter from space. My hand, I remember, shot up, and again, as if to say "Wait" or "Hold on a minute," but she was eight places at once in my office—picking at the knickknacks I'd lugged with me through the years, trophies and goodies and inspirational speeches, plus a pile of newsclippings that confirmed, more or less, what purpose and direction I could give youngsters—and then, settled at last in an easy chair, she said, "I hear you're smart. Let's have lunch."

She had a smile that involved the whole of her face, plus a bent-forward posture that said she could be lively on a million other subjects, and before another second went past, I said, "Hell, yes."

Maybe I fell in love with her on another day in a different restaurant when she said, almost clinically, that she liked the way I attacked my food, which was like the way her dogs—a boxer named Lucy and a foundling Dane-like monster named Luther—went at theirs. I was de-light-ed, a word it takes both mouth and heart to say correctly. I was delighted to learn that she was from Shreveport and that her daddy, by whom she was still enthralled (though he'd been dead for five years), was the sort of man who climbed into his pajamas at six-thirty in the evening, a man who liked *Ivanhoe,* a quarter horse named Nellie First and the happy company of fellow millionaires. I was delighted by her age, thirty-six, and the years she'd worked as a waitress, or as a bartender, or as a public relations gofer in Hermann Hospital at the Texas Medical Center in Houston. I was as well delighted by the tragedies that had struck her, age-old troubles like alcoholism and a passel of brothers and sisters as swamp-infected and priss-minded as any creation from William Faulkner. I was charmed by her drawl and the singsong my whole name became when she thrust open my door to declare that one player I had was, regrettably, dense as igneous rock. I took delight, which is mental pleasure that does not lessen over time, in how damned intelligent she was, in the way she could just stand up and say, "This is shit, this Shinola." She knew, and I let her teach me, what texts are and how we are better for losing ourselves in them. In lunch after lunch, Bubba, who was "Cecil" to her, learned what slips of the tongue meant and how, through manner and word, we act out the horrors and miseries of our youth. In one hour, I learned the two words we have from Old High German; in another, what politics have to do with the art we consume; in another, how pride is related to sloth, gluttony to greed, and the several things that goeth before the fall.

One day, in addition to the palaver and eye-looks that are part of love, came the actual making of love. We had gone to her house, a ranch-style stucco on Bennet off Menaul, a house she cherished as if it too knew about fear and failure and human wishes, and in the middle of looking for something—a book, I think, whose thesis concerned the personality sloppy handwriting reveals—she said, "Cecil, it's time we had sex." Miss Mary Louise Tipton was serious and laughing at the same time. She had done all the thinking, I realize now, as she always did the thinking for the two of us: in her mind, where there was already so much about males and females and what they've done to each other, she had seized the subject of us, debated its pros and cons. She had the facts, among them old prohibitions against sin, and she had shaped the pain, or happiness, they might foretell: she had decided, of a Thursday afternoon, that Cecil Fitzgerald Toomer, sometime nitwit, was the man she could best mean love with by making it to.

I, on the other hand, was not thinking at all. Like a schoolboy asked to cha-cha at cotillion, my hands were stuffed in my pockets, and I was doing well not to shuffle my feet or hem-haw too loud. "When?" I said, a question so pathetic I am still embarrassed to have uttered it. "Now," she said. I thought of her room, which she had said was upstairs, and the black lacquer bed she claimed was the biggest in Bernallio County. I wondered too about the amused looks her dogs were giving me. "Where?" I said, the last of my clever responses. I considered her kitchen, which was small, and its cold tile floor, and her dining room, whose every flat surface seemed covered with papers related to the inheritance she was pointedly indifferent to. I saw the corner of a rug that appeared now tattered and certainly too scratchy. And then I came back to her eyes and the irresistible invitation they were. "Here," she said.

Neither was I thinking when Miss Mary Louise unzipped my Levi's and urged me down on top of her, a cane chair shoved sidelong to make space for us. It is only now—in this summer two years later when I am divorced, when Coach Ewing is dead, when my former family has moved back to Deming in Luna County to live with its faithful relations, and when Mary Louise and I are planning the honeymoon Paris, France, is supposed to be—it is only now, thousands of hours removed from the events herein, that I am thinking, really thinking; and what I see, in the film I close my eyes to watch, is a man unaware but wholehearted—a man a bit like Purvis L. Watkins before he fumbled. Silly as it sounds, this man I was, whose body always seemed too big for the indoors, was giving her, like a model sportsman, all the things and conditions and states of mind he was: He was muscle and grit, the greasy foods he hated but gobbled down anyway, the dreams he half remembered, the shitkicker music his boots tapped to, the marvels (good and bad) he was always shocked by, the real and made-up histories he was, the Catholic growing-up he'd had. He, the me I used to be, was giving her, in the square yards of floor they lay on, all he knew: his first kiss and the winter he'd run his fastest, the drunk he'd too often been, the only fist he'd thrown in a fight that had blood in it.

Then we were finished, sweaty and sore and altogether light-headed. Time had started again. The walls went straight again, the roof clamped down like a box. "Oooohhh-weeee," Miss Mary Louise said, like a cowgirl.

Lordy, those next months were weird—those months before Bubba woke to Cecil the way, years and years before, Purvis L. Watkins had awakened to his own peculiar world of woe. Your hero, I say, had two lives. In one I could be seen, say, in Ekerd's drugstore, in tow the versions of myself that are Bobby and Samuel, buying Crest toothpaste or Mennen deodorant, paying from the sixth-grade shop project in leather that is my wallet; in the other, by twilight or noon itself, I could be seen in Vincent's Blue Moon Lounge or Butera's Cafe, the hairier part of a snuggle or the louder half of a ho-ho-ho. In one life, itself not craven or deprived or ruined, I paid a mortgage and bills from Southwestern Bell and Dillard's; in the other, I held a tumbler of Jack Daniel's and lounged most agreeably in a green deck chair constructed by the best hammer-and-nail socialists in Sweden. In one life, itself fine enough and honest, I got to grab an undergraduate by the facemask and announce what it is rover backs are obliged to do on weekends—which is to sunder and to rend and generally to stuff an opponent into the foul middle of last month; in the other life, I was myself snatched by the cheeks or ears and told where the self sits and how meaning is refracted—that was Mary Louise's word, indeed—through the lens of our limited perception. Peculiar to say—yes: strange, strange, strange—I passed nimbly life to life. I want to add, if I can be only sixty percent sappy about it, that in one life I was a fish; in the other, a bird. A rock in one; a tree in the other. Finally, because of the way insight works, particularly that which (as my father used to say) smites us hard and quick, I was nothing.

"Do you have something to tell me?" Stacy Jean asked that week in October my marriage was to stop and I was to find myself blubbering again like an infant. We sat in our family room, Stacy Jean reading a good-versus-evil spy novel she liked and me making the X's and O's and arrows and lines that illustrate what piling on and crackback blocks can do. I had lines scrawled here and lines wriggled there and, until Stacy Jean directed me to tell her what was going on and why I was as distant from her as the moon is from Miami, I was completely beguiled by a vision of football as precious and tidy as college philosophy. "Something's bothering you," she said. My head snapped up as if I'd been clobbered, and I found myself, as if awakened by a siren, in the real world again. I would like to report that she asked me if there was another woman or if I loved her still, but she didn't. I looked ill, she said. Maybe I needed a checkup? I was tossing and turning in bed, I was stumbling into furniture, I was babbling—facts I was totally ignorant of. "I'm fine," your hero told her, mostly not an untruth.

Here it was that I took her in, this longtime wife of mine. I thought of the sixteen years we'd been together, the presents I'd given her and how rough I could sometimes be. I thought of the fancy underwear she looked appealing in and the eight cuss words she used as effectively as teachers use chalk. I thought of her folks, Winona and Bill, and how, as ranchers, they were wholesome as milk. She was good, I thought. She liked to garden. She had patience with the lamebrained and foolhardy. That was Monday. On Tuesday, as she is now someone you are reading about, so she seemed to me to be a person I had only read of, a character out of Hardy or Charles Dickens or Leon Uris. She ate spaghetti with a fork, forsook dancing when the Watusi came in, could make a fist the littleness of which could make you gasp. She was a heroine about whom I knew many things—her birth weight at the Mimbres Valley Hospital in 1948, her green-and-white Wildcat cheerleader outfit, the Yamaha motorcycle she once liked to ride, the enduring contempt she had for Richard Nixon, the ups and downs she suffered; but except for the final chapter, those pages having to do with her dumbstruck, wayward husband and his bye-bye to her, I had, Lordy, finished my reading of Stacy Jean Richards Toomer.

On Wednesday, so it has been reported to me, I assembled my players on the practice field to harangue them about love. Our opponent that Saturday was Colorado State, so there were many, I gather, who were befuddled by a speech that never once mentioned valor or the digging down victory comes from. I don't recall any of this, I confess. Not the slightest word. But even now, from boys who are Juniors and Seniors, I hear how I climbed the tower to holler down at them, how I used a bullhorn and appeared deeply angry. There was fall sunlight and a bell ringing and New Mexico noises elsewhere, and there was, I am told, this crazy man shouting about affection and what a withered landscape we wander in. There were linebackers and nose tackles and defensive ends, and there was this fellow dressed in shorts and a UNM Department of Athletics T-shirt bellowing about the swell and warp love could be in those the bushwhacked victims of it. This exhausted an hour, I hear. Coach Toomer, I hear, talked about sapsuckers and dipsticks and those who are mollycoddled overmuch. I hear that Coach Toomer, wearing dark glasses and a baseball cap that looked slept on, made fists and pointed in the high and low directions wisdom comes from. He called for reason and its antithesis. He called for a breaking apart and a putting together again.

Geez, he called for sowing and reaping.

These were boys from Alpine and DeWitt and Forest City, boys who majored in poly sci and bio and comp lit, and they were urged to consider all that stood apart from elections and paramecia and foreign gobbledygook. They were introduced, instead, to creatures named Stacy Jean and Mary Louise. They got to hear about Little Leaguers named Robert William and Samuel Beck. These players, students big as refrigerators and violent as hailstorms, heard about dreams, which are the waste of you; and actions, which are not. They heard how much greater they were than the sum of their no-account parts. The word "spirit" was used, as were the gestures said to be occasioned by it. A cloud whisked by. And a second. You could hear

raspy, shallow breathing and watch athlete eyeballs shift round
and round nervously. The bullhorn clicked off, clicked on.
Then it went tumbling in the direction of Section H, Rows 9
through 15. Coach Toomer called for a glass of Gatorade, I
understand, and one was brought him.

"Coach was loco," was what I heard later; is what, in fact,
I still hear from time to time. Coach was off his rocker, his
marbles spilled, the inside of him fractured and collapsed.
Coach, in his tower and wobbling, was most out of touch, as
cut loose and moil-minded a human as is possible in sunlight.
He mentioned rain and related elements from the sky, and
screamed down at one huh-faced boy, "See?" And that boy,
who was from Espanola in the north and was no smarter at
football than was Daffy Duck at dancing, went "yes" with his
head in a fashion that made you fear what muscles "no" used.
In the next minute, Coach talked about the body, which was
vehicle and medium and incarnation of the goo your mind
invented. "Do you dingleberries see?" Coach asked, clearly
displeased they did not. "You understand, Bigmouth?" And
Bigmouth, a spoon-faced safety with feet the size of pontoons
and a three-speed brain shaped, it was believed, like a loaf of
bread, said, "Hell, yes, Coach!"

And so commenced another paragraph, the sharpest points
of which were Coach's opinions about dress-wearing and the
miracle hips are, plus what we are inclined to feel when spring
rolls around. "I am trying to account for things here," Coach
said, now using a second bullhorn so those still asleep in North
Dakota could hear. Another hour had gone by, in the tick-tock
way time can, and noboby had moved a lick. Even in the silent
seconds, when Coach seemed especially cockeyed and heaven-
sent, his players, all ninety-six of them, were paralyzed, a contraption he had built, dismantled and flung the makings of all
around.

"Love," Coach Toomer said, giving the word eight syllables
and half the color wheel. Why not call it hair, he wondered.
Or teeth. Or the food you had for breakfast. What was wanted

was a new word, one shook free of the la-la-la Romeos swoon over. For that purpose, he said, football was a fine word too, and a fairer approximation of what havoc happens between boys and girls. Foot-goddam-ball. Love needed some rules, he declared, along with impartial folks in stripes whose job it was to say when, and how badly, you messed up. Hell, some structure was called for, some cheek-popping whistle-blowing that signaled you had a half-minute to conjure up new plans for going headlong at it. "Ha," Coach said, in what may or may not have been a laugh. "Ha-goddam-ha."

Later that evening, much as I had on another evening in the "yore" I spoke of earlier, I tried to explain to Stacy Jean what had happened to me. I described how I had climbed down from my tower, the going up an exercise I did not remember at all. I mentioned how I'd suddenly whipped into wakefulness, finding myself walking through a clot of my players, theirs the faces you see on those who've witnessed a car wreck or similar calamity. I used the word "goggle-eyed" to describe my own expression and mentioned the roundabout path I'd taken to my Toyota in the parking lot. I used the word "tired" to say how I'd felt; "nothing" to say what I knew. I had regarded the sun, which had been orange as a flagman's vest, and wondered how love is lived in paradise. Stacy Jean was being herself solicitous, asking if I wanted a drink and what would I say to a visit from Dr. Weymann, our GP. I had her one hand in mine, and in my mind three-quarters of a sentence in regard to the bags I'd pack in a few minutes, and then—about the moment, I think, when Stacy Jean plainly understood what I had not yet said—I heard it: that blubbering me.

As I had been years ago, I was again cold. And cogitating too. I was wondering about the rattling insides of me, the clatter my hooks and hasps made breaking loose. Wait, I told myself. Consider. I had a "why" question, and a "how" and a "when." "Bubba?" Stacy Jean said, a name I could not for the life of me make sensible. As before, the it in me was crying: a tear on one cheek, a second on the other. Its mouth dropped open and its face, I suppose, was like Purvis L. Watkins's own, wonder-filled and baffled, the victim of ten or ten thousand ideas at once. As before, it, the me I was, desired answers. To questions about the forward movement of living life. About what to do with weakness. About why it is we have the hearts we do, and how it is they work.

THE WHO,
THE WHAT
AND THE WHY

Only sixteen months after our daughter's death from, improbable as it may seem in the nowadays and hereabouts, mononucleosis, I began breaking into my own house, as expert a sneak thief as if I had taken to the trade as a toddler.

The first time, I burst out of sleep as if crawling up from the deep end of our swimming pool, breathless and arm-weary, a man—if you'd seen him splashing and kicking—who clearly had not been exercising for pleasure. It was two A.M., dark as dark gets in fairy tales, and I remember that from one state of being to the other, from sleep to wakefulness, I carried nothing, as if whatever I'd stumbled upon in my dreams—the who and the what and the why—had broken free of me, as gone from me as was our daughter, Harriet. I remember slipping out of bed, my wife, Jimmie Sue, as imperturbable as a log; it was Thursday, which meant in the spring this takes place that she had school tomorrow (two dozen fifth-graders whose job it was to learn from her some long division and when to use "who" and "whom"); for me, as I went downstairs in my robe, this day meant that only hours from now I'd drive down the valley to the airport and fly to Dallas to find myself, more hours later, in a studio, its walls acoustically perfect, saying, for enough money to buy a Toyota truck, what is scrumptious about Fritos corn chips.

I am, you see, a "voice," meaning that if you have been watching TV at all or listening to the radio in markets served by what ad agencies in Dallas or Phoenix or sometimes L.A. can accomplish, then you have heard me, in the "warm and fuzzy" tones I am hired for, say what is written in regard to United Airlines, or Buick LeSabres, or the symphony of Columbus, Ohio. But on the morning I am now telling you about, I was only and thoroughly me—Robert "Bobby" Patterson, a once-upon-a-time Rice University political science major, a U.S. Army reject (bad feet and a heart murmur), a husband for nearly two decades—the kind of guy who at too many liquor-fueled parties over the years has tried the backflips and handsprings people probably ooh over at the Olympics.

I rose, I have since said to my wife, as if I'd heard a voice calling, and wandered a time, not disoriented entirely but in fact a little bit slack-minded, as if part of me—the parts, scientists say, that still belong to reptiles or what we share with even less-scaly scraps of life—was putting off for a time what it knew it had to do, the way you put off the Brussels sprouts till you've finished the baked potato. In my office, a big room with lots of shelves and plenty of space to build the model airplanes I like, I sat at my desk, fiddling with the light switch on my lamp. My insides, I say, were not knotted or otherwise distressed, but I was, well, anxious, a man either early for a date or, like the White Rabbit, very, very late. Then I was up, out my sliding glass doors and around the cool deck, the pool waters undisturbed, our corner of the desert here in El Paso as clean-smelling as wind and emptiness can combine to be. Behind me reared one hump of the Franklin Mountains, atop which is nothing except radio antennae that go blink-blink-blink, and below me, down the curvy gravel road we own, sat the big homes that belong to the Coronado Country Club, where I sometimes go to take a drink in the men's locker with the far-flung neighbors I have up here (men like Forry Bell and Tubby Walker, who wonder good-naturedly how it is I can make so much money and usually not have anything productive to do before eleven in the morning or after two in the afternoon).

It's funny, I believe now, but you can think many things when you are dressed in your pajamas and slippers and you are walking over terrain that awfully much resembles the moon and there are hostile creatures that live mainly in the dark and don't much like whatever it is we are too near wherever it is they hide. So I was thinking about that—snakes and rabid coyotes and lizards whose unexpected lefts and rights can make you piss your pants—and I was thinking too about an affair I'd once had with a flyweight redhead who could yodel and could herself go unexpectedly left and right with visible vigor; and about a conquistador treasure said to be buried in the Organ Mountains north of here, and about what it must be like to leap out of an airplane with nothing to save you but a sack on your back, made from silk and rope, and considerable good faith in the fellow who'd packed it. And then—this is the genuinely spooky stuff—I was not thinking any longer. I was, in fact, not even me, not Bobby Patterson at all: as transformed as Jekyll was to Hyde, I was one Tom H-for-Harding Butters, a felon, a man with three ex-wives, a Harley-Davidson tattoo on his forearm, and passing ability to pluck the guitar country-style. I had drunk poison, the goo chronic grief is, and I had become Tom Butters—from Cobb County in Georgia, I think, an eleventh-grade dropout but able to add and subtract enough to know when he was being effectively diddled—and I was strolling up a road in the hills west of El Paso, muttering, "Well-well, easy pickings tonight."

So it was that Tom Butters went easily into your hero's almost paid-for house (through a sliding glass door that some dumb ass must've left unlocked) and thereupon helped himself to what Jimmie Sue Patterson, the wife, later held was trash the criminal element was most welcome to: namely, a 32nd-scale model of a USAF Flying Fortress and a gag jewelry box with half a Wilson golf ball glued to the top, plus an armful of books having to do with Wild West gunslingers and perhaps sixty dollars in pesos from a jam jar on her husband's desk. All in all, Jimmie Sue would say in the morning (and later to the police that State Farm insisted upon), it wasn't so much the "valuables," as it was the weirdness of the whole shebang—the way she'd arisen before the alarm and without disturbing her snoring husband, and how she found everything strangely out of order: a couch moved, the refrigerator open, pictures re-hung, the heat lamp glowing in the guest bath, Bobby's new pitching wedge on the glass coffee table in the living room, all the Tanya Tucker tapes rearranged.

Sure, I had a memory of this, but not first-hand. I felt I'd seen Tom Butters in a movie, not necessarily a fine one either, and while Jimmie Sue stormed around that morning, saying "Jesus H." and "Can you believe this?" I went around too, also as open-mouthed and astounded as my offended wife, remembering this or that about Tom Butters. I remembered Tom Butters going into my office and playing with the doohickeys he found there, and how stupidly depressed he was to discover that the only items worth taking—computer and TV and VCR, for example—you'd need a truck and certainly another villain to get away with. I remembered how he slumped in the easy chair my mother had given me for my fortieth birthday, his feet put up exactly as I do mine, and how he wished for three fingers of Seagram's red-eye to sip while he made up his mind. Tom Butters was thinking about a song he liked, a sighin'-dyin'-cryin' tune that mentioned hope and wings, and what he ought to be doing in life and what sort of Nashville cowboy star he'd be; then he roused himself, semiburdened by the goofy curios he had my sense of humor for, and thought to mosey around this house for twenty minutes, pretending he lived up here in the foothills with distant neighbors you'd have to use a bullhorn to get the full attention of.

And then this ended, the movie my memory was, and I, entirely myself, told Jimmie Sue to do what had to be done, law-wise, and that I'd call from Dallas that night. I was stand-ing in my kitchen, something in me rattling like a marble in a tin cup, and I was promising myself—just as I have promised here to tell the truth and nothing but—that I wouldn't think again about Tom Butters, or who in me he was, until much, much later, until I'd told you and you and you out there, in take after take after take, what it is about, oh, Whey, Gum Arabic, Malic Acid and Disodium Inosinate that Kellogg's claims is such a cotton-picking delight to eat with bananas for breakfast.

I know you're probably skeptical about the daughter business, about how likely it is to die from a disease you get from kissing or running yourself down. But, I say to you now, it is possible in America for someone—let's say, for argument's sake and without personalizing overmuch, a child—to feel bad, and then worse, and finally rotten in a way that will require machines and catheters and not enough dollars in the world to fix, and that all your high school pals will find themselves in a Presbyterian church listening to J. S. Bach's "Sheep May Safely Graze" and attending to what can be learned from Old Testament lessons out of Ecclesiastes. Notwithstanding your nice manners and how gifted you are around the piano, or the color of your favorite horse, it is possible—hell, I have Autopsy #A88-216 to prove it—to get Epstein-Barr virus and to have your immune system degraded and so acquire, against whatever odds doctors earn a living from, acute interstitial pneumonia, and thereafter find yourself the victim of "purulent exudate" and "pelvic venous plexis"; and soon enough you become a child who will in twenty days curl up and turn yellow and finally go somewhere, according to the beeping hardware over your bed in ICU, where the numbers are all zero and the lines all flat.

It is likewise possible for that child's father to go flat-out crazy eventually and, from the life he'd led or the dreams he'd dreamed, become as many someone elses as China has Chinamen. The second time I was Hector Walls (aka Herkie, Harold, Hank), with a bum leg and three-page list of felony arrests plus a health-nut parole officer who was really fussy about the ciga-

rettes I smoked. As Tom Butters had, I went in the sliding glass
door by the pool, rested in Bobby Patterson's leather chair and,
once I got my night vision, fed myself a plateful of chicken
salad from the Amana. I had a girlfriend named Peggy (whose
do-what-I-say face came to me two or three times while I crept
throughout this place), not to mention a pound dog named
Cannibal that I had no problem at all seeing in residence here.
As Bobby Patterson reconstructs it now, Herkie Walls must've
spent several hours on the first floor, turning over cushions,
peeking behind paintings (maybe for a wall safe, I don't know),
lying for a time on the bed in the guest room, leaving dirt from
his workboots on the quilt Jimmie's granny had made her for
a wedding present. And then it was morning, sharp and bright
and blue as poster paint: Jimmie was up first and yelling at her
lazybones husband to get out of bed and see this.

Herkie, it turned out, was a vandal, and, sad to say, when I
beheld what he'd wrought, I was for a minute scared, my heart
banging in my ears. Something was being asked of me, I
thought. Something drastic, or heroic. So I tried to tell Jimmie,
as she stood aghast in our living room, that, well, I had the
feeling I'd seen this before. "Oh, Bobby," she scolded, "just
shut the hell up." I took a minute with myself, thought of my
organs, the chunks and hunks and slabs of them, whirling in
a pool under my heart.

As before, I had no real memory of this, just a prickliness
akin to déjà vu or other sensations I suppose there are fancy
foreign phrases for, but by then Jimmie Sue was cursing, asking
what on earth in the direction of our curtains, which had been
torn, and of the junky clutter that was once expensive, even
fine Mexican pottery. Hers was behavior that scared me too,
and so it was easy—as easy as reciting lines strangers have
written down for you—just to keep quiet and make my way to
the phone to complain to an ear at the other end of the line
that the Pattersons, Bobby and Jimmie Sue, had been again
robbed and maybe a little bit terrorized.

That day I had no obligations, no product or service to be

sincere about, so I followed the police around and watched Jimmie Sue kick at the mess Herkie Walls had made—the broken this, the smashed that. I was trying to be generally helpful, plus not too much amazed when tracks were discovered that went uphill a ways and at last disappeared where the ground turned to rock. Only one time did I think to confess what I knew and that was when the police were gone and Jimmie Sue was saying for me to call Rosalita, our cleaning lady, and then to call Carl Probert, her principal, to make apologies for being late: I was looking at the screen to our front door, how an X had been slashed in it, and, suddenly, when I opened my mouth (my eyes squeezed shut as they do when it is your job on earth to concentrate and nothing more), knowing Jimmie Sue had stopped on the stairs to hear me, I "saw," as if on film, Herkie Walls go out the door and wheel around to face me. Instantly, day became night—Jimmie Sue not on the stairs but still in dreamland, all that had happened yet to be discovered—and there was your narrator as Herkie Walls, me awake to myself, ours the evil eyes truly bad guys see the world through, ours the grin thoughtless ravaging can make. I felt something tear free and, like a boulder, go tumbling and crashing downward toward the bottom of me.

"What?" Jimmie Sue said. Apparently I had spoken, or blurted "uh" with shock, but I waved my arm to say it was nothing, and a part of me in the here and now watched a part of me in the then and there go limping slowly into the darkness.

For a time after this, no one in me came to burgle at night. Summer rolled round with many parties to go to and many art-worthy sunsets to shout about. Jimmie Sue was taking a course at UTEP—recertification credit, I think, more words and handouts about, hell, playground management or what to do when a third-grader tells you to take a flying fuck—and I flew off every week or so to this recording studio or that to utter for hours and hours sometimes what would only be twenty or thirty seconds in actual airtime. That summer, I was doing lots of characters. "Be a grit," the producer would say, and for a morning I was, a hayseed's hayseed, a clodhopper in bib overalls with mud between his toes. One day I was a PM, as British and merry-old as kidney pie; the next, as Swiss as chocolate. This was fun for me, I tell you, to put to work an imagination I didn't often use and then use it to urge you to fly to St. Croix or to buy your love seat from the White House on Pisano Street.

Jimmie Sue and I were in good spirits, time putting between us and one hideous memory many new and better ones: we were going away from Harriet, going forward while behind, like a stretch of road you are relieved to see the last of, there remained only no-account markers—a fight you shouldn't have had, a drunk you shouldn't have been—to say what had befallen you way back when. Except for moments the words for which always began "Remember when," Jimmie Sue had recovered, and I too was mostly whole, only a little bit like a crybaby when I was alone for too long or when I had to go into Harriet's room to find in the closet something we'd stored there. Still, this was a good summer, filled with folks like Forry Bell and his wife, Marty, who sold me stocks that did right well (as promised), and a vacation we took to the Yucatán peninsula to see how it was when, as the foolish song goes, the world was young. We were like youngsters ourselves, Jimmie Sue and I, courting ourselves anew, bathing often enough to be conspicuous, phoning at odd hours to say one or the other was missed, and making love in the way Tubby Walker claims is mostly funny bone, kneecap and satin sheet.

And then they came back, our nighttime visitors, the legion of men I was and was and was. Unlike Herkie Walls, they were not cruel but peculiar, even sad, taking a cookie or watching TV. They were named Tunch and Philly Dog and A.T., and they arrived from such places as Wyoming and Yorba Linda, California, men who had once been fine but were now not. They ate with our silverware or helped themselves to my blue jeans and sometimes wrote a note with my typewriter to say thank you. More than once, after it became clear that really no danger was involved, Jimmie Sue volunteered to stay downstairs, to keep watch. "I'm gonna catch one of these jokers," she said, "find out what the deal is." The first time, I woke to find her fully clothed on the living room couch, a pot of coffee handy, curled asleep with a flashlight held to her chest, on an end table a birthday cake, in the center of it a candle you'd use in a blackout. Another morning, all her shoes, high-heeled and not, were lined up in front of her, like soldiers on parade, and another time our laundry was folded and sorted and set in stacks to be put away. "Jumping Jesus," she said, laughing about it, this as much a joke to her as what passes for humor in the headlines. "Jumping damn Jesus." And, of course, through it all we told nobody, as there didn't seem any way to explain, short of theories too bizarre and hokey to be believed, that Jimmie Sue and Bobby were, well, being trespassed upon by ghosts or hoboes or whatevers that liked to spirit away with them such goodies as golf tees, Tupperware jugs and every copy of *House & Garden* magazine.

In September, when Jimmie Sue had to go back to school, it fell to me to stay up nights, to keep watch. I felt foolish, like a chicken in a bikini, but I was a good boy and, having been told what to do, I did it. So every night after Carson, after a kiss or two, and if I didn't have a morning appointment or work that required a plane trip, I'd stay up, arrange myself in my study, acclimate myself to the night and become reacquainted with the sounds that come up after the sun goes down. But they didn't come, the men I was. Not a one. At first, I was relieved, content to have myself back as myself, but then, owing to restlessness and ordinary fear, I was lonely, even sore for companionship, a little bit angry that I—so I backasswardly reasoned it—had been abandoned. I felt bony and broken off and too clumsy for the indoors, a man composed of coat hangers and galvanized roofing nails. And then he returned, Herkie Walls.

I had been standing at the door, blue-hearted and somehow

mournful, and when I said as much to my backyard, he was there again, in a T-shirt and jean jacket, already angry and mean-minded. "Howdy, partner," he said, his smile too toothy to be life-lifting, and, feeling half of me wander off and dry up, I stepped aside to make way for him. He was me all right, a man with my hair gone whichaway and no concern at all for posture, a me as I might have turned out, a me with no wife or pals or dead daughter to dwell on.

It's an unsettling feeling to be in- and outside yourself at the same time, but—and one reason this story's being told—I was, Bobby watching Herkie, Herkie going headlong about his business. This time he went upstairs, in a manner that suggested he'd had lots of practice since last he was in my house, and I followed, not at all surprised that he headed straight for our bedroom, the door open, only my wife in there and whatever heaven she was dreaming of. For a minute or two, he stood at the foot of our bed, his expression sidelong and cocked, like a dog that has heard something far off and perplexing, and then he touched her, his finger to her foot, and I understood he was thinking clearly about what a choice item she was and how, if he pulled back the covers, which he did, he could study her in her nightie and maybe know fifteen or twenty things about himself and what he'd returned for.

Breathing shallow, his face twenty percent improved by shadows, he didn't move, just peered and peered, something about this woman vital to him, and then she stirred, mumbled, "What?" still mostly sleep-soaked, and Herkie, his voice mine, said, "That's okay, baby," and not another thing until, in the hall, I put a hand to his shoulder and told him no.

He was about to go into Harriet's room, and so we had a moment then, me and me. Time was spreading, I could tell, running out of groove, my house a jumble of angles and corners and nooks to hurt yourself on, and I was overtaken with the need to speak in a hurry, three words at once almost, to say that there was nothing in that room that he'd want, not a thing, the valuables and mementos given away to friends or donated, even the clothes gone to be useful elsewhere. He seemed confused, maybe split inside himself, and so in a strangled whisper I tried to tell him how it was and how I just wanted to be left alone by him and others like him, those who were the sour and vicious and lowlife in me.

"Go away," I told him, the center of me frozen to a point, "just go the hell away." But he didn't move, the son of a bitch. A little time went by. And, in the drip-drip way time can, some more. We were there, eyeball to eyeball, Herkie and Bobby, a fellow and his counterpart, and then an alarm was going off too loud, and I had nothing but sunrise to face.

"Slow the dickens down, son," my father used to tell me, an instruction easy to give when you're, as he is at sixty-six, rich and civil and have several girlfriends to coddle. But it was instruction I saw the wisdom of after that encounter with Herkie Walls, instruction I seemed to take so completely to heart that by the time I ran into Tom H-for-Harding Butters in Harriet's room nearly a month later, I was almost at a complete stop, inert as a stone and only a little bit more sentient.

Tom was clearly sad, ruminative and thrown back on himself, and so was I, this being the anniversary of Harriet's death and thus an occasion which calls for much recollection though very little chitchat. I had awakened, I have told Jimmie Sue, not with a start but nevertheless all at once, coming to life after midnight the way you see runners cross the finish line, exhausted and absolutely through with themselves and normal stuff. As before, I had gone outdoors, seemed to spin round three or four times and then returned, approaching Bobby Patterson's house the way you see people go up to doors they expect to be shooed away from. This was the end, I guessed, and nothing to do but have it.

Time had not been kind to Tom Butters: he'd had, as it is put in the fat novels I like, reversals—a sweetheart lost or too smart for him, not enough money to go when beckoned, some work he was too proud to do well—and right now, in memory, I see him collapsed on my daughter's bed, too lanky for the thing really, his hands behind his head, eyes open to what the ceiling might reveal. Plainly, he felt hollow that night, somehow less than the three that one and one and one come to, and for a time he was bitterly amused by the idea of himself as a contraption with not much to do except eat and drink and repeat the penny-ante hopes he had. He was dreaming about going somewhere—the South Seas, Timbuktu, Oz—and then he was not, knowing there was nowhere to go that was not itself already too much like this place and time. He did wonder, however, why this room was so—well, "emptified" was his word, sterile and cell-like, perfect for thinking as it turned out but at the same time a room that nearly leeched your thoughts right out of your head and left you too breath-defeated to argue about it.

At this point in the movie of me that I told Jimmie Sue about, Tom Butters heard a noise and got up to find it, indifferent to the creaks the bedsprings made. In the center of the room, he turned his head a little but often, and got himself straight with east and west. A party was going on somewhere, he believed, and if the noise kept up, he'd find it soon enough and so make some sense out of the whoops and ho-ho-hos reaching him across the dry, windswept hinterlands. At Harriet's window, the one from which she used to yell down to us at the pool, the Tom Butters in me stood gazing, near then far, adjusting his field of vision, making notes to himself about what was and what wasn't. He was singing another song, I think, this one echoey and twang-filled and heart-thumping, and then he wasn't: what had sharpened into view were two men under an extremely bright yard-light about a hundred yards away—the Forry Bell and Tubby Walker that Tom did not know—smacking golf balls into the desert.

They were happy men, all right, a bit under the influence but more like animals in their joy than like humans who should know better, and so for the next half-hour, he watched them,

as pleased with them as they were with themselves, the picture
of grown men being juvenile and heedless under a lamplight
as good for Tom's insides as water is for thirst. They whacked
and flailed and swatted, sometimes stumbling about to get
their balance, and Tom Butters could see that though they
weren't good or even remotely athletic, they were indeed en-
thusiastic, not mindful at all regarding any of the do's and
don'ts daylight seemed too full of. They were average as dirt,
he decided, just more blessed by happenstance, and so there
didn't seem to be any reason—not one, at least, that couldn't
be wished away or laughed right in the fat face of—for him not
to join them.

"Go on over there, boy," he told himself, and then waited
for his legs to work. He was having a debate with himself,
clearly, taking up this idea and that, weighing what had weight
in him and what didn't. He scratched his chin, brooded seriously over himself. He'd get a haircut, he was thinking. Maybe
do four or five thousand sit-ups. Later get a tuba and learn to
toot it. Then, nodding affirmatively and putting down the
ticky-tack he'd arranged to steal (a map of the North Pole and
a shoehorn and a shamrock suspended in glass), he whirled
around fast, eager to get going and not mooning over himself
any longer, and—poof!—it was only me again in the world.

Just like that, like presto and abracadabra, it was me throwing on my robe and slippers, heading toward the garage for a
bucket of balls and my three-iron. They were forever gone,
these men I was, and I, hollering happily, was charging out the
door, aiming to wake West Texas with the noise in my heart.

LIVING AFTER MIDNIGHT

FOR JEFF H. AND BILL C.—
FROM THE GUY
ON THE THIRD FLOOR OF CLARK

IN THE MIDDLE OF THE NIGHT,
WITH YOUR COVERS PULLED UP TIGHT
IT'LL COME TO YOU.

—JOHN HIATT

LARRY, CURLY & MOE

DESE ARE DE CONDITIONS DAT PREVAIL.

—JAMES FRANCIS DURANTE

Reed met Hoffman in Gephart's freshman Intro to Comp Lit, a M-W-F lecture as notorious for the old fart's life-is-hell worldview as for its twenty-pound reading list of what Hoffman called deep-thinking European riffraff: bearded and self-absorbed sourpusses like Heidegger and Kant and Schopenhauer. By the end of the hour, after Gephart had thoroughly defaced every blackboard in CLK 202 with scribbled insights from everybody but Superman and Betty Boop, Hoffman and Reed were best friends.

"Being and nothingness," Hoffman said. "Awesome line."

"Killer material," Reed said, trying to keep pace: he'd felt it too—the way the words had gone in like fishhooks, barbed and bent enough to rip coming out.

"Hoffman and Reed," his new buddy said. "Natural damn philosophers."

A week later, they rushed the same frat, Phi Delta Gamma, the one with the most venal view of scholastic life. They learned the rules, the secret handshake, how a Greek greets a Greek coming through the rye. Jumping Jesus, Reed would think later, what a semester. They did the cornball pranks—a Zeta Tau panty raid, the diaper dash across Mather Quad, the pimple pop, merely the most adolescent shit in America—and

celebrated their change from pledge to active status by crashing a nitrous party at the dental school, where they found
amusement by saying "tee-hee-hee" and by articulating,
H-man's word, what pleasures might be discovered at the intersection of the raunchy and the lurid.

In the middle of the party, Hoffman rose, snatched himself
up on what he described as his high horse. He looked around
as Reed believed Caesar had.

"I'm thinking of the material world," he said, "which is
emblematic of a higher reality. What're you thinking?"

Confusion filled that room like a rank smell, all the doctors
looking sideways at one another.

"Me too," Reed said at last. "I'm thinking what he's thinking."

"We only have three choices," H-man said.

There were seven strangers in the room—Grumpy, Sleepy,
Dopey, et cetera—and so there were seven facial expressions
that more or less said, "Who the fuck is this guy?", a question
Reed guessed could best be answered by fists and by jumping
feet-first into the midst of them.

"Move, ascend or vanish," H-man said. "Otherwise, we're
just picking cotton."

By Thanksgiving, they'd gotten a class-C license, and had
gone on WRUW, a Sunday earlybird show called "The Mike
and Ike Turf Club and Surf Shoppe," two hours of dawn-
related, if obtuse, music and revelations of the sort heard in a
riot. They were into dope now—pot, black beauties, whippets,
X, white crosses—narcotics that encouraged introspection expressed in sentences that went whoop-whoop-wham. Their first
morning on the air, they told stories. They were foundlings,
they claimed, the offspring of Ohio white slavers from Youngstown and Medina, respectively. Reed told about his first girlfriend, a puerile piece of work named Harvelina Vanderbilt
Jax. She'd chopped his heart out with a garden trowel. Fed it
back to him chunk by bloody chunk.

"Now I have Mindy," he told his audience, "the sweetest
girl on earth."

Hoffman was waving his arms, calling time-out, punching every button he could reach on the control board. He could go that one better, he declared: His first, swear on a stack, was a Shetland pony. Named Isabel. These boys were a hoot, Reed said. Batman and Robin. Scylla and Charybdis. Minneapolis and St. Paul.

"All together now," H-man wailed into the microphone, and that morning they ended the program by singing what Johnny Cash had known about that better home awaiting in the sky.

By sophomore year, they were roomies, their double in Cutler approximately two hundred square feet of rubble and circus noise. Shit-fire, they were too untidy even for a frat house: stop signs; the manifold, headers and exhaust system of a Harley-Davidson roadmaster; enough Z-fold to accommodate every word thought or yet to be invented. Very Possible and Nearly Likely: that's what H-man said they were. Reed was still seeing Mindy; H-man a duke's mixture of coeds named after plants or the spring and summer months. Later, Reed remembered this as the prelude, the pray-the-Lord-my-soul-to-keep part of the dream you could smile through before the demons and serpents harried you into the terrible cold that waking up was.

This was before King the dog. Before the pistol. Before the Yalies and the cocaine.

In the fall term, after they'd endured Zubidoo himself and several weeks of no-fault, karatelike instruction in *español* nouns and verbs, they started a magazine, *The Satyr*, photocopying of the most renegade kind, text that advocated anarchy and rapture. They'd taken to introducing themselves as *escritores*, "writers." Ar-damn-tistes. Moody types without much to be solicitous about. But already something was wrong with H-man. Depressing stuff about his mom, who was dangerously obese and had to have her hip joints replaced at the Cleveland Clinic. Plus, his dad, now retired from the navy, was just hanging around the house waiting for a hobby to show up. H-man was distraught. Every night he was smoking sinsemilla. A three-pack-a-day habit of Camel filters. He was using acid—blue cheer, windowpane, a microdot that put you in touch with

God, that forced you to talk Hebrew: You could see through your hand into the next week, inanimate objects followed you home. Moreover, H-man's own weight had shot up.

"I look like Porky Pig," he said. "I got to lay off the Oreos."

"And the Twinkies," Reed told him.

"Wrong," H-man said. "Never underestimate the medicinal value of yellow dye number six."

Throughout the semester, Reed worried. His pal—screw that, his numero uno—was coming undone. Link by link by link. One night he found H-man in the broom closet next to the gang showers at the end of their hall: besides a bucket and some mops and the usual liquids useful for wash and wax, the other thing in there with him was a girl, maybe fifteen, naked.

"See what he's done," she said. She was two parts happy, one part scared, one part shit-faced, and Reed leaned in to study the black scratches on her butt cheeks. He recognized several words, "ibid." and "op. cit." and "quid pro quo," then she indicated her back and what rose into impressive focus was a half-dozen remarks he recognized from the assigned reading in *The Wilson Quarterly*.

"Who's this?" Reed said.

H-man searched near and far, hand shading his eyes à la Lawrence of Arabia.

"Who's what, Ace?"

Slowly, Reed backed out of the utility closet. Up and down the hall, the dorm was a Friday night as practiced by statistics majors and would-be aerospace engineers.

"This isn't funny, H-man."

"You're telling me," he said. "I don't even like Warren Wilson."

Over spring break they published their last issue of *The Satyr*. What a mess, Reed admitted, as attractive as hair on a woman's lip. They named names. Pointed fingers. Espoused a John Birch approach to crime and punishment. Ragged on those acres of the world that Uncle Sugar owned: Israel, South Africa, Cambodia. "Sport," H-man remarked. "A goof," Reed put in. Still, H-man was falling apart, a rickety tower in a hurricane, a vampire without the noteworthy sleeping habits. When he did sleep, a horrible hour to witness, he mumbled and shouted. You couldn't get a "howdy" out of him without twenty minutes of "why" and "wherefore." His cheeks were hollow, his teeth brown as tree bark. His gums bled. He was taking the bullet in all his classes, F's many and absolute enough to foul what should have been a classy transcript. In April, he stumbled into his macroeconomics class from the fire escape, his wallet and keys and change in a Frisbee.

"Go to the health service," Reed told him. "Man, you're a disaster."

H-man rolled his eyes, pounded himself on the chest like Tarzan.

"You've dealt with those people, amigo. They're reptiles, honest to God. Not a mammal among them."

H-man was yammering about himself constantly. He'd had a cat, Fletcher. He'd learned to swim at eight, sucked his thumb till grammar school, collected beer bottles. He'd read everything, he said. *The Jail Diary of Albie Sachs. Ivan*-fucking-*hoe*. He knew how waves worked, particle theory, what made all the little birdies sing *tweet-tweet-tweet*. As a kid, his best friend was Walt, a genuine delinquent. Broke into the Elks club. Vandalized. H-man had played Pee-Wee football, Pop Warner, really liked the thump one body could inflict on another.

"I'm meant for something," he insisted. "I have aspirations, dreams. I just got to discipline myself. Stop being so raggedy-ass."

Reed agreed. They'd pump iron, he said. Play basketball. Eat asparagus, rack out by ten-thirty, lay off the stimulants, say their prayers. No more escapades.

"Tomorrow," Reed said, "we clean this hole, get haircuts. We got about eight million people to apologize to."

H-man unwound himself from the position he'd been fixed in. The Lotus. The Bar-b-que. Something. He was eyeballing the squalor they lived with.

"Affirmative," he said. "I roger that, Capcom."

Damn fine plan, Reed thought. Could've worked too. This was the early eighties. Plans were afoot then, and succeeding. Citizens got up when the alarm buzzed, brushed and flossed, and went forward with deeds to do. All over the world—except in those misery pits where nothing could be done to help—people roused themselves, shook off a fetter or two, and just flat-out pitched themselves headlong into the hubbub. Reed had words for it: "optimism," "confidence," "direction." That's what he told Mindy one night before he went back to his room to study for o-chem. You had to be a go-getter, he said. He'd learned that from his father, a shop steward everybody at Republic Steel knew as Mac. You had to get a fix on, buck up, find out what the code was and cleave to that sucker. You had to be a straight shooter, upstanding in all regards. You couldn't afford to take friendship too lightly. He had a relationship with H-man, soul brother. They were Frick and Frack—another phrase the old man had brought back from the union hall.

"Are you finished?" Mindy said.

Reed felt he'd run out of breath about fifteen minutes ago. "Yes."

Code or no code, Mindy said, Carl Hoffman was a rodent.

Reed took a step back. He'd been slugged in the heart, he thought.

"Someday," Mindy said, "you're gonna have to choose. You have lousy taste in friends, sweetheart."

An hour later Reed stood at the door to his room. A new sign was up, obviously the result of hours of effort with a ruler and industrial-strength markers: it was a story, roundabout and semicheerful, CONTENTS UNDER PRESSURE: DO NOT INCINERATE. Its heroes were Tjorg and Meek, in breastplates and carrying cudgels, theirs a quest into the long-lost and never-was. They liked to go places and hear themselves talked about, the language in reference to them too full of g's and y's to be less than uplifting.

Mindy had been wrong, Reed thought. H-man was just

fouled up, blue-hearted maybe. But you made allowances for
H-man. You bent a little. H-man was steadfast, inflexible as a
ramrod. He was a Boy Scout without the short pants. He had
a photographic memory, could make a corpse laugh. He was
going to amount to something, you could see that. A doctor,
a life-saver. He could stand on his head, yodel. He was merely
going through a bad period, a slump. You could see these
things: if you were zig to his zag, whiz to his bang, you could
see these, and you knew, in the truest place to know such facts,
that he'd pull out. Hoffman was Tjorg; Reed, Meek. Jesus, they
had a whole story ahead of them.

Then Reed threw the door open and noise came rushing out
of there like air out of tomb.

"Welcome, earthling," H-man said, and Reed heard in
H-man's voice a note or two that said his buddy was still gone.
He was in a closet somewhere. On a moon.

"I was thinking about dinner," Reed said, making conversation. He had chosen, he understood. He really, really had.

"I ate," H-man said. "I had gruel. Porridge. Fatback."

"What about class?"

"Dropped it," H-man said. "I had a vision. It was a musical,
lots of tap-dancing. The narrator held up a sign, told me to bag
natural science."

In one corner huddled H-man, ragged, his hair an angry
storm cloud, his shirt shredded. In the other corner crouched
the dog, and Reed had one thought: if there were canines on
Mars, this was one. This was definitely one.

"Say hello to King," H-man told him. "King, speak to the
man."

There'd been a fight, clearly. The beast was mangled, an ear
dangling, its coat plucked out in patches. Plus, it had too many
teeth and too much blue tongue to lick them with.

"This animal has had a past life," H-man said. "Two years
ago, it was a retired State Farm executive with a Volvo."

Reed tried to follow the words. He saw himself collecting
them, like playing cards, a large number of which you'd need

to understand what the hell was going on; then, after he
noticed the pistol at H-man's feet, he let the cards go, all of
them, as if a hurricane was blowing down on him. It was a .22,
he thought. A Colt, maybe. Hell, he didn't know. But it was
shiny—chrome or nickel—and the realest thing he'd seen in
twenty years. His heart had slammed into his stomach like a
fist—Whomp—and he knew instantly that this was no room
to which he could ever again bring somebody as sweet and
wrong as his girlfriend Mindy.

"This dog can read," H-man was saying. "You don't want
to frustrate a dog like this."

Reed could believe that. Frustration. Literate canines.

"This animal can tell time," H-man continued. "You also
don't want to say anything, for example, about its heritage or
country of national origin."

He could believe that as well.

"Most of all, if you're a normal person, you just want to ease
on out of its presence, leave a dog like this and its master to
their very own selves."

Reed was concentrating on the pistol. He had an impression
of himself turning away on his heels and bolting headlong out
the door, arms flying above his head in fear.

"Tell me I don't see that," he said at last.

H-man regarded the weapon, pulled his blanket over it.

"Out of sight," he said, "out of mind."

For Reed, catching his breath was like fielding a baseball
dropped from the top of Terminal Tower.

"Where'd you get it?"

"Barter," H-man said. "Goods and services. You'd be surprised what folks'll take in trade."

"I'm worried about you, H-man."

"That's your nature, buddy. Inside you is some little old
worrywart, Aunt Bee or some such. That's why I love you."

Reed tried watching the dog. It appeared to be having
thoughts now, perhaps fetchingly complicated thoughts—
about the stranger he was, say, and his exact relationship to

these less-hairy beasts as well as the significant silence separating them.

"Reed," H-man said finally, "I believe a line has been crossed here. Most definitely."

When he spoke again, Reed knew he would sound like a tire going flat. "You want me to leave, I guess."

H-man looked like an overwatered plant, droopy in the extremities.

"I got some shit to work out," he said. "I'll catch you on the go-round."

Reed spent the next week at Mindy's, an inconvenience to the five other girls living in her suite. He saw H-man often: at Thwing Hall, on Guilford House steps, once at the Mather Dance Center, where he was watching two guys in leotards express their back-and-forth appreciation for Spring. Reed wanted to go over, say happy trails. Without H-man, the week had been long, no high jinks whatsoever. Mindy was making him sleep on the floor. She liked to turn the lights off at ten-fifteen. She did sit-ups, jumping jacks. She used a nightshade and earplugs. Reed had to knock before going into the bathroom. Still, with H-man, that dog was always around—a snarling, sullen, vile creature. It had other lives, Reed was hearing. It had known Dwight Eisenhower. It had spit on Jesus. It had been Eve's backdoor man.

On Thursday, during Mindy's quiet hour, the time she used to meditate on beauty and beauty only, he said he was going back to his room. Check on H-man. Pick up some clothes.

"Wash your hands before you come back," she said.

Reed stood in front of the mirror, checking his appearance. For some reason, he felt he had to make a good impression on H-man, and to that end he'd chosen a T-shirt and surfer shorts. There should be humor involved here, he thought.

"I won't stay long," he told Mindy.

"You look like a toad," she said. "I don't know why I put up with you."

On his way over, Reed put together a speech. H-man, a

devotee of Omar Bradley and George S. Patton, liked speeches. He liked hearing the truth, he'd said, liked it as much as horses liked oats. He liked to see individuals swollen with conviction and impossible to shut up, exactly the image Reed carried in his mind when he took the elevator up to his floor. You had to be the sort of guy, he thought, who would just fling open a door and begin to bellow, not stopping until whatever hung on the wall—posters, pictures, parachute silk—had fallen off.

"Hey, man, what do you think?"

The door was open now, but for a long time there hadn't been anything to bellow about: the place was pristine, shiny enough to require Ray-Bans, and, Christ, there was H-man— suit and tie, wing tips, as ordinary as a Mormon. He looked like he'd been standing at attention for a month.

"You've been busy," Reed said.

Idle hands, H-man assured him. The devil's workshop.

The window was cranked wide, and Reed could smell rain. A springtime Alberta clipper was coming down, wet air out of Canada and farther north.

"Where's the dog?" Reed wondered.

For a second, before he recovered himself, H-man appeared downcast, weepy.

"Split," he said. "Wore out his welcome, I guess. Not even a good-bye note. No manners in the afterlife."

In the closet Reed's clothes were pressed and hung and arranged according to function—everything sanitary and laun-drylike that could be done to wash-and-wear. His shoes, even his tennies, were polished.

"I wonder if I might ask a favor?" H-man began.

He was smiling—that old, toothy, cheek-popping thing that would haunt forever—and Reed reminded himself of the forty thousand notions he had aimed to ask about or get straight between them, but all that came out, two having been put together with two, was, "Dope."

Again, H-man smiled. "I hate being so predictable."

It seemed to have been uttered now, the word, and Reed

knew a few minutes remained to hem and haw before he had to say yes. This is the way it would always be, he understood: Reed might propose, but H-man would always dispose.

"You have a car, I gather."

"I do indeed," H-man said. "A Ford, courtesy of Univac on the third floor."

Here it was that Reed identified the smell in the room—close and sticky and warm as bathwater.

"You're wearing cologne," he said.

"Eau de Whatever," H-man said. "Gives me a lift. I put this on, I love everybody."

"And you'd like some company?"

"What can I tell you, good buddy? I get lonely. I start to cry a little."

Reed took a moment with himself. He could hear his dad talking, Mac. On the one hand was the law regarding possession of controlled substances and all the law might do to you; on the other, this Hoffman character, H-man. To the father in Reed's head, this situation bore only a passing resemblance to friendship. But Reed wasn't listening to that man. He was, instead, imagining that this might be the moment where he put aside the very content of himself. At this moment, he thought, it was possible that he was storming inside the most private room of himself to take out, stick by stick, piece by piece, whatever he had been even five minutes before.

"What is it this time?"

H-man wasn't smiling now. "I'm nearly ashamed to say."

"Shame? You?"

H-man shrugged. "A figure of speech, buddy. My attempt at understatement."

Instantly, Reed felt himself split in two, half of him walking across the room to sit and watch what remained shiver and go stonelike with fear. He had thought they were talking about weed. Maybe Thai stick. Now they weren't.

"This is serious, I guess."

H-man looked beautiful, fifty points above the curve.

"Depends on your point of view," H-man said. "For a straight-arrow, it's serious. For others, it's just the CBS News with a laugh-track."

Reed reviewed the true things he knew. H-man knew how to eat an artichoke. He laughed too hard at stupid jokes. He would treat at the movies at Severance Center. If asked, he would carry your sorry ass up five flights of stairs because you had drunk too much vodka and lost completely your ability to stand erect. Then, very suddenly, Reed was out of truths to know.

"It wouldn't be cocaine, would it?"

H-man nodded—"Very modest amounts," he was saying, "a token really, symbolic value"—and Reed watched the distant half of himself shrivel up and vanish. Thinking about cocaine, even in token amounts, was like thinking in practical terms about incest.

"You got money?"

H-man's hands were busy in his pockets for a second before a wad came out so soiled and crumpled you might only touch it with a ten-foot proverbial.

"Six hundred and twenty-three dollars and eighty-one cents," he was saying. "I sold my books. My Smith Corona."

"I'd like to think a minute," Reed said. "Oh, boy."

H-man shook his head. "No can do, partner. Time's awasting. An appointment. These chaps like to sit around, hear me on a variety of subjects. It's like seducing a carload of sixth-graders."

Many words went through Reed's mind—"pathetic," "pitiful," "miserable"—the theme of which he discerned immediately: No matter anything—his old man, his girlfriend, anything he was as recently as one second ago—it was now time to say yes, the shortest speech anywhere on record.

"I drive," Reed began. "Ohio has a thing about maniacs behind the wheel."

That was when H-man literally danced, mentioned Butch and Sundance, Laurel and Hardy, Heckle & Jeckle.

"This is against my better judgment," Reed said.

H-man had stopped hugging him, a twinkle still in his eye.

"You don't have a better judgment," he said. "We're like sheep that can fox-trot a little. Judgment has as much to do with us as range rot and cockleburs."

In the car, H-man yattered like a speed freak, all spit and run-ons. They went up through the Heights, into Beechwood on Fairmount Boulevard, Reed very grown-up behind the wheel.

"I got it all worked out," H-man was saying. "This summer I land a job—house painting, the light company, productive employment. I take next year off, get my head together. Next I reapply for admission. They see the new me, no more H-man. No squirrelly shit. A scholar, that's what. I demonstrate my earnestness. The ways are mended, I tell them. What do you think?"

They were at SOM Center Road, waiting for the light, and Reed wasn't thinking at all until it occurred to him that this wasn't a Ford at all, it was a fucking Plymouth Fury.

"Who'd you say you borrowed this car from?"

"Ears," H-man said. "That geek over in Staley. The Buddhist. The one with the finger cymbals."

"I thought you said Univac, remember? A Ford."

"What difference does it make? It's a car, transportation."

It was dark and raining, and in a minute they'd be in Gates Mills, then Chesterland, then all the way out in West Geauga. An hour more, they'd be in Pennsylvania. Fucking Keystone State. Another line to cross.

"I'm going back," Reed said. "I am definitely going back. You lied to me."

"C'mon, buddy. Don't be a pussy."

For another mile, Reed had nothing to listen to except the tick-tick of the wipers, then, dammit, H-man started whining, all the me-and-you stuff just spilling out his yap: *honest, man,*

it's a done deal, no problem, c'mon, man. He said "lookit" this
and "lookit" that, bolt upright the whole time, remarkable
sitting posture, his voice a squeak of tragedy and woe-is-me
crapola, making this promise and that promise, pushing this
Cisco-Pancho idea nearly as far as it could go.

"Shut up a second," Reed said. "I gotta think."

The radio was on, a tune Reed couldn't find the beat to, just
stupid guitar scratching that might irritate you right into something ugly, and with a tremor, Reed thought that he was afraid
again, his fear wheeling inside him like a bat in a house.

"What's the deal, Carl?"

"You're mad, aren't you?"

The rain was coming in sheets, and Reed believed he was
closing down inside—a valve here, a gate there—as mad now
as he'd ever been, anytime, anywhere. He felt he was being
taken apart with a crowbar and a blowtorch, the scrap of him
lugged away to be pitched on a pile no bigger than a potty-
chair.

"This is not fair, H-man."

H-man shook his head, scornfully. He didn't have time for
fair. Fair was an out-and-out luxury. Fair was like heaven—a
place you could ruin your knees getting to.

"So what do you have time for?" Reed asked.

The deal was this: they'd go out to Fowlers Mills, a street
named Londe or something—you couldn't really say they had
streets out here, more like lanes or trails, very ritzy—and
there'd be this big house, monster domicile, the snowbelt Taj
Mahal, belonged to a lawyer—Thrall, Hibbard and Maloof
maybe—and Reed could stay in the car or come in, his choice,
just that H-man would handle the business part, the transac-
tion, which really wasn't all that big, currency-wise, strictly
penny ante to these guys, a self-indulgence on their part, the
white-collar equivalent of wearing jeans, slumming; there'd be
small talk—how ya doing, what's your sign, what about the
Cavs?—then bingo-bango they, Batman and Robin, were history.

"Bingo-bango?"

"Right," H-man said. "These are educated folks, refined. They do this as a hobby. Like model airplanes. They get high, talk about eschatology."

Reed rubbed his eyes, sought to come up with the best insult. The knife was in him; now he would stick it in someone else.

"So how do they know you?"

Slowly, the air between them grew icy and thin.

"Christ," H-man started, "you don't want this adventure, fine. I'll go by myself. I just wanted you to come along. I missed you."

"And you knew I'd show up."

H-man looked around himself, an Isaac Newton clearly obliged to point out where the apples lay.

"Sun gotta shine," he said. "An article of faith."

Reed was thinking about his insides, what a stew they must be, what a shock they'd appear to a life-saver familiar with what the hell insides were supposed to look like.

"This is the last time, H-man."

H-man said his word again, "affirmative," to which he added about a minute of okays.

"Jesus Christ," Reed said. "A fucking stolen car."

"Borrowed," H-man suggested. "A loaner. Euclid Avenue is full of them."

A truck went by in the opposite direction, one headlamp cockeyed, and Reed, briefly blinded, worried he had lost the road entirely.

"You're a mess, Carl. I mean it, I don't want to see you after this."

"Me neither," he said. "Even I don't want to see me."

The place was humongous, landscaped like a Holiday Inn, a circular drive to front doors that Smokey and the Bandit could race through. The rain had stopped, and the whole area—which was dense with evergreens and maples and flower beds that Reed's mom would have flipped for—looked like richness as envisioned by Midas himself.

"Wow," Reed said.

"Impressive, huh?" H-man told him. "Some Swede did it. A hot tub in every bedroom. Got a bathroom, no shit, with its own zip code. We could drive a bunch of the brothers up here, play floor hockey."

Reed thought about what one Swede had wrought—levels and angles and far-flung corners, like a pirate ship breaking up in a typhoon.

"I met them at an Indian game," H-man said. "Next box over. Yale guys, I think, mid-thirties, boola-boola. Treated me like an exotic pet, an orangutan maybe. I treated them like ruling class dickweeds. An accord was reached."

So it was a social thing, Reed guessed.

"Right," H-man said. He had knotted his tie Windsor-style and seemed very proud of it. "I get narcotics at a deep discount, they get half an hour with the offspring of Joan of Arc and Attila the Hun."

Reed thought about that as well, how it was possible in America for folks with disparate backgrounds to find a common interest in the bizarre and the bewitching.

"You hungry?" H-man said. "They got a black maid or whatever, cooks a world-class enchilada."

And then they fell out, the words that had occurred to Reed the instant he steered into the drive, a sentence that had barreled at him like a runaway train when he braked the car to a stop and all that could be heard was brassy cha-cha music, or calypso, and all that could be seen, high up and forever, was blackness as deep as the cape a witch wore.

"I'm sorry, H-man. I missed you too."

"Yeah," he said, "ain't it a bitch."

A porch light had come one, and H-man was smoothing back his hair.

"You want to come in," he asked, "shake the hand, dance the dance?"

Reed thought of all he'd experienced in the last hour—a discussion, a ride, a night thus far divided by ruin and rain.

"No thanks," he said. "Just hurry up, okay? I got class tomorrow."

So he was out, jaunty, as if he were picking up a date, as if he'd brought a gardenia wrist-corsage, as if the Mister would answer the door, scowl for a second before he stood back to marvel at the 165-pound phenomenon that was H-man: *Good evening, sir, my name is Carl M-for-Malone Hoffman, son of Sam and Rosalie of Medina, a pre-med at Case Reserve, and I sure hope the lovely Debbie is ready, because if we don't hurry, we'll miss the first dance—a box waltz, I believe—and maybe most of the apple cider.*

After H-man disappeared inside, Reed fiddled with the radio. The Tribe was in Toronto—Large Lenny Barker the loser this time—and Pete Franklin on JMW was reaming Phil Seghi and the dipsticks in the front office. Reed couldn't imagine Pete. Yelling like a banshee five nights a week. You couldn't fake that. No way. You had to be the sort of guy who took offense, a guy who knew his ABCs and wouldn't tolerate any funny business—that was Reed's dad's phrase, "funny business."

Reed turned his mind to other subjects, general weirdness: the Hundred Years' War, Henry David Thoreau on the issue of perseverance, the slimy shit Stephen King wrote. It had begun raining again, a comforting pitty-pat on the roof, and Reed felt his frame of reference shift, like a camera panning left until the landscape stopped. It was still Thursday, he guessed. May something. Finals were next week. Several all-nighters, then a summer of yes-sir, no-sir at Gathy's Hardware on Coventry. He'd see H-man, sure. But no more of this dope business: it was just too funny. No more reefer. No more anything. Beer, maybe. Old Grand-Dad. Southern Comfort. Keep the highs and lows manageable, exercise personal discretion. Moderation and simplicity. No more synthetics, honest Injun. Only stuff grown—more or less organic intoxicants from corn and barley and potatoes, for instance. Nothing you had to own a lab coat to understand.

And then he heard a noise, like a hand smacking a wall or a table, and he noticed the front doors were open, the hall behind H-man as bright and wide and long as a shopping mall.

"Glib sophomore puke."

It was a matter-of-fact observation in regard to a condition you could do little about, like the day and date, and Reed felt the center of him rattling, his heart a rock in a plastic cup.

"Being," H-man was saying, a look-before-you-leap recitation of ingredients to a recipe that might take a century to cook up. "Grief. Happenstance. Fortune."

"Good Lord, get him out of here." The voice had all the charm of gravel and glass. "Get him out of my face."

Then it was H-man's turn again: "Compromise," he said. "Error."

When it was over, when he had survived this and a million other close calls with and without H-man, Reed was still amazed: time didn't shrink or warp, no slowing down or speeding up. There was no noise either: no thumping and banging and shrieking, no boom-boom-boom from H-man, and, best of all, no hollering from himself.

This was the way it happened.

H-man appeared on the steps, and Reed knew there had been difficulty, a failure dreadful enough to occasion sharp dialogue. There had been a misunderstanding, clearly. Umbrage had been taken, feelings bruised. Later, he learned that H-man had offered to piss on them, just unzip and let go right on the living room rug. Pissing on the furnishings, H-man would later argue, had been suggested as some sort of proof, a demonstration, an exercise of principle as it attached to action. But Reed didn't understand. He only remembered H-man coming backwards down the steps—deliberately and, given the givens he seemed consumed by, too slowly—the only item of real interest in evidence that awful, awful pistol from the week before.

"What's the matter, Carl?"

"Change of plans," H-man said.

Silhouetted in the door now stood three men—"Bozos," H-man would say later, "total dildos"—not one of whom resembled Reed's idea of a gangster. Or an Ivy Leaguer. Dressed in sweaters and slacks, they could have been golfers, one guy a dead ringer for a young Gerald Ford. To Reed, they looked like the executives his old man talked about, pencil-pushers called "Chip" or "Nick," citizens able to drop fifty dollars in the plate on Easter—the immediate ancestors, H-man might contend, of King the dog. Reed didn't know how he knew this; he only knew he had one unhappily silly question to ask so he wouldn't start sniveling.

"Are we going now, Carl?" Reed said. "I mean, is this it?"

"In a jiffy, hombre."

H-man had his arms crossed, the pistol in hand as almost an afterthought, his weight shifting from one leg to the other. He appeared to be ruminating, balancing options Reed knew he himself couldn't conceive of, the merely grave against the possibly deadly.

"I'm upset," H-man said.

They could appreciate that, one man said.

"I mean," H-man began, "I had expectations, certain desires. I'm disappointed now."

The same man—the tall one, maybe the homeowner, the one with the Woody Allen glasses—hastened to agree. Everybody was disappointed.

For an instant, that seemed to be enough for H-man: dis-ap-point-ment, some language courtesy of the lungs and lips and tongue that Reed thought he once upon a time knew the precise meaning of.

"Carl," Reed said, "I really would like to go now."

But H-man, already two steps closer to the men, was speaking again, so low at first that Reed could only pick up pieces of the monologue: "Immutable principles," he heard plainly. Then: "Conditional acceptance." Then burst forth a sentence that mentioned "privations," "largess," "human contaminants," a grammar there didn't seem to be a positive ending to.

"What is this?" the Jerry Ford guy was saying to his pals. He looked helpless, and in genuine pain. "I mean, I thought we had consensus here, closure. I thought the asshole was going away."

But H-man was still talking—no, babbling. He seemed completely unwound, nothing in the bottom of him but dust and char and rubble.

"Animus," he was saying, his gun-free hand sawing the air. "Parable, the outskirts of desire, solemnity, macro-commands—"

It was mishmash from Gephart's class, Reed thought. Then it wasn't. These sentiments had not come from a book. You got them somewhere else, Reed knew. You got them standing in a downpour in front of a house you could bust ass a whole lifetime for and not pay off. You got them when you possessed a pistol. When you were outfitted in your cheapo high school graduation suit. Drugs had as much to do with this situation as did hang gliding or World War II. This was about your best friend sitting in a fucking Plymouth Fury you'd stolen on Euclid Avenue and maybe where you'd be in forty million lousy years.

But it was over.

The men had drifted inside, the Jerry Ford look-alike first, followed by what H-man would later call the Larry character, the slick who'd kept his opinions to himself. When it started raining, the third one—the Curly guy, Mr. Sympathy himself—remained in the doorway, his expression exactly the combination of charity and good will Reed hoped to see if he ever needed an uptown lawyer.

"Go home, Carl," the man said. "You'll feel better in the morning."

"I felt pretty good an hour ago."

"Yeah," the man said. *"C'est la vie,* partner."

They were speaking French, Reed told himself. That was a good sign. Mindy spoke French. *Le chat,* the cat. *Le bras,* the arm. Then, watching the pistol, Reed found himself wondering who Mindy was. Mindy was nobody.

"What about a sandwich for me and my buddy?" H-man

was saying, more or less harmless again. "I haven't eaten for a week. Let's kiss and make up, all right?"

"Sorry," Curly said. "You gotta learn some manners, Carl. More sugar, my friend, less vinegar. You just can't deal with people in this outrageous fashion."

Reed had the impression H-man was nodding, perhaps being reasonable. Then Reed had the impression there was something more to account for. The pistol. *Le canon.*

"What about this?" H-man said. "I get some credibility with this, right? I mean, aside from the fact that it isn't loaded."

The Curly guy, Mr. Sympathy, came down the steps a little, a teacher visiting the playground, and Reed could hear Jerry Ford in the house hollering about how damn offended he was, about going to hell in a handcart.

"Grow up, Carl," Curly was saying. "You're—what?—nineteen, maybe?"

Reed leaned over to check what H-man was doing. He could see rain, diffused light, legs. With a sigh, he leaned back. H-man, it seemed obvious, was reaching closure. An asshole was going away.

"You've got a great act, Carl. Real talent. Take some time off, my friend, back to the fundamentals. You give me a call in a week, we'll start over. No harm, no foul."

H-man took a moment settling himself in the car, his face nearly ruined: rain-splattered, his hair slapped across his forehead like leaves, his suit coat and pants drenched. He seemed exhausted, as if he'd arrived here from a long way off.

"You got a handkerchief, Alex? I'm a tad overcome, good buddy."

Sorry, Reed said. Very carefully, he had started the car. The engine came alive with a clatter, the wipers flapping again, and Reed put his hands on the wheel at ten and two o'clock, textbook driver's ed, his gaze riveted on the hood ornament, not for anything about to acknowledge the weapon on the seat between them.

"Know what?" H-man said.

He was nodding, a gesture Reed understood to include the two of them and this place and whatever else in the here-and-now that had to do with misery and fear and time.

"Someday," he said, "this shit's got to stop."

CAPTAIN KANGAROO

''AIN'T NOBODY GONNA SAY AMEN?''

—HOWARD FINSTER

Alex Allan Reed didn't marry Mindy. That business, Reed would say later, ended the following fall when she returned to school with a fiancé in zoology named Etienne, a Frenchman who could do fifty one-hand pull-ups. Instead, after he graduated, Reed married the other sweetest girl on earth, Carole Bashaw, from Rocky River on the west side, a theater major. He had wanted H-man to be his best man, to deliver a forward-looking toast about them, but Carl hadn't come back for his junior year and soon enough he seemed to have disappeared. Stories circulated about him, of course. One frat brother, a fatso named Squid from Baltimore, claimed to have spotted H-man at the Springsteen concert at the Coliseum; and Juli Lund, the chatterbox from Wallace's poetry class, believed she'd run into H-man at the CSU job fair. He used a cane, she said. He was at Michigan. Maybe Michigan State. A Spartan. He was doing accounting, she believed. A practicing Christian.

That first year, Reed thought about H-man a lot. Too much. In April he received a package at *Northern Ohio Live*, where he was the listings editor—recitals, dance concerts, restaurant guides, busywork that required the vigilance of a monk. Immediately, Reed knew the handiwork of H-man: the package was covered with stickers—Goldilocks, a picture of Brezhnev, a Mighty Mouse decal, R2-D2 dry-humping C-3PO. In his office there on Magnolia, he could see a corner of the Phi Delt house, a touch-football game loudly going on in the field between it and the law school. He didn't want to open the package. Opening it might mean something. Half of him didn't even want to know it existed, that it sat in front of him like a request or an order, or an idea that had taken three years to concoct. Half of Reed desired to be home with Carole Bashaw. Half of him—the goody-goody self that wore pajamas and thought it looked sharp smoking a pipe—wanted to be in their living room watching "Days of Our Lives," content to have a villain or two to root against.

In front of him, on the VDT, glowed the movie listings—*The Man Who Would Be King, King Kong* and other royal jokes whose presence Reed also didn't want to know about. He watched, instead, the Jiffy bag, a number six, adequate for a can of cookies or a manuscript. Adequate for whatever in H-man's mind stood for the moon, the sun, the stars. Were it a book, you couldn't guess it. Preaching by John Milton, possibly. Another bedtime tale from Richard Nixon. You could have thought all day, you could have thought everything it was possible to think—you could have remembered, for example, that he was right-handed; that he was an Aries; that he'd broken an arm; that spiders and roly-polies gave him the heebie-jeebies; that he'd scored double 800s on his SATs; that he'd hollered cusswords into the Grand Canyon; that his blood type was O—you could have thought all this, plus more and more, and just when you'd decided that inside was either H-man's tribute to the Rolling Stones or his idea of an EYES ONLY communiqué from the Count of Monte Cristo, you might remember that H-man, Carl M-for-Malone Hoffman, was allergic to chocolate, and so, obviously, he would have sent peanut brittle wrapped in detailed instructions for surviving a massive thermonuclear exchange.

It was Carole Bashaw who opened the package that evening.

"Oh, Reed, for crying out loud," she said, and tore into it, gray packing material flying like fur. H-man wasn't a big deal to her; he was only another smart-mouthed world-beater Reed had palled around with before she'd entered his life. "Here," she said, and, the kitchen table between them, there it was, a T-shirt that said MY MOTHER WENT TO FT. LAUDERDALE AND ALL I GOT WAS THIS CRUMMY UNDERWEAR.

Carole Bashaw was smirking, shaking her head. She stayed home to study soap stars—"professional training" she called it, "picking up pointers"—and Reed could tell she was imitating one now: Veronica or Rachel or Mrs. Dunworth Lindsay, one of the shrews. Part of Reed was really touched by the effort Carole Bashaw was making, but the other part, the ghost of himself that dreamed and wandered the house in the dark, that part was busy with the realization that, unbidden and without reason, he'd heard from his erstwhile buddy. A message, indeed, was being conveyed—maybe simple, maybe not—and most of it had to do with the fact that H-man, his sense of humor intact, was loose in the world somewhere. Most of it.

A year went by.

Another.

Carole Bashaw worked at the Bolton Theater now, in the business affairs office, a type-and-file sort but still gung ho enough about drama and what could be learned from it to drag Reed to a production every month. *Hedda Gabler. Love's Labour's Lost.* Three excruciating hours with Alan Alda. Reed had moved over to the *Edition*, the free weekly published on Thursday. He could use his mind there, he said. Actually write something besides addresses and the dollars and cents of feeding yourself. He did a piece on biker bars, twenty-five hundred words about picaresques named Flyer and Shorty and The Prince of Fucking Darkness. You could use language like that: Fucking. You had a special freedom: you could allude to the pope, Yosemite Sam, Dr. Filth and the Leather Cup. The readers were hip: they ate up his piece on strip joints—the Carousel, the Toy Box, all that humanizing prose about astrophysicists who, between the hours of ten at night and two in the morning, liked to be called Ginger or Aspen or Rockin' Roxy; the public ate up his I'm-a-guy-who-cares piece on the Hispanics on the west side, a cover story that afforded him the chance to use his *español* again. He used the word *"balazo,"* the word *"cabrón,"* managed to work in references to Honduras, Salvador, Cuba. "Coo-ba," he told his readers, a lesson in pronunciation. In that piece, he'd been creative: he'd shown the reading world what life was like after midnight. It was after that piece, after he'd been a celebrity for half an hour, that he met Sylvia and started sleeping with her. She had words herself: "frolic," "no harm, no foul," "ha-ha-ha." She intimated that she was wearing a garter belt, and a name occurred to Reed. Carole Bashaw. She was at home, he assumed, pretending to be Audrey Hepburn. Or Meryl Streep. He bought Sylvia another drink. What the hell, he thought. Ha-ha-ha.

Another year.

In those days he wasn't thinking about H-man much. H-man was data from the long ago, the far away. H-man was the block you'd grown up on, the lawn you watered, the hoods who'd beat you up outside the Loews on Spring Street. Nor was H-man on his mind when Reed surprised everybody by taking an associate editor's job at *Cleveland Magazine.* Carole Bashaw wanted a baby now, but Reed wasn't sure: He was twenty-six, making good money, could eat free at any of the advertisers'. The bosses had sent him to the men's department at Higbee's, spent two thousand dollars making him look like an adult. He had a Ford Escort he could take home, enough steno pads to transcribe *War and Peace.* He had a girlfriend with a charge account at Victoria's Secret. No, a baby wasn't in the picture. Absolutely not. He wanted to play a little more, misbehave some. He wanted to stay out late, the way you could when you weren't obliged to drive the sitter home at a sensible hour. He wanted—with a capital *W.*

Sometimes at the office, his window looking over Playhouse Square from the eighth floor of the Hanna Building, he could feel himself come apart inside, grommet by hook by rivet, the snaps of him popping loose, a spring going boing-boing. It was desire, he figured. The world had a door, Carole Bashaw believed, against which you could pound and pound with no guarantee that it would ever open. It was a simple-minded concept, he agreed, but the simplest parts of him wanted that door to swing wide, wanted to see what was laughing behind it, to see the smoke and mirrors and blinking lights that the dizzy to-and-fro was known by. He wanted and wanted and wanted, and one day, when he found himself in Medina and the sun was beating hot, every building a blur of edges and glass, and he had little to fret about but a deadline he'd ignored, he understood, Jesus, that he was thinking about H-man again.

His skin had gone clammy, his hands trembling in his lap, and he realized, as if he'd been clubbed, as if the ringing he heard were real, that all he'd been thinking about—thinking with a capital—was Carl Hoffman, boy wonder.

Finding the house proved no problem, a matter of lefts and rights and ten minutes driving like A. J. Foyt, and he was there, an aluminum-sided split-level with detached garage, a place the Beaver and Wally probably lived in now. Up and down the street, the middle class was imitating itself: mowing lawns, washing cars, playing baseball. Reed felt select. This was H-man's place. This was H-man's cracked sidewalk, his scrawny willow tree; in there somewhere—at the kitchen table, probably—H-man had typed his college application essay, "How to Save the World, Man." Reed felt good, not rinky-dink in his tie and black shoes, a feeling that stayed with him when he rang the bell, a feeling he almost didn't know he had until H-man's father—Sam, husband of Rosalie—came around the side of the house and said, "I don't want any. You got it, you keep it."

The man looked like Bob What's-his-name, Captain Kanga-roo. Same moon face, same lame whiskers. But not robust. Not a guy who should appear in bermuda shorts. Not at all the sort who should be carrying a golf club.

"Mr. Hoffman," Reed began. "I'm looking for Carl."

The man's face did something funny then, but there was a smile afterwards—H-man's grin: loopy and too wet—and Mr. Hoffman told Reed to come around back.

"I was practicing," he said. "Days like this, I like to come outside, whack a dozen. Gets my blood up."

For a time, Reed watched H-man's old man belt a few. Not real ones, but Wiffle balls. Optic orange. He took a half-hour to set up, it seemed. Wiggled his butt hula-style before lashing out. "Oooommpphh," he groaned. Reed thought it the most unattractive swing imaginable.

"Till I started doing this," the man said, "I was lost. Pitiful, actually. Lay in the sack, watched Donahue, Oprah. God-awful stuff."

Reed had seen where the talk was going: "Carl put you onto golf?"

Mr. Hoffman took another swing, an effort the Eyewitness News I-Team might have had an interest in.

"Drove me up to Acacia Country Club," he said. "Don't know how he got us in, but there we were anyway. Felt like a million bucks. Sunshine, water, Bloody Marys—all the virtues."

Reed recalled the feeling: You knew everybody, everybody knew you. Your wallet was full, your car paid for. Feeling like that gave you a running start and a fresh twenty-four.

"You want a beer?" Mr. Hoffman asked. "Got every brew in the Western world."

Inside was decor that facilitated conversation. Books were everywhere. The *World Book Encyclopedia. National Geographics* to the ceiling in three unstable-looking stacks. Metal sculpture that seemed the product of despair and dynamite. Pictures dominated one wall: H-man astride a two-wheeler, Mr. Hoffman on the deck of a ship, H-man shaking hands with Rocky Colavito. Reed found himself looking at plaques. H-man had held a position of leadership in DeMolay. He'd been commended by the Jaycees for accomplishments recorded in engraving so small that Reed couldn't make it out from his chair.

"You're Alex," Mr. Hoffman said. "Carl told me you'd be around."

Reed supposed that Mr. Hoffman had heard pretty recently from H-man then.

"A year ago Christmas."

They were drinking Royal Dutch brand beer, a solid white bottle, by appointment to His Royal Highness Prince Bernhard of the Netherlands.

"You know where he is?"

Mr. Hoffman didn't take any time at all to answer.

"Oklahoma," he said. "But he was talking about Africa. Said he was writing a novel. That boy has the imagination of an iguana."

They had another beer, Dos Equis, and a third before Reed learned that H-man's mother had died, coronary thrombosis, but that Mr. Hoffman wasn't crushed from it: she'd led a good life; besides, everybody had to go eventually. You took the long view, Mr. Hoffman said. Get that view sufficiently long and nothing meant squat.

"I learned that from Judge Wapner," Mr. Hoffman said. "He's way out in front on these issues, take my word for it."

It was less hot now, the sun at the other end of the house, and Reed remembered what he yet had to do today. He had a muny judge to interview—an hour's worth of Q and A you'd feel grimy from afterwards—and he was supposed to stop at Lee Road Beverage to pick up a bottle of Australian wine. Carole Bashaw had invited the Zants over. The Zants, Boyce and Ilene, had entirely too much money. The Zants flew to New York to buy their toilet paper. The fucking Zants had a point of view, albeit indefensible, about everything.

"Got to run," Reed said at last, but Mr. Hoffman was already up and moving down the hall.

"Wait," he said. "Something for you."

While Mr. Hoffman was gone, Reed considered the furniture. A couch roomy enough to snooze on, a La-Z-Boy he had no trouble seeing himself slumped in. You could relax here. You could, whenever the urge struck, put down your solid white bottle of beer and wander out through the sliding door to smack a bucket of balls to kingdom come.

"I didn't peek."

Mr. Hoffman had handed him a Bass Weejuns shoe box sealed with filament tape, and immediately—judging from its curious weight and the thunk you heard when you shook it—Reed knew what was inside.

"Came parcel post about two years ago," Mr. Hoffman was saying. "Strict instructions: 'Present for Reed, no peeking.' In point of fact, there was a whole page of instructions. I got it around here somewhere, if you want."

In the car, Reed cranked the air conditioner up to frosty. His blood, he decided, was up. Uppermost, in point of fact.

Except for a few kids several porches down, the neighborhood had vanished indoors. In a couple of hours, he figured, he'd be bullshitting with the Zants. An hour after that he'd be telling the Cajun jokes he'd swiped from Justin Wilson. Still later, he'd be in dreamland, its vistas as flat and unremarkable as this. "Take care," Mr. Hoffman had told him; and now he was looking at the box, knowing the pistol was inside, and that's what he was doing, all right: He was taking care.

He was taking real good care.

JANE FONDA

CONFESSION OF OUR FAULTS IS
THE NEXT THING TO INNOCENCE.

—PUBLILIUS SYRUS, MAXIM 1060

The girlfriend after Sylvia was Marsha, a neonatal nurse at Metro—another sweetest on earth. So was the woman after her, Nikki with an *i,* a barmaid at the Sweetwater Cafe. There was no Carole Bashaw now. She had the house in the Heights, the stereo and the knickknacks he couldn't care less about. She had a new job, project coordinator, quote unquote, for Dance Cleveland, and every now and then, for his birthday and when they weren't drawing the crowds they needed, she'd send him freebies: Alvin Ailey, Trisha Brown—moderns you needed a PhD in voodoo mechanics to understand. Sometimes he'd bump into her in the lobby. "Michelle," he'd say to his date, "meet my ex-wife." In the last three years, he'd orchestrated an embarrassing number of such introductions: Felice, Ann-Marie, a rueful redhead named Vita or Veeta.

He was working hard, twenty-four or thirty-five hours non-stop, a lunatic who could give you 150 words on the new giraffe at the zoo. His was prose of the bump-and-grind kind, sentences that trafficked in words like "egregious" or "whipsawed" to make their point. In those days, he would think later, he was making points. He made a point regarding AIDS and another regarding such mixed drinks as the mimosa, the rum collins. He made a point about auctions: "Bidder Enemies." An impressively cogent point was made respecting microcomputers, in which he wrote about "flip-flops" and "master/slaves" and "AND gates." That's what he told H-man when he appeared in December: You had to admire an artiste, Reed said, who could make a point about Aquamar Gourmet American Sturgeon Fresh Caviar and still shake the world's hand with a straight face.

"How straight?" H-man asked.

"Scary straight."

Reed didn't know how H-man had avoided the rent-a-cop—much less how he'd gotten into the building itself, late as it was, to say nothing about the battered footlocker he was dragging—but there he stood, rapping on the door like one of the cleaning crew: for a heartbeat, a million miles of time and memories stood between them, and then, almost as quickly, nothing stood between them, nothing whatsoever, and they found themselves marching like drum majors up and down the halls of the magazine, in and out of every open office, jumping off desks, singing "The Battle Hymn of the Republic" and "In a Gadda Da Vida" and "I Feel Pretty," pledge songs the hotshots in Phi Delt had punished them for not learning.

And then, as if a whistle had screeched, as if he'd been trapped in a spotlight like a rabbit on a highway, Reed came to himself. That's the phrase he would use ever after: "came to myself," a way of suggesting that the universe, heretofore settled and meet, had inexplicably tilted a little, each of its dire but eternal laws a teensy bit in error.

"There's not going to be any trouble, right?"

H-man stopped playing the trashcan bongos and was endeavoring to look like Little Lord Fauntleroy.

"Me, Ace?" he said. "I'm aghast. That's what I am."

Reed had the image of checking himself as if for leaks. "Hey," he said, "you can't blame me for asking, right?"

In the car, on the way to Reed's condo in the the warehouse district, his footlocker jammed in the trunk, H-man was more than aghast. He was "mortified." Then: "peeved." At Reed's door, he threw some phlegm in his throat, affected a teary-eyed demeanor, and allowed as how he was, sniff-sniff, "in-damn-sulted." But after Reed shoved open his door to show, proudly, the little he owned and the much he'd done with it, H-man was happy. De-fucking-lirious.

"Think of me," he said, "as a Guernsey cow in a gently rolling field of clover."

For a time it was not possible to think of H-man any other way. Cross-legged on one of the two lawn chairs that, besides a Futon, were virtually Reed's only furniture, he told stories. He'd been in Chilpancingo. In Mexicali. Fished tuna out of Astoria, Oregon, mouth of the Columbia River. Holed up in Ravenna for a while, snapped some killer photos of the dome of the Basilica of San Vitale for *Smithsonian*. He'd worked cruises for a year, he said. The Royal Viking Line. Caldera. St.-Nazaire. Flogged Chevys for Bob Tartone of Harlingen, Texas. Sales Associate of the Month, twice.

But Reed had realized H-man was lying: when the dope appeared, H-man was cohabiting with an L.A. Lakers cheerleader named Cindi.

"You want some?" he said, holding the vial in the air.

"I do booze," Reed said. "Lots of it."

H-man took a snort, looked twenty percent better.

"Me too," he said. "Hooch has spectacular properties."

Something else had invaded the room—a presence annoying and indelicate, not the least bit propitious—then H-man said, "Man, they must've cut this shit with Drano," and Reed excused himself to find the bourbon and two glasses. When he came back, H-man was standing, his pants in a heap at his ankles.

"What can I say, man?" he began. "I've been in prison, the joint."

Later, when H-man was asleep and Reed could hear him fidgeting, Reed believed he'd had important thoughts at this hour of the evening. But he couldn't remember them. He could remember H-man's legs, how pale they were, how skinny and too hairy; and he could remember the thunk in his chest before his own words came out.

"What's prison got to do with the pants?"

Before he looked genuinely hurt, H-man seemed confused. "You're being superior, aren't you?"

Reed said he wasn't being anything, he just didn't savvy the logic, didn't see the connection between pants and prison, but H-man, more sad than angry, was already talking.

"I'm trying to make a point here, and you're being Mr. Shit-Don't-Stink. My feelings are hurt, really."

And now, while H-man, hunched over like a tailback, was pounding on his thighs, thumping them for emphasis on each word, Reed wanted to know that point. He cautioned himself to listen attentively, as if failure to do so were an ethical concern. He thought of himself bent over a math problem, a now-or-never calculation the answer to which might be zero.

"I fucked up," H-man said. "Really bad."

Reed said yes, his question mark soft but as real as the blood beating in his neck.

"Track marks," H-man was saying, and with a twitch Reed noticed that the pimples on H-man's thighs weren't pimples, not ingrown hairs, not scratches you could get from itching yourself, not cherry moles. They were scars, divots and slices and nodes you didn't want to look at too closely. "Skank," H-man said. "Speedballs. Meth sometimes. I can't begin to tell you."

"Try," Reed told him.

The usual, H-man said. A little lamb that lost its way. A period of panic. Then acceptance. Time goes by. The lamb adopts a point of view. Pretty soon the lamb is lying around with needles sticking out of it and hanging out with guys named Tuffy and M. C. Killer.

"This is sad, Carl."

H-man was in full agreement. This was the saddest shit on earth.

For too long that information hung in the air as well—

another aspect of the nasty presence that seemed to have barged in the door with them.

"But you're clean now? That's the word, clean?"

H-man had his pants up and was sitting on his footlocker.

"Pure as the driven," he said. "I do recreational shit now. I take vacations. A little flake. Some hash. You ought to try C. S. Lewis with a toot on. The man makes sense."

Reed had another issue to get clear.

"A line has been drawn, I take it."

"Cross my heart," H-man said, and here came that grin again, a decade old almost and still bright as a flash cube.

For a moment, neither had lines to cross a heart about. Reed knew it. H-man seemed to know it. Instead, they just looked at each other, nodding as if they had the same thoughts, as if they were again in the back row of Gephart's class; as if they stood again at A, gazing ahead to where Z lay shining and gold and true.

"I'm guessing," Reed said, "you're looking for a place to stay."

H-man looked sheepish. "If it's no bother."

"What if I had plans, stuff like that?"

For a moment, H-man seemed to debate with himself.

"I'd beg, white boy. I really would."

"I don't embarrass easily."

H-man went down on both knees, clasped hands held aloft. He looked like a Hollywood idea of a peon going uphill for faith.

"You're a hard case, Reed."

"Wrong," Reed told him. "I ain't no case at all."

Something had occurred to Reed, but he wasn't sure what. Still, it was there all right: nettlesome, pesky, a bother you couldn't laugh your way free of. When they went to bed, he believed it would come to him—not all of a sudden, sure, but slowly, like a puzzle arriving in the mail piece by piece by piece.

In his room, Reed spent an hour reaching for sleep. "What?" he asked himself and heard the word come back at

him from the ceiling and the floor. He imagined himself thinking, all of the associations pertaining to H-man swirling down
a drain over his heart. What he felt he was hunting for was like
a splinter in the finger; only it was in the brain this time, and
deep, ugly deep, down where the rags and wishes of you were,
down where you couldn't go without having told yourself a
hundred stories that you were the swashbuckling hero of, so
deep that the journey back was perilous too.

An hour later, Reed was up, in his bare feet and considering
H-man's footlocker: the splinter was working itself free. When
he awakened H-man, Reed had it exposed: the splinter was old
and huge and wicked as a knife.

"You killed the dog," he said. "King, you killed him."

"Killed," H-man allowed, was not a word he liked.

"What do you prefer?"

"Dispatched" was a nice word, as were "eliminated" and
"terminated." Some phrases also seemed relevant.

"You must've been feeling bad," Reed suggested.

Curled, H-man was still down on his blanket, the covers
clutched to his chin as if he were expecting the bogeyman.

"He wanted me to," H-man said. "We were stoned, really
rocked. He was miserable. I wasn't much of a pal to him. We
squabbled all the time. Plus, he was sorry he'd come between
us. King implored me."

Reed had reached a decision regarding mankind: about what
a curiosity it was; about how—on a snowy night, say—it could
lie in the dark and from the feeble bundle of itself reveal to you
the oddest truths.

"Something bad's gonna happen, isn't it?"

H-man didn't speak for a long time, but when he did, his
voice had little of the enormous burden Reed thought appropriate to past lives and what you'd done in them.

"This is the twentieth century, Ace. Bad is its middle
name."

* * *

The next day the furniture arrived. H-man had had the car all afternoon, and when Reed walked into his place that evening he felt he had entered a world where the only exclamations to be heard were "lo" and "behold." What had been spare and ascetic, the quarters of an individual who tried not to be home four nights out of seven, was now cluttered and overrun with gadgets and doodads, end tables and throw pillows, the vibrating and reclining and hideaway that his Sunday *Plain Dealer* was full of, low and space-age, chrome and glass as nerve-wracking as boredom.

"Senor Alex Reed," H-man began, leading him by the hand toward a wood-and-glass thing against one wall, "meet your hutch. Its name is Billy. As in Shakespeare."

Reed had been thinking about badness all day: war, pestilence, famine. He'd drafted a piece called "The Inn Crowd," and between 'graphs about stuffed artichoke bottoms Mornay, between dashes, between semicolons, between cans of Diet Coke and trips to the toilet and breathy phone calls from what presented itself as another sweetest woman on earth, he'd been assessing the truly foul things you could fall victim to—poverty, indifference and loneliness, as well as the affliction that was all-purpose woe—and now he was home, bushed, even his arms tired from having to type provocatively about bananas Foster, and here stood H-man introducing him to a blender named— let's see—Fred, to the love seat Inez, to the dinette Geoffrey Goddamned Chaucer.

"And this," H-man said, facing a sofa, "is Miss Suke Tawdry. She hails from Antwerp, I believe. A Libra. She has a list of pet peeves a mile long—men with beards, answering machines, perfumed soap—"

"You're stoned," Reed said. "Clocked."

H-man threw his arms out wide: What could he say, birds gotta fly, bear got to visit the forest.

"So where'd you get the furniture?"

"Ask me no questions," he said, "I tell you no lies."

H-man had stretched himself out across Miss Tawdry. He

was wearing a silk smoking jacket—later to be known as Sir Galahad, after the yahoo progeny of Lancelot and Elaine—his hands behind his head, his hair slicked back like a seal. He needed a beret, Reed decided. A rhinestone cigarette holder.

"You want some, don't you?"

Afterwards, Reed contrived not to think about this moment too much. He avoided thinking about the hour and the date, the way the sunlight roared through the windows, that you could hear nothing from the outside—not traffic, not airplanes, not a peep from the city. He tried especially hard to forget that he'd said, "Sure, what the hell," and that in ten minutes, fifteen tops, he too was addressing his home furnishings, in particular a glass coffee table calling itself Carole Louise Bashaw.

"How'd you know about her?"

"I snoop," H-man said. "An inquiring mind."

Reed felt light-headed, the work of poison on his nerve ends.

"Wanna tell me about it?"

"What's to tell?" Reed started. "I liked light bondage and leather underclothes. She was a Methodist. Basic incompatibility."

H-man looked pleasantly taken aback. "Surely you jest."

Right, Reed said. It was a metaphor.

They each did another line—ragged and bitter and full of winter wind; H-man fetched the Jack Daniel's and for a while they went up and down. Side to side.

"Ponca City," H-man said. "Oklahoma."

Another second passed before Reed understood that H-man was telling how he ended up in jail.

"A home," he said. "Very comfy, very spacious. Much in the way of consumer goods. I go in through a bedroom window. I'm a cat, I'm a mouse, I'm a ghost. Quiet is the thing I am. The place is Ming City: VCR, silver table settings, cash in the cookie jar. I'm in heaven, I figure. I'm at the pearly gates. I got my passport out, my harp music selected. Alas, I figured wrong."

"Alas," Reed said. "Alackaday."

He'd been stupid, H-man confessed. Need occasioned bone-headedness, dumbness of epic proportions. Need, he'd concluded, was absolutely the most unbecoming characteristic of the species. That, plus a conscience.

"Red-handed, so to speak."

H-man was nodding, vigorously.

"Ma and Pa Kettle, so to speak. A Remington eleven-hundred shotgun, so to speak. Twelve-gauge, semiautomatic. Up to five shells."

Reed could imagine it: quiet then not; simple joy displaced by its sensational opposite. Oddly, he found himself thinking about the soul: in his mind's eye, he saw it resting atop a bed of chipped ice, like a single cocktail shrimp. It was the dope, he figured. Dope, like the intimation of gunplay, made you more religious.

"I negotiated," H-man said. "Pa would have none of it. He had the high ground, weapon-wise. Wrong casa, I told him. Wasn't this the Dunwoodys', Mary and Jay-T? Ma was on the phone—kerchief and cap, the whole bit. Eeeekkk, I believe she said. Practical joke, I said. A college prank, I was bringing it back in the morning."

Reed thought that amusing, and said so.

"Five years," H-man said. "Less than three with good behavior."

This Reed could not imagine—not one blessed minute of it.

"Sooners," H-man was saying. "A very direct people. Very forthright. Not like, for instance, New Yorkers. Take my word for it: you do not ever want to have a powwow with authority in New York."

They shared another line, too profligate for one hit, and Reed, suddenly ten miles away from himself, felt moved to tell his own story. It lacked panache, he knew. It lacked the drama of H-man's—no Wild West showdown, no scintillating repartee—but it did, all things considered, feature a confrontation with equally direct, equally forthright people.

"My parents and me," Reed started. "We don't see each other anymore."

"This is not another metaphor, is it?"

"I don't think so," Reed said. "It's just a story."

H-man appeared sympathetic, even eager for news from the domestic pages, so Reed went on. There wasn't much to report, really. After the divorce, he'd driven to Youngstown for a week. Helped his dad rebuild an Evinrude outboard, saw some know-nothings from the ancient history that was Cardinal Mooney high school. Hung out mostly. Watched the tube—even went bowling, for crying out loud.

"An underrated pastime," H-man said. "You can learn a lot about fashion there. I like the shoes."

Anyway, it was a bitch of a week. Reed guzzled too much *cerveza*, slept till noon, didn't tidy up after himself. There were arguments. One night his father called him a supercilious prick.

"I know that word," H-man said. "I really do."

Yelling entered the picture, Reed said. Nobody had ever yelled like that before. His mother stayed in the kitchen, yelled at the cupcakes she was icing. Turned out they liked Carole Bashaw. Maybe fonder of her than they were of him. Their own son, his dad said, was too selfish for his own good. He had too much money. He was inconsiderate. Irresponsible. His dad didn't recognize him anymore, not anything about him. Not his hair. Not his eyes. Zilch.

"Irresponsible," H-man was saying. "Oh, boy."

Then his old man slugged him, suckerpunched him, and Reed could feel himself now tumbling back as he had then, the air whooshing out of his middle, up becoming down, the room rotating in such a way and with such velocity that he found himself collapsed on his side, the light breaking into whorls and puddles, and little in his ears but the hollow clomp-clomp of his heart and a cartoon voice that could have been his own, moaning, "No, no, no."

H-man had set up another line, a white rail almost, this the one you had to crawl to reach the humming end of.

"You want to watch TV?" H-man said.

The news was on, he'd noticed. They could see how America was doing. Amber waves, the oft-cited purple mountains.

Much could be said about his dad, Reed thought. He was a Republican. He paid cash—no Visa, no MasterCard, none of that. He'd served in Korea, shaken hands with General Douglas MacArthur. The old man knew the purpose of every tool it was necessary to own—the stilson wrench, the adz—and had a basement workshop out of which appeared three-legged stools and a rocking horse.

Suddenly, Reed had run out of things to think: zilch. H-man, like a terrier, was digging in Miss Tawdry's cushions, trying to locate the remote control. H-man was whistling "On a Clear Day." H-man was having a face-to-face with the armchair, which was Pepe LePew, and the ottoman, Popeye the sailor man.

"Can I tell you a secret?" Reed felt workworn, as if he'd slept a week on chicken wire. "Someday I'd like to do something really important."

H-man told everything—the fork he was using, the Salisbury steak TV dinner he was toying with, the crowd of curious consumer goods—to *sssshhhhh*.

"Me too, Ace," he said. "Someday I'd like to win the Indy 500."

When they opened the footlocker, H-man made an exceedingly complicated ritual of it: candlelight, Grateful Dead music, a half-hour of jumping up and down, mumbo jumbo to ward off the evil spirits that were beat cops and prosecutors and tax accountants and investment bankers and stuffed-shirt dick-steppers with precious nicknames from joints like Choate and Exeter. You had to be watchful, he warned. John Lennon had been an evil spirit, no kidding, as were the San Francisco Giants and the Keebler elves. These spirits—in disguise, of course, and smoothies of the highest order—were everywhere. The Tri-Lateral Commission. NATO. David Letterman.

"On the other hand," Reed prompted.

"Exactly," H-man said. "Flash Gordon, now there was a righteous spirit."

Reed was enjoying himself, truly. That day he'd told his subscribers about Kitty Allesandro, shampoo girl at the Mademoiselle Beauty Salon, a graduate of Normandy High School, a blonde thought to possess the most dextrous fingers in Cuyahoga County; and now he was with H-man, attending to the names that flew by him—Marcuse; the Marxes, Karl and Harpo; Thomas Jefferson, slaveholder—and watching H-man paw through his footlocker, coming up first with a Hawaiian shirt that took considerable energy to explain the pedigree of, as busy and hothouse an example of ticky-tack as Reed had ever seen.

"Given to me by a wahine," H-man said, now red and green and blue, covered from the waist up in grotesque pineapples and coconut palms and several furiously erupting volcanos. "She was a princess. Brown as a walnut. Her name meant 'sunset in the arms of the one you love.' Or 'sunrise,' I forget."

It didn't matter that this too was lie. Nothing mattered. Reed had been enjoined to kick back, relax, take a load off. A treasure chest was being opened, he'd been informed. You didn't want to sit too close. You, inadvertently, didn't want to reach inside. Something might rise out of there, beastlike, and bite you on the hindmost. No sudden movement, please. *In-* or *ad*vertent.

"It's very complicated, isn't it?" Reed said. "I mean, my letting you stay here and all."

"What it is," H-man began, "is downright baroque. I shudder to think."

Indeed, Reed said. Thinking about it was very hard work.

They were drinking Cuervo tequila—also, according to H-man, a spirit at the righteous end of the political continuum—and Reed was trying to imagine what it would be like to have an expert like Kitty Allesandro, shampoo girl, wash your hair. Flash and Kitty. Magic fingers and ray guns. That's the sort of world it was.

"I should make you go live with your father," Reed said.

"No can do, Ace," he said. "Where do you think I've been for the last month? We parted. Tearfully. He thinks I'm in Yellowstone. A park ranger."

"So why me?"

"I drew straws," H-man said. "You got lucky."

In his treasure chest, H-man had a shovel, a U.S. Army entrenching tool, and with Houdini-like fanfare—"Presto!"—it was revealed, as were a rotary phone, a pea coat that might fit a child, a Coleman cook stove, long underwear, a tin of Turtle Wax, *Roget's University Thesaurus;* next, with more hocus-pocus, came one, two, three—finally, six cans of Weight Watchers vanilla malted milk mix, pine-scent spray air freshener, enough Levi's for a Nebraska farm family, a Totes umbrella: Oh, H-man allowed, it was a peculiar but cunning collection of whatevers, each item selected in accordance with an agenda whose particulars, subtle but vital, he was not finished formulating.

"Whatevers," Reed said. "Very specific."

H-man waved him quiet: he'd found his novel, a slab of typing paper that even from where Reed sat appeared too slapdash and beleaguered, even too vicious, to be intelligible.

"What do you call it?" Reed said.

"*Chaos and Desire,*" he said. "A working title."

Reed watched it shift back and forth in H-man's hands—over a thousand pages, it was alleged, of the worst boy-girl moral-to-the-story, theme-dripping prattle this side of the first fucking grade. It needed work, H-man said. Too specious for its own good, it needed to be beaten with a ball peen hammer. One day it might make a camp fire worth roasting your wiener over.

But it was gone now, and a stack of credit cards thicker than a poker deck had appeared, and instantly Reed knew where the new furniture had come from: H-man's lighter-than-air personality, plus his flair with a department store fountain pen.

"Wait a second," Reed said, rising and finishing his drink.

"Show and tell," H-man said. "I approve."

A minute later, Reed was back, and they both had their guns out. Chaos, he'd told himself. Desire.

"You kept it," H-man said. "I'm touched. Honest."

Reed was amazed by H-man's weapon. Sitting on the coffee table, half-wrapped in oilcloth, it seemed huge, big as a chair. It seemed to absorb all the light in the room, all the light that could be turned on anywhere in the city. Looking at it required enormous will, like looking at your mother naked.

"This is a Combat Commander .45 autopistol—a real hog," H-man was saying. "Makes a terrific noise. A bona fide attention-getter. I got to use both hands."

On the stereo, Jerry Garcia was describing the virtues of wonderland, who diddled whom, how the land looked from the high hill he defended, the walk that was walked, the talk talked. It was still early, Reed knew, eight-thirty or thereabouts. Another handful of hours lay ahead of them, time enough to explore the bottom of H-man's treasure chest, hours enough to eat and drink and complain about the upside being down, about the bittersweet that living life was, about the moil and whirlwind you could sometimes find yourself in if, for instance, you were poor or otherwise inept at getting attention.

"No bullshit, Carl. What's the story?"

H-man put himself together then, as fascinating a process to behold as old-fashioned watchworks.

"You won't get crazy on me, will you?"

Reed thought to pat himself down. He imagined himself as little more than rind and ganglia, too incompetent to be crazy. "No."

"I steal," H-man said. "That's what I do. A thief. It's a calling, a profession. I'm an itinerant. I do a dozen or so jobs—convenience stores, Gas 'n' Gos, H&W Root Beers— then vamoose. Accumulate enough capital, then take a break. Got a house in Taos, no joke. Jane Fonda lives down the valley. Dennis Hopper. I got a Vanguard fund, zero coupon bonds. I ski."

The gun had sharpened into view again: big, blue, alive.

"I'm good," H-man was saying. "Well, good enough. No more homes, though. I'm like a—what?—a pediatric hematologist, say. I specialize. Places that deal in cash, small bills, no denominations you have to explain. Establishments where armed robbery is a factor of the overhead. I'm probably the most circumspect felon in criminal history."

Reed found himself looking at H-man's shirt again, the brash it was. He found himself studying H-man's head, his skinny arms, his body like a pipestem, his little guy's feet, his thinning hair, his common eyes: they could belong to anybody; notwithstanding what was in your innards or your private thoughts, these features could even be your very own.

"What's the matter, buddy?" H-man asked. "Your face is all runny."

Presto, Reed had thought, the word flying through him like a pinball toward tilt: That thing was in the room again, the presence that had rushed in with them the evening before, and Reed understood he had a question for it, an inquiry into the exact nature of its mission.

"So where do I fit in?" Reed said.

"Why, same as it ever was, good buddy," H-man told him. "You're my partner."

For several nights thereafter, they went to nightclubs. Shooter's. Rick's Cafe. Every watering hole on the river. H-man sought to instruct Reed in the latest dance steps, hip-busting moves of his own invention: "The Wandering Jew," "Some Enchanted Evening," "Search and Destroy." Watching H-man was like attending graduation exercises at Clown College. He liked to invade the busiest place on the dance floor, throw his arms skyward, and move thirty ways at once, exuberance evidently a condition best arrived at by shimmy and shake and by hugging all the sweetest girls on earth.

At the Aquilon, a club on four levels, a fun house of chrome tubing and floor-to-ceiling mirrors, H-man, wearing yet another Technicolor outfit from his treasure chest, convinced nearly forty fun-lovers to form a line, boy-girl-boy-girl, and off they charged, hands on hips, open-mouthed with glee, H-man at the front, a card-carrying rabble-rouser: they were doing either a manic cha-cha or the hokey-pokey, a snaking, twisting, giggling line of arms and legs that, all together now, went one-two-three-Ooommmpphh, one-two-three-Aaaahhhh.

Reed stood at a window looking east to a downtown that was lit up and Christmas-like: Lego-land without the miniature "ohhh"-arousing engineering. A minute ago, he'd had his own sweetest girl—the Queen of Sheba, he believed, from North Olmsted, a secretary at American Greetings—but he'd given her a little coke and aimed her toward the ladies' room to entertain herself. He'd tried to impress her with some thoughts he'd newly come to, the foremost being that most truths, in particular those having to do with boys and girls, were utterly unremarkable. "Sweetheart," she'd said, "I think all day long. At night I just like to sweat and go in the direction I'm shoved." More badinage ensued. He had skills, he assured her. Talents. For example, he could name the presidents in order. "Hold it," she said, her hand up. "I got a point of view too," she said. What, Reed asked. "Don't sweat the little shit," she said. Oh, Reed said. "Everything, fella, is little shit."

Now he felt good—anointed, special, fluid, at the center of whatever splendid gear it was that turned one world against another. It wasn't the blow. Definitely not. To be sure, the blow lent a certain luster—a glow, a cast, a radiant hue—but it could not touch the most creature core of you: You were on holiday, indifferent to time itself, disconnected and untouched, just another carnivore in shined Italian shoes.

Reed held a hand to his chest, pleased with the thump he heard. His name, he reminded himself, was Reed comma Alex, a welterweight now too thick-waisted to run for a cab. He liked fettuccine Alfredo, the wise give-and-take sometimes heard on NPR. He could dress himself passably well and knew when an "excuse me" was called for. He read Updike, voted Democrat;

he could play bridge, dribble with the off-hand, make a kite out of a pillowcase. And now he was smiling. Most heartening of all, he'd discovered, when he stood up straight, when he huffed himself up with a deep breath and squared his shoulders, he understood, more with his heart than with his head, that he wasn't wanting anymore: the door Carole Louise Bashaw had so often blabbered about was creaking open now, its hinges big as boxcars, and what resided in there, in a palace white and infinite as heaven, was Reed himself, every nail and knob and screw of him, a Reed as composed and felicitous as an angel, a Reed with a place to be in the world and brave business to do there.

"Carl," Reed said, catching up to him at the bar, "let's go be naughty."

Sweaty, his hair sticking up like a wheat field, H-man was an advertisement for exhilaration, and across the way the Queen of Sheba was moving toward them, hers a dress with enough lamé for a doo-wop Klingon. Reed was convinced she probably had affectionate names for her breasts and how she used them.

"You sure, Ace? We're talking permanence here, commitment."

ALICE C.

BE USEFUL WHERE THOU LIVEST.

—GEORGE HERBERT

The next night they sat in Reed's car in a lot at West Ninety-third and Madison. "Lurking," H-man called it. "Skulkitudicity. Skulkation of a large magnitude." This was the part of town, Reed thought, where junk went. A well-dented refrigerator, tires, two seatless ladder-back chairs, a hubcap, railroad ties—it had ended up here. A transshipment point, perhaps. Maybe it would reappear one day as antique Americana. Across the street was a Dairy Mart, spaces for eight cars in front.

"You're not stoned, are you?" H-man said.

Reed shook his head. For the last twenty minutes a tune he couldn't get rid of had rattled in there, "The Girl from Ipanema." The old man's favorite. It was weird.

"Good," H-man said. "Remember, this is capitalism, we're entrepreneurs. Safety first, good buddy. 'Brisk,' that's our watchword."

Strangely, Reed was comforted by the way they were dressed, like Fuller Brush men—off-the-rack conservative business suits, clip-on ties, broganlike clodhoppers you had to wear a week to get the squeak out of. Plain. That was another watchword, H-man had said. Nondescript, the two-legged equivalent of Quaker oatmeal. Shirts with collars, no jewelry, no watches. Reed felt he could overtake himself on the street, even bump shoulders with himself, and not know Alex Allan Reed from Humpty Dumpty. "Perfecto," H-man had said, seeing him in his outfit. "You, Ace, are one grade-A outlaw."

Now H-man was explaining about zone cars. Cleveland was like everywhere else, he was saying, a passel of bad guys, a paucity of good. Hence a lot of body fat with *pistolas* riding around in monster Fords with too many acres to patrol, inadequate hospitalization, and a kazillion mouths to feed back at the trailer park.

"You're shaking, pal."

"Nervous," Reed said. "Pumped, I guess."

Here it was that H-man, from his position behind the wheel, backhanded Reed in the gut, thumping him in the same spot his father had. Reed felt his belly tighten, his mouth drop open, and clearly heard himself gasp "oooohhh," as though, in addition to the pain, there was astonishment involved.

"Don't romanticize," H-man was saying. "This is no more glamorous than changing your socks. Doing laundry. This is work, means to an end."

Reed could feel his breath coming back, his eyes watering; H-man should not have hit him.

"There's no context, Reed. No ideology here. We're *bandidos*, get it? We take the money—'abscond' is the word—we spend it. We clothe ourselves with it, pay the electric bill. This is not political. No fucking metaphors here."

Reed nodded. Assured himself he had not wet his pants. The guns were in evidence now, his on the seat between them, and he was clearing his mind. His mind was a jungle, mysterious and dense and endless, and he was pushing through it, machete in hand. His point of view was being extended, he told himself. Like any other undertaking, this required rigor, concentration, internalization. You had to apply yourself. Application betokened action. Action, in turn, betokened consequence. Consequence could be dealt with at a later date.

"You go in," H-man was saying, "with your piece out. A

piece is an eye-catcher. The civilian looks at it, doesn't see you. Later, Deputy Dawg discovers that Dudley Do-Right was held up by a six-foot silver thing that could say *buenos días.*"

"Deputy Dawg," Reed said. "I like that." In fact, he told H-man, he found himself in the position of liking everything.

"Me too," H-man said. "I got a big heart."

The Dairy Mart lot had been empty for ten minutes, the clerk occupied behind the counter. With the exception of the glass doors, all the windows were covered with posters: DOZ. AA EGGS 98¢, FOOD STAMPS ACCEPTED, PLAY THE LOTTO. H-man had allowed as how he preferred women behind the counter. Contrary to popular belief and whatever was printed in the pages of the pointy-headed, women were less troublesome, more socialized to say "How high?" when you said "Jump." Moreover, these places always instructed their help to be cooperative, to bring no sorrow either to themselves or to their employer.

"Women and sorrow," Reed had said. "I can dig it."

There had been more observations, portions of which came back to Reed as he watched the store, the streetlights, the nearly desolate street itself. These places hired kids, teenagers. A teenager acquired its basic understanding about behavior through kung fu movies and music videos. Being stuck up was like being on "Saturday Night Live," an experience worth three days of feeling like a big shot. Plus, at a place like this—a Starvin' Marvin or a 7-Eleven—there were rarely any security cameras. Should there be an aforesaid, H-man had advised, buy a Fudgsicle or a six-pack of Pepsi and skedaddle. There were— "abso-goddam-lutely"—rules in effect here, rubrics. Safe, for example, was immeasurably better than sorry. Sorry, you could never be. Sorry was for spilled milk, for forgetting your birthday.

"Gotcha," Reed had said. "Skulkitudicity."

Another guideline concerned weapon discipline. You must never fire your gun. Never, never, never. Discharge boosted the crime into another felony class. At that point, were you perchance apprehended, sentencing minimums kicked in. At that point, ladies and germs, you were up shit creek.

"Ready?" H-man asked.

H-man already had his surgical gloves on, his coat buttoned.

"What if something goes wrong?" Reed said.

"You're trying to depress me, Ace. That's not funny."

Reed had his own gun out—in both hands, in his lap. For a minute, he hadn't been able to move.

"Nothing goes wrong." H-man could have been talking about the speed of light, about a fact of nature. "We're blessed, Reed. You and me, man, we're un-fucking-touchable. Besides, we're college men."

H-man had started to open his door, but Reed grabbed him at the shoulder. He had a desire—one of many, he realized—to get something straight between them.

"Carl," he said, "don't hit me again, okay?"

Afterwards, they called it, quote, the caper, unquote. The caper, they agreed, was like a long time in a dark place with a woman in love.

H-man strolled in first—led, it appeared, by his pistol.

"I'm assuming you know what this means?" he began, and the girl behind the counter said, "Please?" as if the two guys in front of her were the instant personification of her job application, specifically the fine print wherein it was grudgingly revealed that the world was, after all, a mool of gloom and doom for which management, those in the shiny high-rises miles and miles away, assumed no responsibility or liability.

"This is going to be very easy for you," H-man was telling her. "You gotta trust me now."

According to her name tag, she was Alice C., at most nineteen, with hair so frothy and ropy and tangled like seaweed that Reed knew immediately how her morning hours were spent. She had been reading *The Star*—the article, Reed noticed, in which it was alleged that Brenda A. Sorvino, a Redondo Beach, California, coed, had been made the love slave of Venutians—which Alice C. put aside forthwith. She was trying to catch her breath, quick and shallow, but she otherwise appeared more shocked than frightened by the interruption.

"Open the cash drawer," H-man ordered, now using a dumb Spanish accent. "Cash-o, drawer-o, *amiga*," he actually said.

Reed was to watch the doors and the rest of the store— sometimes there was a second clerk—and he did so, pointedly ignoring the sinister upward flight of his heart. He'd lost his legs, he thought. His fingers. The fluorescent light, he would remember, was stark and unflattering. It made the skin look unhealthy, putty-like and pitted, and seemed to have everything to do with the word "ache" and the word "scream." Hydrox Sunshine cookies, he discovered, were on sale. If you had the inclination, you could browse in the magazine rack, learn the salients about professional wrestling, about how to improve torque in a 280-Z, about how to shed unwanted pounds. More fine print.

And then, with some urgency, Reed realized he was counting—"Ninety-nine bottles of beer on the wall, ninety-nine bottles of beer"—concentrating very diligently as he subtracted his way out of this place.

"You okay?" H-man wondered. "Snap out of it, compadre."

For too long, Alice C. couldn't get the cash register to work, then, relieved and pleased with herself, she could: "Well?" H-man said to her. He was being courtly, a beau brummel, and a second later, when Alice C. could see that too, she nearly giggled before starting to stuff the bills into one of Dairy Mart's own paper bags.

"*Muy bueno,*" H-man said. "You're my kind of date, senorita."

Afterwards, Reed wished he'd brought a camcorder, or pad and pencil, to keep a record, some evidence that he'd not melted or split in two. He liked Alice C., the way the light spun off her in chunks, in shards. She had red fingernail polish— significantly, even startlingly red polish—as if a statement were being made, and Reed amused himself by thinking about how much he appreciated statements, even those uttered by fingers.

Statements were ubiquitous. The obvious were tedious—
"Don't walk"; "Keep right"; "No shirt, no shoes, no service."
No, he preferred the clever ones, those artfully articulated by
things like hair color and posture, those assertions that were
possessions and places to go; from one point of view, you might
contend that the entire culture was hollering at itself, a constant, fractious dialogue that comprised cars and high-heeled
shoes and where you lived. All you had to do was heed them,
Reed figured. If you had gleaming red fingernails and complex
hair and dangly, jangly earrings, all you had to do was listen to
the statements being made by guns and preacherlike black suits
and size eight surgical gloves that came one hundred to a box,
and subsequently you would understand where it was you stood
on the ladder that went up and down forever.

And then Reed heard H-man say, *"Gracias,"* his accent still
full of hot sauce and chile peppers.

"Yes?" Alice C. said, nothing in her eyes to indicate that this
event was over. "One more thing," H-man announced. He'd
said it "ting," like an elevator chime, and Reed congratulated
himself for not laughing.

"What?" Alice C. asked, and H-man told her, *por favor,* to
lie on the floor. She was not to move, *comprendes?* She was,
instead, to think about her boyfriend, or her algebra home-
work, or how to bake brownies, but she was not to move until
she had counted to, say, five thousand. There was to be no
cheating, she was given to understand. Cheating, like sloth or
perfidy, was totally unacceptable. Were one to cheat—by, for
example, not counting all the way to the predetermined figure,
or by peeking—then one was in for a world of pain. *Un mundo
de dolor.*

"Okeydokey?" H-man wondered, and for the only time that
night Alice C. answered without a "huh?" in her voice: *"Yes,
sir."*

A second later they were out of there. Alice C. went ladylike
to the floor, H-man grabbed the bag—"ill-gotten gains," he
would call it in the car—and now, a little snow coming down,

Reed was making his way in the night with what might be called a corncob shoved up his butt.

"Very calm," H-man was saying, advice Reed accepted as reasonable, even wise. *"Muy tranquilo."*

"My legs aren't working," Reed said. "I'm gonna fall over."

Mind over matter, H-man said. They were ordinary taxpayers with four packs of Juicy Fruit and some Hostess cupcakes, walking insouciantly to their automobile, okay?

The adrenaline had hit him, Reed thought. That would account for the zinc in his mouth.

"We are vets named Fred and Barney," H-man was saying. "We have wives. Yours is Betty, mine Wilma. We sell widgets."

"Wilma." Reed held the word on his tongue like a bolt. "Married."

"We are Episcopalians, I believe. I've had an affair with a secretary—a blonde, let us say, with a breathtaking way of climbing on and off—and you, too bad for me, don't approve."

Reed tried to imagine Fred's secretary but could only come up with the usual—lips and hair and hips, a libertine's feckless imagination.

"You like to write letters to the editor. You're fretful about your cholesterol. Once upon a time, you used to, as is often said, shake the tailfeathers."

"The tango," Reed guessed.

"The rumba, Barney. The bossa nova."

So they were in the car, the heater rattling, a number of miles—five thousand, it was possible to believe—between them and what they'd recently accomplished.

"I'd like to say something," Reed began. Mind over matter.

Behind the wheel, H-man looked like Gomer Pyle, a complete transformation to innocence.

"Go ahead, Ace," he said. "It's a free country."

Reed had felt that the cogs and springs and bearings of him were scattered there and there and there, and while the car turned this way and that, he scrambled to bring them under

control, the wayward widgets he was. He needed these fittings
and toggles and gauges. Without them—without every tissue
and bone and clattering organ they were the correlatives for—
he would be unable to ball his hands and pound on the dash-
board or stomp his feet and bounce in his seat and shout, using
the breath he'd been holding for a year, "Yes, yes, yes!"

"Feel better?" H-man asked.

Reed ordered himself to nod. He felt that, unbelievably,
he'd squeezed himself through a keyhole, emerging on the
other side of a door into a room whose weather was wind and
dust and desert heat.

"—my first time," H-man was saying, "I blacked out. No
kidding. Earth, fire, water—the total experience. I couldn't
complete a sentence for an hour. Went to a bar, ordered
hemlock."

At home, H-man chose not to count the money.

"It'll only depress you," he said. He had dropped it on the
kitchen counter, the bag now soiled and not as heavy-looking
as it once appeared. "I prefer to save up, count it in a week or
so. Astound myself."

For a while, before Reed announced he was going to bed,
they watched Arsenio, hoping Madonna might show up in her
bustier and garter belt.

"You did good," H-man said, his voice without any hee-haw
in it, not a bit.

"You feel all right, H-man?"

He'd put down his drink, Jack Daniel's he hadn't tasted: he
appeared pent up, a visage Reed thought familiar from their
early either-or days.

"Getting a cold, I think," he said. "Fever."

Reed could tell that more was to be heard. Arsenio had made
a joke about George Bush, a fifty-percent truth-filled insight his
studio audience went berserk over, while Reed wondered
where he'd misplaced his gun. For a moment, he felt cold and
inert, a stone with a bachelor's degree and a deluxe Rolodex the
size of a rump roast. He remembered having the weapon. In
his coat pocket. Heavy enough to tip you over. Heavy enough

to pull you down and keep you there. And then Reed could see himself conveying the pistol to his closet, putting it in the Weejuns box, closing the door very gently and backing respectfully away, not concerned at all what it would do in there by itself.

"I'm going to be moving on soon," H-man was saying.

Reed understood: "moving," "on," "soon"—words like numbers to be astounded by sometime in the future. He wondered what it would be like not to have H-man's treasure chest to trip over. Not to have H-man himself.

"Nothing personal," H-man said. "It's like the man says."

Sure, Reed agreed. What man?

"The way is the way, and there is an end," H-man said. "That man."

The next day, Reed would decide, there had been two of him in America. One—"Let's call him, oh, Jekyll," Reed told himself—was natty and pin-striped, an *escritor* with straight A's in the major spelling arts. Jekyll was working on a piece called "You Think Your Job Is Tough," which featured a diener from the county morgue, a diver for the Great Lakes Dredge and Dock Company, an ironworker dancing around the reactor walls over at Perry. Jekyll, fashionable and friendly as a lap dog, ate chicken salad, ordered his tea with lemon, washed his hands before and after. But there was the other, ah, the rootin'-tootin' sort, the humanoid with the deviant outlook: Hyde. According to the song, Hyde was working on the chain gang. Hyde hailed from the underlife, a being called into being by fears and dry hopes that nobody from the wakeful half of living life would recognize. Hyde, slope-brained and sly, packed heat. Rough'n'tumble described Hyde. Theoretically, this one went upriver to the Big House, did his bit without complaint, wouldn't let himself be hosed around by some flunky turnkey. Hyde was Jekyll's secret, not deep and dark as might be expected, but goofy and flat-out improbable.

"Show time," H-man announced that night, and out they

went in their costumes: a beverage store on Lorain Avenue. Reed felt himself at the hot end of the wire, loosey-goosey and swivel-hipped, able to leap the tall, more powerful than whatever they'd find speeding through the night.

They didn't do suburbs, H-man explained. Suburbs had higher tax rates, which meant more revenue for the forces of good, which in turn meant poorer odds for the forces of blah-blah-blah.

"Evil," Reed said.

"Depravity, the whole nine yards."

Stick to inner cities, Reed learned. Inner cities were the incorrigible's analogue for Disneyland. Corruption, greed, self-interest, irony, feather-bedding, crookedness of Homeric dimension—comparatively speaking, inner cities were the milieu in which one was less likely to swap wits, not to mention gunfire, with a hero.

"You're a cynic, H-man."

"Wrong, Ace. I'm a Visigoth who doesn't pay Social Security."

This time, during the amble back to the car, they were Alphonse and Gaston, earnest boulevardiers with the meager dream of making it big.

"Your wife is Babette," H-man said. "A brunette, very comely."

"I bet she can cook," Reed said. "I love food."

H-man had his hundred-watt grin. "Crepes, Beef Wellington, a soufflé to sleep on. Mine, on the other hand, Clarice, excels in the carnal crafts. We have kids, as well. Yours are Vera, Jock and Dave. Vera, that's the heady one, you have to watch her every second. What an imp."

"Ooohh, oui-oui," Alphonse said.

Gaston, it turned out, had an army of kids—William the Conqueror, Emma Bovary, Yves Montand, Madame Defarge—kids he didn't quit talking about until this bag of money sat on the counter next to the other.

"Let's get high, H-man."

But H-man was already in the pajamas he'd taken to wearing—roomy, silky apparel that made him look like someone you could find on matinee TV talking British to a prole-like gofer named Edmund.

"Go ahead, Alphonse," he said. "I got a headache."

Reed didn't like the too tragic self-regard in H-man's voice. "You're a party-poop, Carl."

Now it was H-man's face that went runny and gray.

"I feel old, Ace. Inside me is a guy in bib overalls, with straw in his teeth."

In his room, Reed did a couple of hits, dope that went nowhere in him, firecrackers that fizzled. That tune was back, "The Girl from Ipanema," as annoying as a leaky faucet. On his desk was mail he had not attended to: his maintenance fees were going up, Higbee's had raised his credit limit, AMEX was offering him an annuity. Life, he thought, was a cher of bowlies. That was his mother's phrase—Marjorie—and he saw her now in her Sunday best—hat and heels and hose. She liked Sergio Franchi and Julio Iglesias. She could dive from the high board, make no splash at all. His mother. Wife of Mac, he of the fists.

Reed did another hit, spilled a sprinkle on his chest. "Shit," he said. He wet his fingers, dabbed at the cocaine, rubbed his gums. What was needed, he thought, was a plan. But there was a problem: that girl was walking again, that girl from fucking Ipanema, her feet big as buckets, hers a path in the sand that Godzilla would leave behind. What's more, his leg had started shaking, ticking back and forth as if it, now autonomous and rebellious, were in a hurry to be making decisions on its own. He imagined himself in a tunnel, crawling, a kerosene torch flickering, noises reaching him from the darkness ahead. He ordered the leg to stop—to cease and fucking desist—and when it ignored him, he reminded it that he, Alex Allan Reed, was a certified badass with a devil-may-care attitude—enough attitude, at least, for some, no pun intended, *grave* mano-a-mano if impelled to that.

He was holding the wire again, he thought, and the only thing to do was to follow it back, hand over hand like a climbing rope, until he got to its source. As a consequence, he found himself going round and round in his room, a tourist. He'd bitten into a cinder block, he felt, and for a time it was pleasant to watch the air in front of him spread and tear like taffy. He did another hit, sucked it into the attic of his head, heard a dozen distinct explosions, but the leg was shaking again, more vigorously than before, and Reed knew the time had arrived to ask that offensive limb if it knew who the hell it was messing with. He had a gun, he reminded his leg. *Una pistola.* Perhaps Mr. Leg-o Left-o was unaware of the serious damage such a sterling example of machine skills and wantonness-related know-how could inflict. Damage of the irremedial kind. Damage in the maim range. Damage, in fact, it might not be possible to withstand.

"Reed," H-man called from the other room. "What're you yelling about?"

So he was ripped, he thought. Positively clobbered.

"Sorry," he said. "Go back to sleep."

He tried reading some undersea Tom Clancy, but the words—composed, unfortunately, not of letters but of unruly microscopic dots—kept running into each other, a Chinese fire drill, until even the simplest sentence was no longer a vehicle for sense but, when read aloud, was the kind of rasp and buzz and squeak he imagined filtered earthward from Mars. These were imps, these Martians. Varlets and rascals.

For a time, he stood in his doorway to listen to H-man asleep on the Futon. H-man didn't snore. Even in college he hadn't snored: in college, he'd shouted, he'd barked, he'd chattered in a manner that had to it more music than meaning. But now Reed didn't know what was going on with H-man. Carl Hoffman, thief. H-man was leaving soon. That much was apparent. "Soon," however, was a relative measure—like "fast," like "bad"—too much in the eye of the beholder. "Soon" could be anytime. Tomorrow. Next month. In a blue moon.

Back in his room, Reed wondered where the dope had
landed in him; he imagined it as a mist settling over the
landscape of his organs, some winter inside to match the winter
out. "Soon" was like "perhaps," he believed, too conditional
to bet on. You could go loco waiting for "soon"—provided, of
course, you were waiting for it. Carried to extremes—and, to
be sure, it could not be carried to any other end, right?—you
could wrench yourself inside out, a consensus intergalactic,
first-team wild man. He did another hit, the maraschino cherry
on top, discreet and ceremonious. The possibilities were limit-
less, he guessed. But there was this night to get through,
minutes and hours to climb like molehills and mountains. He
could pretend, he thought. He could creep up on another's life,
try it on like a warm winter coat. But who?—a question he
repeated so swiftly it finally came out as baby talk: ba-doo?

He didn't know anyone at work, not really, but the names
flashed through his head anyway, like leaves, like junk in a
drawer to be cleaned: F. Lincoln Todd, What's-his-name in
sales, the know-it-all in the red suspenders, Betty built for two,
Gladys with the fringe on top, Choo-Choo from Chattanooga,
the other sweet Betsy from Pike. Negative, he told himself.
You couldn't be those people. They had no H-man, natural
damn philosopher. You could be, therefore and only, yourself—which was Scorpio and left-handed, somebody with a
grudge against the cauliflower family of vegetables; which was
somebody with a thirty-dollar haircut and no living grandparents; which was somebody—a Martian, say, a varlet—who in
his youth had been a Thespian, who'd risen to the rank of
webelos in the BSA. Reed heard himself laughing, a very
healthy sign. His was a self, he'd just discovered, that had
learned to play "Lady of Spain" on the accordion.

He dosed himself again—his last, he promised—and waited
for the drug to arc through him, its truant, potent chemicals
to collide with his own. The self: now there was an interesting
concept. He stopped, waited for the last of him to catch up.
Reed tried to imagine it—like a marble, or goo as jiggly as jelly.

The images for the self were manifold and myriad—ice and rock and paper—and before long he was thinking of David Hutto, a friend from junior year in high school. "Whoa," he told himself. "What the hell." His was the cerebration, he decided, of a squab—a thought here, another there, no sequence, no order: a bug; a worm; goodness gracious, a thread for the nest; peck-peck-peck.

He waited a second, took a breath, then, nothing in him to say no, it became clear there was little else to do but take up the memory of David Hutto. They'd been drunk one night, riding around fancy-free in David Hutto's Honda, seeing what could be seen under the helpful influence of a six-pack of Iron City and a joint of red-dirt weed, when David Hutto revealed that he wanted to change his name. "David" was inconsistent with the image he had of himself. "Daaa-vid" was the shout heard in the neighborhood at dinnertime. "Daaa-vid" was white bread and mayonnaise and burgers on the grill. So Reed had asked the inevitable: To what? And here, David Hutto, already balding and easily too tubby to be a success, cracked open like an egg to let the self within come wriggling out: Lance, he'd said. *L-a-n-c-e.* A self blond and hale and carefree as any Beach Boy. A self with a Mustang V-8 convertible and three bikini-clad girlfriends to pay for gas. Lance Elroy Hutto.

Now, lying on his back and watching the ceiling shift, Reed wondered who his Lance was. He was waiting, he understood. His leg, chastened, had wandered off to sulk. It had begun snowing more heavily, each flake going splat-splat-splat on the street below. For a moment, the walls of his room held very still. A siren could be heard way off, and going farther. Be patient, he told himself. In the quiet, so complete a silence he could hear the click of his blinking eyes, he pictured himself suspended like a hurdler between his past and the remaining years of his life. Back straight, he contrived to remain alert. A sentinel. He wanted to be sharp: he wanted to be see the tiny hole his Lance oozed from.

His mouth set hard like a doorknob, Reed tried to pull

himself free of the wall he seemed lashed to. He was pecking again, he concluded. Several adjectives had come to mind—"shorn," "riven," "denuded"—and he promised himself that one day he'd go back over this chapter in his life with a dictionary. With tweezers and a Shop-Vac.

Then he was sober.

It would be necessary, he understood, to be properly dry-minded when his Lance, using a corny Mexican accent, picked up the phone and told whoever answered—a male, tool-wise relative: his father—to get down on its knobby knees and not to get up until it had counted its way to a billion.

DIXIE

NOWHERE TO GO BUT OUT,
NOWHERE TO COME BUT BACK.

—BENJAMIN FRANKLIN KING, JR.

B riefly, Reed felt himself an expert in everything awful or stupid or bogus that had ever happened: swine flu, Wrong Way Corrigan, Piltdown man.

"Think," H-man told him. "What day is it?"

In his getup, Reed had his gun at the ready. He was disposed toward mischief.

"Friday," he said. "Why?"

He had dotted many *i*'s, crossed many *t*'s, but he had written exactly one line all day: *Peter Cook and Dudley Moore as Faust & the Devil in bizarre tale of unrequited love for a waitress*—a sentence as much in need of a verb as it was something substantial to be about.

"Many people," H-man was saying. "Much frolicking, much gamboling. Lucre of the filthiest sort."

Reed couldn't agree more: lucre, moola, bread, the legal tender. So?

"Many Marshal Dillons," H-man told him, a confidence that apparently obliged him to whisper. "Check your crime statistics. Consult your FBI. This is the lying low part, Reed. This is the subsection about not falling into a pattern, about bad habits."

H-man was flipping through the channels: WUAB, TNT,

CNN. All that seemed to be on was war. You observed a range of emotions: terror, bewilderment, hysteria, enormous jubilation when one horde vanquished its motley counterpart.

"I knew it," Reed said. "You have a theory."

Oh, H-man fairly squealed. Did he ever.

It was a theory, Reed later concluded, that could have come from anywhere, from everywhere—*The I-ching,* Jeane Dixon, Hi & Lois, Dear Abby.

"Pay close attention." H-man had cleared his throat, a senator with Congress all to himself. "The Day of the Week Theory, very arch reasoning. Friday and Saturday are for amateurs, dilettantes, infants with cheesy moustaches. Monday's a low turnover night—few from the right side of the tracks but little in the way of coin of the realm to get sweaty about. You with me so far?"

Reed was with him. All H-man needed was a pointer and an overhead projector.

"Am I boring you, Little Beaver?"

H-man's voice had hardened dramatically, frighteningly: for an instant, Reed imagined he could see in H-man's eyes what H-man himself had reported seeing years ago in the eyes of that forthright Sooner with the terrible shotgun. A crater, Reed feared, had opened between them, deep and noisy and steamy, and he was frightened to go to the edge to look down.

"No," Reed said. "Go ahead, please."

"You gotta pay attention," H-man said. "No attention, no reward. No reward, no point in dressing up."

Right, Reed said. No reward.

Every day, H-man said, had a value, a ratio, a coefficient. Tuesday, for example, was primo: boredom hadn't set in, nor had anger. Wednesday, the night they'd popped the Dairy Mart, was ennui, a veritable Eden of disaffection, of discontent itself. Thursday, on the other hand, was ambiguous. A weekend without the cover charge. Could be, could be not. Ambiguity was a slut. Ambiguity could crush your nuts, or make you hum. Ambiguity—a word which had come to the present world via

Middle English and Latin, you could look it up—was raunch, pure and simple. Beaucoup X there.

He had his substance now, Reed thought. X: *equis.* His verb would come along later.

"The unknown, Ace."

Reed wondered about the night before, Heck's beverage store, Thursday: "We were lucky then."

"Indeed," H-man said. "Ambiguity was humming our song."

For another five minutes, Reed tried to follow H-man, but it was like chasing Br'er Rabbit through the briar patch—even H-man admitted it. His theory had to do with origin, he said. Plus various factors associated with diurnal conduct. "Concatenation" was a word used, as were "conflation" and "febrile." You had to puzzle it out, scratch your noggin. You had to account for the wind, for low-grade ionization, morbidity rates, for the relative weight of the dingdongs and dipshits in the world. But a solution was possible. You turned your vast intelligence toward the problem itself. Isolated it. Advanced your hypothesis, computed your abracadabra and—voilà— epiphany.

Reward, Reed was thinking. Dressing up.

Then H-man admitted he was stoned.

"Shit-faced," he said. "Destroyed, pounded, deracinated."

"I should've known."

Si-sí, H-man said. He should've.

Reed had his verb now, a form of the infinitive "to know," as in being fully aware: You could look it up.

"So what now?"

They were both staring at the TV, its lights throwing up a crowd of flickering, vaguely disconcerting shadows in the room. Sport was on, the International Barefoot Skiing Championships, and armed robbery—clearly—was out of the question.

"We clean," H-man said.

For only a second was Reed befuddled, then he saw that H-man meant "clean," as in soap and water and LesToil and

Easy-Off, and Reed himself started laughing, the crater between them quiet and closing over. "Clean," he decided, had
certain associations with such words as "virtue" and "hope."

"Why not?" he said. "Let's do it."

For an hour they worked like coolies, moving garbage from
one pile to another. They stripped the linen, attacked the
throw rugs with the vacuum. "Change the bag," H-man reminded him. "You need maximum suck to get the grit out of
the nap and weave." H-man did the bathroom, scrubbing the
tile and digging hair out of the sink trap. He was in great spirits,
magnificent dope spirits that argued in behalf of universal weal.
He used bleach on the grout, polished the enamel on the tub
to a shine bright enough to blind. They played Roy Orbison
on the CD, debating good-naturedly the blue-ribbon merits of
hillbilly versus shitkicker. Shitkicker, they decided, was exceptional on account of its hormonal—nay, inguinal—link to
mirth. And dangerous love.

In the kitchen, H-man bemoaned the dearth of necessary
supplies: Windex, Dobie pads, steel wool, Lux liquid, no frigging scrubbing bubbles. He washed the dishes by hand.
"Never, never, never," he said, "use a dishwasher. Too many
working parts, too much margin for error."

Reed understood the analogy completely: In important
ways, man was himself a machine—many moving parts and a
margin of error big as Kansas.

"Where are the trash bags?" H-man called an hour later, and
Reed went in to discover his pal in an apron, a dishtowel
around his head like a do-rag.

"Man," he exclaimed, the refrigerator open in front of him,
"when was the last time you ate from this thing?"

With a scrub brush he was poking at dozens of half-finished
milk products—cottage cheese, butter, yogurt—all of it in in-
sipid decay.

"Dismaying, huh?" Reed said.

Wrong, H-man informed him. Fucking outrageous. There
were diseases to be avoided. Bacteria. Fungi. Creepy-crawly
shit for which science didn't have the slightest. H-man looked

him square in the eye, a brilliant idea in the making: "Got any ammonia?"

By midnight Reed was being taken on a tour of the place, another hello-how-are-you introduction to the goods, as well as the nooks and crannies, he was hereafter responsible for. "An ounce of prevention," H-man said. "Et cetera, ad infinitum." In addition, he had hints—as many as the vaunted Heloise herself. Salt was dandy for wine stains. Peanut butter was good for chewing gum. Baking soda for odors. Always run the water for the disposal. Never put off till tomorrow, look both ways before crossing, and so forth—a host of yamma-yammas central to epiphany. And then it hit Reed, waylaid him.

"How do you know all this?" It was a question Reed believed essential to get an answer to.

"Marriage," H-man said woodenly. "I was a husband once."

H-man had his apron off, folded neatly and laid on the counter, and Reed hoped to hear the whole of it—where they met, her dress size, what she looked like getting up: the Carole Bashaw stuff—but that instant vanished and Reed could tell, voilà, that more was involved here than a pair of I-do's.

"Her name is Martha," H-man was saying. "Another story of woe and lovecraft."

Again, Reed found himself waiting. He was standing in a kitchen so sterile he could belly flop on the floor and eat from it, and he was waiting, H-man's face at the moment not well or thoroughly lived in.

"I have a toddler out there," he said. "A boy."

On Saturday, Reed endured spells when he was convinced that Sunday would never arrive, a mirage. The world had stalled, repeatedly and without warning, and if you listened closely, you could hear it start again with a bang and a shiver, staggering, as if the engine of it, infernal and jerry-built, were sputtering, oil and sparks flying from its cables and chains and cams in eye-stinging, stinking, smoky showers.

A movie was being made of his life, he thought. But whole

sections had been snipped out: the loyalties, the way the hip bone connected to the leg bone, the past a mess of words and actions coming at him like trash in a tornado. The movie, too cockeyed and fuzzy, didn't show his first girlfriend, Lisa Werner, fifth grade; not his first bike, a Huffy too dorky to pedal to school. Nor did it show him as a sack boy at Kroger. It ignored his first car, a Chevy Nova with a frame so twisted you could look out the passenger window to drive. He was another man, it seemed, limping and leering, a blabbermouth, a disorderly spoilsport, an ingrate who crushed his cigarettes out on the floor. Worse, the creature who played him was rough and pugnacious, cocky and foolhardy, a dufus that strutted and tooted its own shiny horn, a coward: He was being played by fucking Daffy Duck.

He couldn't abide the movie. It showed only what he did, what he mumbled about what he'd done, not the sizzle in his head, not the hiss in his heart, not that spear of fright shooting into his brain. It showed only a man—call him Reed comma Alex—on the eighth floor of the Hanna Building, hunched over his desk like a jeweler, in his hand a blue pencil, in front of him, spread carelessly all around him, pages and pages of what he'd managed to type on the subjects of weddings and brides and how to look your best when someone gave you irretrievably away. *Lace,* he'd written. *Veil, bodice, train, bouquet.*

That was in the morning.

At noon, he drove down Superior to the Sohio Building to park in its garage so he could go into The Arcade next door for lunch. It was cold—air that slapped and scratched at him, cold that strangers felt compelled to grumble about—but Reed couldn't feel it. He was too angry, he thought. Or too scared. That's the way the morning had gone: a whipping back and forth between rage and fear. The car hadn't started, just a grinding and a clicking that for all he knew could have been the whatchamacallit or the thingamajig, any of the zillion parts cars could fail from; then, unaccountably, the engine turned over, and, out of sour gratitude and to whatever was empowered to hear such outbursts, he muttered, "Thanks for nothing." On Carnegie, he'd hit an ice patch, and for too long, the steering wheel a stupid circle of plastic evidently unneeded in the Milky Way, he drifted sideways, the cords in the middle of him snapping free one wirelike strand at a pop. In the building, the elevator wouldn't come. He punched the buttons; he kicked the doors. "Motherfucker," he said, liking the echo of it so much he shouted it again. "Mo-ther-fuck-er." When at last the doors opened, he cursed them and the hall and polished floor, and he rode up telling himself a story, a fairy tale almost, about two guys riding free in the Wild West, guys who ate out of cans and made friends with the wildlife. Still later—tenish, he thought now—he'd heard a hollow crackling, voices in a can, somewhere down the hall from his office, and here came that kicking in the gut again, a tongue-swelling surge of fear that left him shaking outside Choo-Choo's door, listening to her answering machine record a call from a Rupert who was getting back to her after she, Christ, had failed to get back to him.

Anger.

And fear.

He bought a roast-beef sandwich at Arabica; and at the same moment he found a table overlooking the well of the mall, he realized that what he deep down wanted was not coffee but cocaine, and for an instant he was tempted to say "oooppps" over himself as if he were scrambling to get out of his own way. He wanted a mound of the stuff, a blow so high and peaked he'd need a rope and pitons to climb it. That's when he saw her: when the first snort of the blow he did not have hit the ledge of his brain and set him ablaze like a three-star combat zone. Alice C. From the Dairy Mart. Another oooppps-worthy fact of life that commenced with a *C*.

At first, he wasn't positive. She was too distant, on the lower floor and moving away from him, up the steps toward the Doubleday's at the south end. In addition, she was wearing a parka, fur-trimmed and big enough across the shoulders for a fullback. But, in a second, that was her hair, a bushel basket

of twigs and leaves and vines, and that—the kid next to her in
the jeans and the Indians cap and the screw-you slouch of a
dropout—*that* must've been the boyfriend, perhaps the self-
same one whose virtues she'd been persuaded to ponder less
than a week ago when she hugged the floor behind her counter,
a victim of dutiful churchgoers married to the comely Betty
and the winsome Wilma.

Reed felt smart—in possession of private knowledge. This
was a minor but genuine miracle. In the narrow world H-man
had talked of, such developments were possible. Such, indeed,
had become essential: coincidence on a scale at once personal
and grand. In that world—the lopsided planet on which,
H-man had argued, the sapient were goobers and gods both—
water ran uphill, mystic signs were delivered and correctly
interpreted and insight arrived like a right cross to the throat.
In that world, pearlike and inevitably slowing down, clerks with
chatty fingernails ventured forth with stooped teenage boys to
bring a breed of bliss to guys who, simply as possible, just
wanted to fly higher and faster.

Reed took a bite from his sandwich, negotiated with himself
to calm down, addressed his organs in the order they troubled
him—eyes, ears, brain. The couple was on his level now, arm
in arm, walking toward him. She looked different, a daytime
female that had dressed itself according to MTV and what was
in its pocketbook. But she was pretty, that was obvious, maybe
a little used for nineteen or whatever—a mouth you wanted to
hear the word "wonder" from, eyes you could imagine closed
in repose—and Reed saw her for a moment as a bride, demure
and coy and smelling like sunshine. She was tight—so tight you
might touch her elbow and she would hum, all the valves and
levers and sockets of her smooth and fit. She had a walk you
could sing to, heel and hip and head, her waist exactly an arm's
reach around, and when she and the metalhead turned into
Arabica, Reed believed he could hear the music of her: the
tinkle and chime and thrum she was when she wasn't eye to
eye with a six-shooter.

He was not angry now.

Or frightened.

A miracle had appeared, nibbling a chocolate chip cookie and on the arm of a hoodlum with DOKKEN stenciled on his ass, and, he would tell H-man later, it was nothing—no big thing at all—to rise when they left the pastry shop and to bump into her accidentally on purpose.

"I'm terribly sorry," Reed said, the p's and q's his mother had taught.

Alice C. was looking at him, and beyond: He was a stranger. In his festive sweater and wool topcoat, he was a Tom, Dick or Harry never seen before. Not in her wildest.

"Please," Reed said. He had his wallet out, a dollar to replace her snack. "Allow me."

"That's okay, man," the boyfriend said. "We're cool."

They were. Reed could see that: cool. With a capital.

"Thanks anyway," she said. "It wasn't very good."

He watched them on the stairs. A cavity had opened in him, and filled, a mass shifting lower, and he feared that something—a plank, a brace, a strut—had fallen free inside him, keen now to hear the creak or groan that would say his heart, jerking with every thump, was ready to tumble. He held his breath, the world wobbled a degree or two, but he knew: It was the Lance in him, in its handsomest duds and grinning. Lance had had an idea—not about Alice C., but about Sunday night, about the who and the what and the why.

At home, Reed found H-man dry-firing his finger into the street, a chair scooted up to the window.

"I got lonely," he said, his voice as fey and flat as his eyes. "I woke up, no best buddy."

"Work," Reed said. "You don't want to know."

H-man squeezed off another round, *ka-pow:* a man entering the Preview Lounge across the way.

He'd suffered dreams, H-man said. Perverse episodes. Escape, nick of time, dark of night, script by Kafka. There was tedium involved, the running of marathonlike distances. Cries were heard, an owl hooting. Cast of thousands.

"I saw her," Reed said, excited. Inside him, in the most

secret room of him, a flashlight was swinging wildly. "The girl from the Dairy Mart, Alice C."

H-man pulled his finger down, uncocked his thumb. He demonstrated interest of the sort cats showed for mice.

"What'd she say?"

Nothing, Reed told him. It was gorgeous, right out of "The Twilight Zone," where peculiar met eerie. He'd been a stick to her, a stump.

"What'd I tell you, Ace?"

"She was with her boyfriend," Reed said. "A real loser."

"Let me guess," H-man began, making an elaborate production of his warm-up before he nailed the boy—the Elvis sideburns, the jean jacket, the wallet with the attached chain running to the belt loop, even the Picway biker boots, the brand that required twenty minutes to lace up. A ruffian. A pogue. A varlet.

It was like everything else, Reed figured: he should've seen it coming. Ka-pow.

"You were there."

"Sheer chance," H-man said. "I told you, I was lonely, bereft. I went for a walk. Winter fascinates with me: the cold, the mukluks, the hacking coughs."

Reed entertained the notion that he should be angry, that it was not possible even H-man could enjoy a mile hike in the wind and blistering snow. He'd been ambushed somehow, he thought. A violation had occurred, a betrayal; but he'd already pulled up a chair, and Reed had no plan for his plan but to speak it.

"Sunday night," he said. "Maximum profit potential. The world on cruise control. Like you said, moola and golf and everybody sober."

H-man had taken aim on nothing, maybe the wind. "Yes?"

"I get to be the Lone Ranger," Reed said. "You get to be Tonto."

Reed didn't know what to expect—negative noises mostly, he guessed—but he went on, half prepared to stick his fingers in his ears if pushed to that. A man had options, he figured. A man could shut down, unplug himself. Or a man could explode. Pick up the pieces afterwards.

"I've been thinking about this all afternoon," he said. "You can't imagine what's been going through my mind. I'm all thought out. I got to do this. Bird gotta fly, I gotta burgle."

H-man was smiling now, his one-of-a-kind, ear-to-ear variety.

"What about me?" he was saying.

"You get to drive, sahib."

They laughed right through dinner, take-out pizza, double cheese, afterwards snorting some of the coke that Alice C. had for a while been the walking-talking substitute for. Reed performed his imitation of Gandhi, lots of bowing and scraping and much singsong in the service of sentences that, as they did more coke, began to sound more and more Swedish. "Yumping yiminy," Reed cried. "Fondue." It was jibber-jabber and used up a half-hour until H-man recounted his Merle Haggard story.

"The singer," he said.

Right, Reed told him. Okie from Muskogee.

"He's a con," H-man said. "Did a concert for us once, a real grit. What a brick. Broke into an all-night grocery. Interrupted two stock boys and an assistant produce manager smoking a joint and eating Wing-Dings."

Reed understood this anecdote was leading somewhere and said so.

"I got a surprise too," H-man said, and Reed, his insides going clang-clang-clang, readied himself for it. "It seems I have made some acquaintances."

Female, Reed said. But he was only guessing.

"Aggressively female," H-man said, and for a full minute Reed had the impression that he was watching himself and H-man from high up in the corner of the room. With great satisfaction, he was noting that below, in sling chairs with personalities enough to have names, sat two men who might, given their crooked state of mind, slap on party hats and moo.

"I'm listening," he said.

His walk, H-man began. A clearing of the head, a sojourn. A tavern was spotted, a bar. Pete's, Mike's—one of those places. He was made to feel welcome. The bartender, Pete or Mike, told Polish jokes, which H-man was good-tempered enough to chuckle at. Drinks were served. Talk was exchanged regarding poontang, the mysteries of same.

"Yumping yiminy," Reed said.

Mike or Pete had addressed him as "Bub." "Bub," it seemed, was crestfallen, even depressed. "Bub" had suffered a divorce, which meant agony and misery, which meant forays into the hinterlands of the spirit. "Bub," as it developed, wept in his beer. Mike, or Pete, whipped out his multifunction calculator. Two was added to two.

"Why are we whispering?" Reed said.

H-man had his finger out again, this time a digit to wag.

"A phone call was made," H-man said. "The long was attended to, the short."

Reed was thinking about it, the mysteries of same. The last woman he'd been with was, for several hours, the sweetest girl on earth. She'd invited him to her apartment in Lakewood, right on the Gold Coast, a manorial layout with goodies in gold and bronze and teak. Many of the Browns resided there, she'd announced. The Cleveland Browns. "Here, tiger," she'd said seductively, handing him a drink, B&B. He was enjoying the view, a moonlit lake from fifteen stories up, when she burst out of her bedroom clutching a tiny fur contraption, like a tube sock, she insisted he wear. They were the perfect couple, he'd decided. She possessed accoutrements, he the alacrity to use them.

"I gotta tell you, Ace," H-man was saying, "they're gonna want to be paid, these girls."

Reed had an expression H-man was certain to recognize: "I roger that, Capcom. That's an affirmative."

H-man looked at him, a little man with a big secret.

"Mine's Dixie," he said. "After the war."

WOLFMAN

THE CHANGES TAKE PLACE INSIDE.

—JOSEPH CONRAD

Reed's had been Amy Joy. After the doughnut.

"She didn't subscribe to the big bang theory," Reed told H-man. "That's what she said, honest. She peels off her clothes, dives in the sack, says if she wasn't there, it didn't happen."

They were parked by the self-serve island at the Sohio Gas Mart on Madison and West 160th, Reed putting in a tankful of premium and talking to H-man through the window. This was the ideal place, H-man had said. Off the beaten. The ambience of moral collapse. A lone, unsuspecting you-know-what behind the counter inside. A cream dot dot dot puff.

"How'd you happen to be discussing the origin of the universe?" H-man wanted to know.

"It just came up." That was right: there'd been a series of wows, each more ardent than the last, before the foreplay went haywire. That's what you get with seventeen-year-olds, she'd claimed. A shit-load of enthusiasm and considerable interest in the meaning of life.

"You liked her, I guess."

Oh, he said. Did he ever. She'd used this phrase: the endless deferral of fun. Rode him like a bucking bronco.

H-man was laughing and Reed thought to return the favor.

"How was yours?"

He'd heard moaning. That's what Reed was recalling while H-man, meticulous as a surgeon, rolled up one sleeve of his suit coat: he'd heard spook-house moaning and the kind of thumping associated with foul dreams or seizures. And laughter—cackling as befit the Wicked Witch of the West.

"Look here," H-man was saying.

On his arm, from wrist to elbow, were bite marks, distinct and surprisingly petite, as if each had involved the laborious instruction and deliberation that attended rocket repair.

"Hickeys, huh?"

"Brutal," H-man said. "I loved it."

Dixie, Reed learned, was the kind of woman who started huffing and puffing when you took off your shoes.

"Intercourse," Reed said, "what an idea."

Now they were ready, H-man easing himself out of the car, Reed putting the hose back in the pump. It was frigid, his breath rolling out in clouds, and Reed was shocked by the volume of air he had inside. An impossible amount, it seemed. As if within were a factory pouring out plumes and billows of steam; as if whatever was required of him necessitated vast, even mythic measures of energy.

"We can do something else, you know," H-man said. "Go to the movies, trip the light fantastic."

Reed shook his head. He'd already conducted an inventory of himself, stock-taking of the most painstaking sort. He'd named all his parts, those whose names he could recall, and he'd told himself who he was in the world, and where, and why. He'd sung himself a song, "Baa, Baa, Black Sheep," and packed his cares, those that could be enumerated, in his old kit bag. For extra comfort, he did something else.

"You're a silly man, Reed."

Reed had made the sign of the cross, a whirl of fingerwork for each station itself.

"I didn't know you were Catholic."

"Indulge me a little," Reed said. "As evenings go, this is one of the biggest."

Like the other jobs, this had a title: Abbott and Costello
Meet the Wolfman. Like the others, this was fifty percent
script, fifty percent improv.

"Rock'n'roll," Reed said hopefully.

"Knife and fork, Ace. Salt and pepper."

The Wolfman had a full beard, enough whiskers for a
month-long revolution, and the first phrase out of his mouth,
when Reed charged in the door following his pistol, was "Oh,
hell," as if—on top of his old lady leaving him and his truck
needing a ring job and his daughter pregnant by a standard-
issue punk named T-Bone—this had been a really rough day.
"The third time in six weeks," he complained. "Jesus H.
Christ." Then, before Reed urged him to reach for the damn
sky, he shook his head wearily, the heartache and inconvenience of this interruption as plain to him as white on chalk.

"Dance," Reed said.

"What?" The Wolfman seemed to be looking high and low,
forlorn, as if he couldn't find his keys.

The idea had just occurred to Reed, a plot turn from a B
western, the kind of dialogue necessary if you wanted to estab-
lish your credentials.

"I said dance, tenderfoot."

Reed felt lost, unsure what silly accent he was using. Then,
like a light in the eyes, it came to him: He was Billy the Kid
and Snidely Whiplash, every stubble-faced, cheroot-sucking
desperado it was desirable to have booed in a lifetime of movie-
watching. And then he said, "That's enough," and Wolfman,
still baffled, wound down like a cheap toy.

"Bad move, kemosabe." H-man was standing beside a dis-
play of Valvoline 30-weight, his own gun at his side. "You're
idealizing again."

Reed tried to look two places at once—at Wolfman, who
appeared now to have a purely academic interest in what was
going on; and at H-man, who seemed, briefly, to have been
offended—then he let the feeling pass. He had options, he
figured. Miles and miles to go before he slept.

"You want the money?" Wolfman said.

"No shit, Sherlock."

Reed inhaled sharply. Unhappily, the job—the fucking caper—had a new title, Sherlock. It, the caper, was evolving, had reached another stage. If the right circumstances obtained, Reed thought, in another minute they'd be sashaying around— Shadrach, Meshach and Abednego—singing "Auld Lang Syne."

"Got only about fifty bucks," Wolfman said. "Lots of credit card stuff."

"A slow night," H-man suggested.

Wolfman shrugged. "The slowest, man. Nothing but hillbillies. I got people going in the toilets to sleep. Guy comes by every night to throw me the finger."

Reed didn't want to hear any of it. Somehow he'd lost H-man, the other half of himself, but the focus shifted anew and H-man reappeared, a jumbo package of Fritos in hand, frowning.

"We'll take it," H-man said. "We do not discriminate, that's our policy."

Wolfman punched the cash drawer open and was carefully—too carefully—picking out the bills.

"I don't guess you want the coin," he said. "Last guy didn't want no coin. Last guy was real fussy."

Reed was concentrating. He could see himself in the reflection from the window, saddened to discover that he appeared bent forward, decrepit, shoulders bunched, his the defeated, woebegone expression of a fish that fed at the bottom. He was thinking about what's-her-face: Amy Joy. He stood in danger of forgetting all she'd taught him about time and space and the banglike noise an intellectual like him could create.

"What's your favorite food, Bub?"

Reed couldn't imagine where he'd gotten that, "Bub." He was now in a vale of tears in which two-thirds of the denizens were named Bub.

"I have to answer that?" Wolfman was saying to H-man.

"Afraid so," he said. "He's the ringleader, evidently."

Wolfman shrugged, did everything but rub his chinny-chin-chin.

"Pork chops, I guess. I like 'em grilled."

That was good, Reed thought. But he didn't know why. "Why" was like "soon": another no-account sound to be made in a big, strange place.

"Last guy," Wolfman said to H-man.

They seemed to be pals now, Bub and Bub. There was something between them, Reed concluded, and if he could only get his breathing under control, he would see what it was.

"Last guy what?" H-man said.

"Last guy had about three teeth in his head," Wolfman told him. "Didn't care what I ate. Had a gun, though."

Reed was stuck, the wheel inside him spinning furiously in place, the checkered pattern on it flickering so wildly he feared he could be hypnotized, wake up as a chicken, wake up suspended in air, his spine rigid, nothing solid to support his middle. Then he could hear H-man crunching Fritos, and only three facts were to be known in the here and now: The money was in the bag, no coin; Wolfman was saying that—the terror and the chitchat aside—this wasn't so bad; and down at the end of Reed's arm a silver object was bobbing, herky-jerky, as though whoever was attached to it, by wire or rope or string, was smack in the middle of brain-misfire.

"How you feel about jumping jacks?" Reed said.

"Costello." It was a warning. From a fucking teacher.

"How 'bout squat thrusts?"

"Lordy." H-man again—a scold, a nag. "This is embarrassing."

Reed was still looking at the astonished eyeballs of Wolfman, the nervous back-and-forth they were; then, no more frozen spots in his chest, Reed offered his advice to H-man.

"Shut up."

Somehow, Reed would think later, an agreement had been reached. They, H-man and his newfound friend, had conspired to put up with him; and he had been enticed to remain a son-of-a-bitch. A supercilious SOB.

"Bad knees," Wolfman said. "I haven't done a jumping jack since the dark ages."

Geez, Reed said. He said it again—and again—unspeakably happy with the tingle it made in his ears.

"Let's go," H-man said. "Amscray, in other words."

Hold your horses, Reed told him. Wolfman was supposed to get on the floor.

"Wolfman?" the guy asked.

Right, Reed told him. Dot dot dot *you*.

Immediately, Wolfman appealed to H-man for confirmation.

"Sorry," H-man said. "It serves a purpose, you know. Identification. A jog to the memory."

The gun wasn't shaking now. Rather, it seemed to float in the air by itself, a special effect, another high-tech enigma to whoop and holler about afterwards in the sweet by-and-by.

"No peeking," Reed said. "Isn't that right, Mr. Abbott?"

Absolutely, H-man said. That too served a purpose.

And now, happily, a final purpose needed to be served, a formal list of do's and don'ts Wolfman was to observe as if, according to the phrase, his life depended on it: no shilly-shallying, for instance; no grab-ass, no farting around; no looking on anybody else's paper; no cutting in line, no picking your nose, no taking the Lord's name in vain; no spitting, no telling the end of the story; no eating with your fingers, no backstabbing.

For a second, Wolfman looked like a tree distressed by lightning. "You're teasing, right?"

Reed made a face right out of Halloween. "Do I look like I'm kidding?"

Wolfman turned to H-man again, the two Bubs.

"We're sophisticates," Reed said. "One of us is a college graduate. One of us, you gotta guess, is a flat-out nihilist. One of us shuns the straight and narrow. One of us does not fly right. One of us, Christ, is on the rag all the time, just whining and bitching, the most sorry-ass shit—"

"That's enough," H-man said.

Reed had leaned over the counter. The fun was gone now, the air out of the balloon.

"Wolfman?"

He was lying on his back, legs crossed at the ankle, the way you would if—the excitement and the hugger-mugger aside— you'd had a bitch of a day and just wanted to take a nap.

"Yes, sir," he said.

"When somebody comes in," Reed told him, "you can get up, okay?"

Next he and H-man were out the door, Reed in charge of a sack of money that threatened with every step to leap from his hand and fly into the sky. H-man got behind the wheel, buckled his seat belt—"It's the law," he'd said a billion years ago—and Reed hoped to hear the words from the beverage store: "Houston, this is Tranquility Base. The Eagle has landed." But it didn't come, and didn't come—zip was coming from H-man.

You were at that point on the map, Reed assumed, where X was before you arrived—a scorched, blank plain full of the old-timey dragons and gargoyles the imagination had put there, a place beyond the horizon, always beyond, unknown in any fashion until, without warning, you woke up there, black against the sun, a speck in a place so barren and deprived nothing could civilize it except the blithe fairy tales you could more or less invent.

"I'm Ishmael," Reed said. "You're Ahab."

Geez, H-man sighed.

"You're the seadog, I'm just a landlubber with too much whippersnapper. You're an interesting fellow—craven, oratorical, eye-catching footwear. I get to hang around belowdecks, swap the shit about bridle-bits and fasces with such as Stubb and Pip and Flask."

H-man had taken a right, and a left, no haste to make waste.

"We get to use lingo like 'ye' and 'thou,' a whole lot of nineteenth-century palaver about the soul. We're looking for a whale, you see, a big fish. It's outstanding—the bounding main, sunshine, all the allegory you can eat. Coin comes into play, I believe."

The headlights of a passing truck lit up H-man, his face at once ghoulish and profoundly tolerant.

"Is there going to be much more of this?" H-man asked.

Reed held on to the door, then himself.

"There's a showdown, of course, a fierce amount of destruction—moral as well as physical. It's a hell of a climax."

H-man appeared to be listening.

"In this version," Reed said, "Ahab gets to live."

The car hit a chuckhole, bounced.

"In this version," H-man said, "your guy is an ignoramus."

At home, they stowed away their gear, changed into their nightwear. That was H-man's word, "nightwear," a matter of buckles and bows and scraps of leather. "Back at the ranch," Reed had announced, unlocking the door. "Where the buffalo roam." He was tired, as if he'd been stretched and twisted and knotted up, and for a time it was diverting to watch a muscle twitch in his forearm. There wasn't much to say, he concluded. His brain had turned off, the factory in him defunct and padlocked.

"You want something to drink?"

"A beer," H-man said.

In the kitchen, Reed gazed into the refrigerator as he thought H-man had, wondering what could be concocted out of Tabasco sauce and carrots and raisin bread. What could be surmised about an individual who more than once had eaten a breakfast of Diet Coke and Jimmy Dean sausage, he at length decided, could take you a week to think through. On the counter sat two bags—"the loot," H-man said, "the swag"—and Reed caught himself staring at them, the word "amiss" now writ large in his consciousness.

"One more." H-man had materialized at the sink, washing

his hands. "We do one more job, then I'm gone. I need to do groundwork, lay plans."

He had appeared so quietly that for a second, long enough to grab a beer, Reed believed he had been beside him all along, insubstantial, a ghost.

"You have a problem with that?" H-man asked.

No, Reed said. He had no problem with anything.

"I got places to be," H-man said. "Men to see, things to do."

So why didn't he go now, Reed wanted to know.

"Good question, white boy. I'll get back to you on that."

In the living room, the TV on to an episode of "The Honeymooners" he didn't think he'd seen, Reed asked what had happened to the other bag of money, the loot from Heck's beverage store.

"Overhead," H-man said. "Expenses."

Ralph and Ed were arranging to play golf. They wore the outfits, plaid knickers and caps with tiny balls on the crown. Very soon, Reed supposed, Norton was going to tick Ralph Kramden off, the direct consequence of which would be a lot of slapstick to-and-fro to yuk about.

"How much?"

H-man put down his bottle, affected surprise.

"You're pissed, aren't you?"

"It'll pass," Reed said. Everything was passing.

Ninety-six, H-man began. Ninety-six, ninety-seven—a number in the n's, pin money, scarcely commensurate with the thrill. Easy come, easy go. Just think of it as shells, as beads. Paper clips, matchsticks, didn't make any difference. It was arbitrary, utterly. Could be fucking body hair.

Wolfman, Reed thought. Sherlock. Moby Dick. The caper was still evolving, adapting and mutating, the superfluous shed, getting simpler and neater. Maybe, if they were patient, it would reach the point where it resembled Tweedles Dee and Dum drinking beer and sitting in front of a TV.

"You got a theory for this, correct?"

"I shit you not, amigo," H-man said. "I got a theory to cover every contingency."

It was over, Reed figured, the movie of his life. He was just waiting for the house lights to come up. Now he would watch the credits, learn who took responsibility for his makeup, his costumes. In the dark, he would discover who'd constructed the sets he moved through, who chauffeured the cars, catered the yummies. These were the details, small but crucial, the sum of which became the organism he was. God was in the details, he'd been told. That man. The one who brought the lights, edited the tape, told you where to do what had to be done, even wrote the foot-tapping la-la-la the doing was done by. That man. You were in the dark, the good reaffirmed, the bad blasted to smithereens, no loose end to tie up: soon you would know who your key grip was, your best boy, your line operator. Still, in a little while—a day or two or three—except for the hoopla, the scenes with derring-do and hit-or-miss, you could forget the bulk of it, including, by chance, who was in it and what happened afterwards.

The next day, Reed called in sick. He had the flu, he said, the rot. He didn't know when he'd be back. What was this, December? Could be March. April was not too farfetched.

"You sure you want to do that?" H-man asked.

He'd had a dream, Reed told him. Venutians had appeared to him, conceivably the same who'd abducted Brenda, the UC–Santa Barbara Sophomore from *The Star* that Alice C. had been reading the night other aliens had swooped down for a visit. It was creepy. They'd sat on the end of his bed, a mommy and a daddy, made outer space yakety-yak, poked him a little, held his insides to a light, wedged back the roof of his skull to hear what was howling in there.

"Sounds familiar," H-man said. "Did they have fingers or just the wandlike affair?"

That afternoon, H-man policed his weapon, a kit from his footlocker open on the dining room table.

"Do this about once a month," he said. "It's a precaution, Reed. You grease a wheel, you clean your piece—it's that simple."

He started pointing at the goodies in the Hopps kit: the rod, the patches, gun oil, a metal brush, the blankety-blank.

"You gonna jot this down?"

He'd remember, Reed said. Mind like a trap.

H-man held up a tube.

"Nitro solvent," he said. "Keeps the action smooth."

Right, Reed observed. That went in the trap too. Like H-man's footlocker, the mind was a respository for the artifacts one ought to have handy in the event one sought fame, and riches, in the darker life.

In the evening, they played Go, Parcheesi, Old Maid— games H-man could win at. Winning, he explained, was, no matter the stakes, head and shoulders above losing. Wasn't anything losing proved. Losing took the lead right out of your pencil.

"I'll write that down," Reed said, and H-man's eyes grew narrow, like slits.

"Don't get weird on me, Ace," he said. "Weird doesn't become you. Not a bit."

After dinner, they did the last of the dope. H-man emptied it on the table, chopped it up fine with the edge of a playing card, the Old Maid herself, shaped it into lines that if laid end to end, Reed guessed, might transport you and a pal and the mealymouthed people in your head to the very limits of Timbuktu.

"Be my guest, senor," H-man said. "Get happy."

"What about you?"

H-man revealed the pills in his hand.

"Sopors, Darvocet," he said. "I'm going the other direction tonight."

Reed took a hit, hoped to count to twenty before the boom went off. H-man was right. Weird was not flattering at all. Weird was infantile, the bully-at-the-beach junk you'd find at the jungle gym, the playroom. It was much better to be cool, orthodox in all undertakings, imperturbable. You ought to imagine yourself an angel peering down, your interest in this or that activity abstract, selfless: a doctor monitoring his monster. Weird was burdensome, too heavy-duty, weight you didn't need to tote when it came time for moving on, or forward. Weird was a drag, classic. Weird absolutely fucked up the action.

Then the boom arrived, as if from one thousand miles away, faint and very likely at first to be mistaken for something else.

"The boy," H-man was saying. "Named Sam, after my father."

The next minutes were filled with H-man's Venutians—Sam and Martha, his mother. They resided in Dallas, with a Santa Claus–like drywall contractor named Sims, in a four-bedroom colonial on Somerset. They'd met Tom Landry, the former coach of the Cowboys. Sam could swim. Martha was going to junior college, paralegal. Boy, could she type. These, Christ, were damned-terrifying Venutians. They even had insufferably cute nicknames for everything—the poodle Skippy, a Chrysler New Yorker called Beulah. Lord. The cat, a calico with one eye, was Pooh. They had sweet names for each other, for pity's sake. Sweet Cheeks. Honey Bunch. Yecch. They even had a name for him. Called him Uncle Carl—"Wonkie Carl, actually"—let him bunk in the guest room under the pictures of Meech and Momma Deedee, the new grandparents. Geez.

"I'm going to bed, H-man."

Carl shuddered as if he'd just awakened.

"Don't blame you," he said. "This is simply too sad sack to be believed."

In the morning Reed drank Coke, ate sausages and watched H-man confront his novel. It, like sleep, was a fitful activity, an enterprise of rapid movement and throat noise, pinched and wet, too calamitous to be done without a hard hat.

"I'm in the section about youth," H-man offered. "I use the

word 'scathe' a lot, too much. The word 'rift.' I got serious diction problems."

In his dream, Reed had asked what the book was about. In his dream, the pages stood ten feet tall and were shiny like sheet metal. In his dream, you couldn't handle it without oven mitts.

"It's big," H-man was saying. "I bite off a lot to chew."

So Reed asked it, what exactly was being devoured, and H-man appeared to chase himself round and round for a second.

"Man versus man, I think. Though nature gets a licking too."

Reed watched TV—argued with Regis and Kathie Lee, won a furnished Florida room and a fully equipped Airstream camper on "The Price Is Right." This inactivity, the lying around thinking, he suspected, was turning him into an ooze you could find lying on the sidewalk in the summer sun: sticky and beginning to sink through the cracks. The morning was passing by in spasms, like a too long train, its separate elements jerking forward before shrieking to a stop. He took a bath, sang a song of sixpence, amazed he still knew the lyrics. His head under water except for his nose, Reed felt the world reach him as a code of bongs and clicks and clanks, the sense of it perhaps decipherable to something less handicapped by a familiarity with English: something—a beast, surely—that apprehended the world only by knowing what it could eat and what could eat it.

A dog, say.

Standing in front of his closet, he saw that he had many clothes to pick from but little passion for picking; and a minute later, when he beheld himself in the mirror in slacks and a sweater with a lonesome pine tree outlined by one vivid mountaintop, he shook his head mournfully. "Rift," he said, his voice irritatingly hollow, as if it were hissing up a pipe from his shoes. He had not shaved, he saw, and understood straightaway that a new regimen was in force, a program consistent with a day whose pieces lay scattered from alpha to omega. A principle was involved here, he decided. A dialectic that embraced, on the one hand, assorted criminal ventures and, on the other hand—what?

He stopped. It was as though he had come round a corner and bumped into himself, seen his head whirling on its root like a cabbage. He exchanged looks with himself in the mirror, watched his jaw go loose and huhlike: he was thinking about King, the dog. In its case, nature had definitely taken a licking. Evidently, nature had had a good talking to, a sit-down that had grown only louder and louder. Nature, quite clearly, had remained its mangy, growling self. Nature didn't know diddly about principle, or about those victimized by it, and immediately Reed conceived of how it might be necessary, given that sort of adversarial but otherwise steadfast companion, to go toe to toe and not find any solution save carnage to resolve your differences.

Then Reed heard the word "death" again and found himself scrambling away from it in a frenzy: it was like trying to run from his own body, like abandoning his bones piled on the sack of his skin, like trying to throw fistfuls of his own flesh into the darkness behind him.

"I'm going out," he told H-man.

"Restless, huh?" He had ink all over his lips. "Pregame jitters."

H-man was in another of his colorful shirts, the one reportedly given to him by Myna Ataful, Waikiki surf-master. This one, he'd said, was ten thousand percent metaphor. It stood for ruin—and wrath.

"It's not tonight, is it?"

"You never learn, do you, Ace?"

Reed thought carefully, even using his teeth. It was Tuesday. A day, one theory held, not governed by boredom and anger.

"A question," H-man said as Reed was leaving. "What's a highfalutin synonym for 'bullshit'?"

He drove throughout the east side, the day exactly like the

sort of snow he hated: brittle and white upon white upon white. But he knew where he was going, and the knowledge of it, like a long-held secret, made the getting there as simple and easy as asking for valuables that didn't belong to you. Knowledge was wonderful, a notion Reed could see the felicity of when he pulled into the wide circular drive in Fowlers Mills. He'd had an interesting experience here, he recalled. Down-right formative. A lesson in interpersonal dynamics. It had been raining, off and on, by turns a drizzle then a downpour, air then water, and he'd met gentlemen named Larry, Curly and Moe. Not much had changed since. Not much could change: gardeners would see to that, handymen, painters, cash.

When Reed got out of the car, he felt fine, a feeling he placed at the orange end of the color bar, then he rang the door bell, a comic jingle he believed he should recognize, and the reds in him, shades associated with alarm and urgency, started to brighten and pulsate. He had no idea what he would say, not an inkling, only the belief, certain as sin, that here was where it had begun, his own section about youth. Closure could be reached here, definitely. Consensus.

"No," the woman said.

She was the maid: her uniform said so, her incredible black-ness.

"A lawyer?" Reed continued. "Tall, dark hair. Works down-town."

She shook her head, so he tried to describe the others—Curly, the one with the glasses; next Moe, the silent guy—before he fumbled his way back to the talkative man who'd told H-man to go home.

"Gerald Ford," he said, thoroughly aware he'd mixed them up, confused their features.

"Don't know no Jerry Ford," she said. "Guy here looks like Papa Smurf."

Reed tried to thank her, was in fact already making his getaway, but she hadn't quit.

"You ought to see the wife," she called. "That's one evil

white woman. You come back in an hour, get an eyeful of that. Looks like Mr. T. Only without the big tits."

Now he didn't know where to go. He had pulled into a turnout on Richmond Road where it crossed the Chagrin River, a place that brought to mind such terms as "fracture" and "disunity." This was where winter was, the snow slushy and streaked, the trees black skeletons with a billion spindly arms, and Reed conceived of himself as a character in an especially tiresome play, all the important action offstage. "You ought to see the honky kid," the maid had yelled. "What a trip. Thinks he's Clint Eastwood. Honey, he ain't no kind of wood."

It was two, two-thirty—a number in the t's, H-man would say—the sun a washed-out disc, more a rumor of itself than any hopeful phenomenon to see, totally corrupt. In the glove compartment, Reed discovered a mostly full pack of Tareytons, his first drag marvelously mild after twenty months of abstinence. A song was playing on WMMS, a moldy oldie that mentioned heartbreak and getting even in the same line, and Reed, drumming on the dash, sang the might-right-fight to it until some loudmouth stole the program to tell Ohio what tape decks to buy. He watched his hands come back to him. Something was happening to time, he feared. A question was forming in Reed's mind, an interrogative independent of any Stooge he knew, and when it was complete, like a hand-lettered banner hung over a doorway, he asked it aloud: "Where can you go when you can go anyplace at all?"

He went to Carole Bashaw's.

"You're romanticizing," he berated himself when he parked. "This is idealization, Reed. Pure and simple."

When she didn't answer the door, he peeked in the front window to say howdy to the furniture he was estranged from. She was at work, he knew. Everybody was at work—making predicaments for themselves and slipping free of them. In and out. Thesis and its anti-. He remembered being on top of her one time, sufficient light from heaven to see by. She had moaned, and Reed had understood he was making love to Jamie Lee Curtis. To Victoria Principal. It was like screwing water. And now he found himself addressing himself in the second person, a "you" importantly related to the specimen which employed it. "You" stood on its ex-wife's porch. "You" was checking her mail, not amused to learn that she was using too much electricity. She had a birthmark like a tugboat on her ankle, an endearing way of mispronouncing any word from German, and once upon a time, "you"—this second person inside and clamoring—had loved her.

Love, he wondered. Doubtlessly a synonym. Doubtlessly highfalutin.

In the car, he felt at once weightless and bottom-heavy, the coils and loops of him pertinent to balance now clogged with grit and grease. He felt himself teetering, on the edge of decisive action. He took out a pad and pencil, found a blank page. Something needed to be done, action simultaneously conclusive and drastic. An appeal was in order, he thought. To higher instincts, to the highroad itself. That's what he tried to tell Carole Bashaw in the note he left her; that's what he meant by the empty pack of smokes and by the serious diction he used.

At home H-man said he needed a lift to the bus station: matters of the practical sort to be dealt with.

"Like what?"

"Like," H-man began, "moving my base of operations."

Here it was that Reed noticed the padlocked footlocker. In his note to Carole Louise Reed, née Bashaw, he'd used the word "scathe," plus he'd poured out his heart to her on the subjects of "now" and "then" and "maybe."

"What about your gun? Stuff like that?"

Hair combed, shaved, H-man had endeavored to look like a banker, very square, whatever the opposite of human was—a citizen with, for example, a wife and a kid and bills to pay in Texas.

"I dump everything," he said. "When we're done, I toss the hardware, ditch the nifty disguise. Caterpillar to butterfly, a veritable transformation. Another NBA head fake."

At the Greyhound terminal on Chester near CSU, they

approached the freight window, the footlocker between them.

"Pick," H-man said.

A list of destinations was ticking through Reed's head: Pittsburgh, Atlanta, Little Rock, a whole continent of inner cities to be anonymous in.

"How about Chicago?"

He'd known somebody from Chi-town, a frat brother named Goonch.

"Too cold," H-man was saying. "I'm thinking warm. I'm thinking rays, doing good for my electrolytes or whatever. I'm thinking leisure pursuits, pool halls, ladies in straw hats."

Reed had a vision that featured cactus, jagged mountains against a valley infertile as a skillet.

"Phoenix," he suggested.

"Too dry," H-man told him. "I get skin like an alligator."

They settled on Houston. It had the requisite elements: immodest size, an ethnically diverse population, few larger-than-lifes, as many ways out as Carter had little liver pills, an inclination toward turpitude, indigenous laziness, mucho mom-and-pop joints, cars of the unattended ilk, no gun shop background checks, peace officers named Jimmy Bob and Cletus, card-carrying rednecks. Tranquility Base.

"Tomorrow night," Reed said back in the car.

H-man nodded. He had the place scoped out: Things U-Need Grocery, a block off Detroit, strictly low-rent, the perigee of rents. A storefront next to a secondhand furniture. Across the street was a Chinese restaurant, Fu Man Chu's, noticed it after the Dairy Mart gig. In bad-guy argot, it was a plum, a peach, a pomegranate—any *p*-fruit you cared to chomp into.

"You're excited," Reed said.

"What can I tell you, senor? I like to travel."

They were downtown, rush-hour traffic as stop-and-go as Reed had ever seen, his only one of a handful of cars moving against the flow. He liked being from Cleveland, he thought. To the rest of the country, the city was an old joke—its river had burned; to go bowling, its mayor had once declined a presidential invitation to the White House, and *his* hair had burned; it had once been bankrupt—but it remained a place in which you could distinguish yourself: you could kick tail here, jump up in a crowd and holler until you were noticed. The rest of America was the gag, too sober-minded and too vain and too Speedy Gonzalez to see that the ho-ho-ho was on it. You had to be tough here. No crybabies. No pissants. No hinky shit. Nose, grindstone, shoulder to the wheel—all the elements.

"I lied," H-man was saying.

They were almost home, Reed thought. Five more minutes they'd be indoors.

"Jane Fonda ain't my neighbor," H-man said. "My neighbors are Apaches named Flat Iron. They like to get drunk, play Hank Williams, the Oak Ridge Boys. Reed, I gotta tell you: Nothing more melancholy than hearing some nasal lonesome-me shit at four in the morning—"

There was more. For six blocks, the sun screaming in at them through the smeary windshield, there was more—Indians and cowboys, animal life screeching, music coming up out of the ground, from the brush, the sun rolling west like a wheel—and Reed, block after block, imagined himself stopping the car in the middle of the road, horns blaring, the door swinging open, and one of them clear of the other, one of them moving very deliberately away.

THE KID

I LEAVE A WHITE AND TURBID WAKE;
PALE WATERS, PALER CHEEKS, WHERE'ER I SAIL.
THE ENVIOUS BILLOWS SIDELONG SWELL
TO WHELM MY TRACK; LET THEM;
BUT FIRST I PASS.

—HERMAN MELVILLE

Tomorrow had arrived like an avalanche, the rocks and earth of it crumbling down on Reed and catching him unaware and slack-witted when H-man rapped on his door to say, "Saddle up, buckaroo."

"Don't come back," Reed said. "After this, no more visits, okay?"

H-man affected to look chagrined.

"You've grown tired of me?"

Right, that was it. He'd grown weary.

And now they were sitting in the car, a half-block down from Things U-Need Grocery, a haggard couple on the morning side of a very tiring soiree. "Loitering," H-man had mumbled a few minutes before. Then: "Dicking around." Then: "Un-fucking-believable." He'd been angry, not sanguine about the amount of come-and-go at the store, in particular a kid who'd walked in and out three times. "Juvy hall," H-man had said. "You develop an instinct, can spot a brother a mile off. My guess is marijuana, maybe a joy ride. One day the training wheels come off and—powie!—a life in the fast lane."

For Reed the next minute had shape and substance, enough character to be in *Who's Who*—a silence that, were it corporeal, would have mange and claws and teeth. His hands were sweaty, so he stripped his gloves off, grabbed another pair from the box on the floorboard.

"Next time," H-man said, "buy the ones with talcum, maybe a size larger."

Reed arranged himself anew, tried to imagine himself in any color but black.

"We can go somewhere else," he said, but H-man was already shaking his head, making like big brother again.

"Always finish what you start, Ace. The half-assed ain't diddly, you know what I mean? We're the righteous dudes."

Reed took it in, absorbed it, followed the advice letter by letter until, in the air between them, was only the weather itself. H-man didn't know how right he was. They were blessed, and Reed understood, with no special relief, that whatever happened, even if there were a major-league snafu, they would be fine. They were charmed. The training wheels were off, and they—Little Carl and Little Alex—would never, not here or elsewhere, fall down.

"You can't go back," H-man was saying. "You've popped your cherry, Ace. You can make up stories, tell a few lies, fudge all you want. You've been to the mountaintop, senor."

Blowing on his hands, the kid had returned, doing an I'm-colder-than-a-well-digger's-ass dance on the sidewalk. He looked twelve, maybe thirteen, in a trenchcoat that could have belonged to his father. He was wearing sneakers, the expensive brand that, according to commercial TV, permitted you to hang at the hoop for hours.

"He's going to pop the place," H-man said. "That's what this is all about. He's going to whack our pigeon."

Reed weighed the irony of it.

"You ought to speak to him," he said.

"I ought to paddle his behind," H-man said, outraged for a moment. "I ought to give him a piece of my mind."

"But you're not a violent man."

H-man appeared to consider it, his fingers keeping the rhythm of his thinking on the steering column.

"And don't you forget it, buddy," he said at last. "I just got an eccentric way of making the mortgage, is all. I am your basic, if more reflective, lone wolf."

This time when the kid came out, he was carrying a soda, most of which he drank in front of the store before walking away.

"Let's go," H-man said.

"Wait," Reed told him. "See if he comes back."

Reed smoked another cigarette, not the best medicine in the world for the cold he discovered he had; but he could tell that, in less than twenty-four hours, he'd developed the habit afresh. He now had a stylish rhetorical tool, stage-business for the hands and mouth while waiting for the brain to engage. In a couple of days, he would reacquire the morning cough; a few more, the wheeze; even more, the flashy personal moves connected with licking and flicking and putting out. H-man was wrong. Old habits could come back.

"What time you got?" H-man asked.

Reed checked his watch: ten-fifteen, the place closed in forty-five minutes.

"We give the kid a little longer," H-man said. "He isn't back in ten, we do the forbidden shake-and-bake."

Reed imagined himself in a roomful of people, what H-man called "interested parties," a room like an operating theater, the gallery at shoulder level and above. He had audiovisual devices—a blackboard, a slide projector, on an easel a cardboard-mounted map showing the block where his car was parked, the corner the kid had disappeared around. *A*, he told the audience, was H-man, the perpetrator, medium height, medium build, the customary etceteras; *B* was Reed, also customary, the incarnation of average. *A* and *B* went back ten years; *A* and *B* had a history.

"Ain't this a fine how-do-you-do?" H-man was saying. "I gotta piss."

A had been struck by the name of the place, Things U-Need Grocery. It was direct, no fancy-schmancy. As subtle as a war wound. *A* had said he expected to find bread and water inside, perhaps a pile of surplus army blankets. But no herring snacks. No canned lobster. No pitted Spanish olives. You'd face a counter, MEAT scrawled above it, the stuff available only in loaves or hunks. Another counter would have PLEASURE spray-stenciled on it, in bins a gravel that in the good old days would have been called lemon drops and Milk Duds and peppermint sticks. "This is the future, *B,"A* had said. "In a hundred years everybody's going to be named X and—what?—Y."

"Stay put," H-man was saying now. "I gotta take a leak."

Reed looked at his watch again. Ten-thirty. The kid, he figured, was home by now, no doubt reading a Marvel Comic or breathing hard at the Playboy Channel. *What do you think the hyphen's for,* H-man had said. *THINGS YOU hyphen NEED.* Reed had thought hard. Even assiduously. *Ignorance,* he'd said. *Or wit.*

"'Tis the season, Ace."

Reed tried to collect himself, stubbed out his smoke.

"I got a drippy nose." He demonstrated. "You have any Kleenex?"

A patted himself down, finally shrugged.

"We'll get some inside," he said. "Time to make a differ-ence, Ace. Strangers in paradise."

Once out of the car, Reed examined his firepower. Thirty-three ounces, round-nosed bullets, smokeless powder, a nine-pound trigger, muzzle flip—the particulars about this, he thought, were fascinating, a fund of information he felt fortu-nate to have come by, as if a unique variety of gratification attended matters that theoretically could become life-and-death.

"What's that you're singing?" H-man said.

She had returned: "The Girl from Ipanema."

"Very cavalier," H-man decided. "I love it."

At the door, *A* declared that he would do the talking. *A* believed in efficiency, in the shortest route between, say, want-ing and having. Wanting, no offense intended, didn't require a lot of parley-voo or extended harangues. Wanting, like poetry, required only the best possible words in the best possible order—provided, of course, once the night was over, you wanted precisely what you had.

"Then you leave, right?"

H-man had his hand on the doorknob, an excellent pose for a practicing poet, and Reed could see that inside was a cramped, nearly tumbledown arrangement of sagging shelves and swivel displays, cases of Squirt and racks of Mike-Sells potato chips, a place that could have been in business since the age of flint and fire.

"Then I go," H-man was saying. "You drive me to the airport, we say *adiós,* I mosey off into the sunset, only a faded memory."

B said something then, most of it better avowed in a better world, one which prized, for instance, sloppy sentimentality and Hallmark-like rhyme schemes.

"Nah, Reed. This isn't too bad. Too bad, as you put it, is a three-hundred pound Aryan Brotherhood sergeant at arms looking for a sweetie in C block. Too bad is a category I avoid like the plague."

So they went in, the air in there suddenly too hot and too wet. At first, no one appeared to be home, then H-man spotted a woman in the near aisle shoving a case of Hunt's tomato sauce, saying she'd be right with them.

"I'm afraid," H-man told her, "it's going to have to be right now, ma'am."

Here her face came up, puzzled initially, then thoroughly goggle-eyed.

"No, you don't," she said. "Oh, no, you don't, mister."

She could have been thirty-five or fifty-five, Reed wasn't sure, only that she'd seen too much sun and maybe eaten a few too many ice cream sundaes, but she was taking care of her face. That was plain. Lots of makeup and eyebrows too theatrical to be anything but Max Factor.

"Oh, Jesus," she said. She had seen H-man's pistol, and all the muscle went right out of her. "Jesus, Jesus, Jesus."

She was *C,* Reed told the crowd in his head, a Caucasian

female in no position, however entitled, to have a temper tantrum. *C* had shoes that were too pointed, and brown hair with too much spray in it and a dress too flowery for winter. These were the "too"s. Otherwise, *C* appeared, under admittedly trying circumstances, to be the sort of woman who might use everything in a fight, even her fists.

"You want the hands up?"

That wouldn't be necessary, H-man said. Just the cash, if she would.

"I'm gonna remember you, Mac," she said. "My ex-husband had a bird looked just like you."

"Please keep your hands where I can see them," H-man was saying, and for a second Reed thought she might thrust them out in front of her stiff-armed, a dummy's idea of a sleepwalker, but she hadn't, so Reed felt he could press ahead with his question now.

"You have any Contac or Protac—medicine like that?"

A and *C* shared an interesting moment then, the latter looking baffled as if she hadn't noticed him before, the former plainly wondering why *B* was not, as per the plan, guarding the fucking door.

"In the back," she said, her chin used to point.

This was *B*, Reed was thinking. As in badass. As in bodacious. As in braggart.

"Fred," the woman was saying.

"Your ex-husband," H-man said.

"The cockatoo," she said. "Had beady old eyes like yours."

In the back, Reed stood in front of the Kotex/NyQuil/Bayer aspirin section. These, he felt certain, were the sundries, most of the cures you needed when you felt rotten, when you were constricted or nearly ruined inside, when you were blocked and sore-minded and addled and bloated and genuinely apathetic—any of the "isms" that seemed a function of the nowadays and hereabouts.

"Larry Joe," the woman was saying, "that's the ex-husband, a dispatcher for the Fairview Park fire department."

"How nice," H-man said; Reed could tell he was just making conversation, being cordial.

"That sucks," she said. "Larry Joe Farmer couldn't find his ass with both hands and a road map."

Reed had a package of Dristan open now, one of the pills in his hand, and he walked to the cold case to get a pint of milk to wash it down. The place was as cluttered and cramped as an old closet, aisles too narrow, teetery shelves too high, cartons on the floor, no discernible order to the displays. You found the Big Chief tablets next to the Kraft noodles next to a wire rack of romance paperbacks. *Love's Pagan God. The Dark Wind of Tyme.* "Tyme," Reed reckoned, was a setting—"a venue," H-man would call it, "a locale"—some crossroads of moors and moated castles and passion-swept bluffs where heiresses like Lady Agatha and Malinda Twogate met their doom at the hands of nimble-minded roués named Yancey. Or Larry Joe.

Then *A* was talking again.

"I like you, lady," he was saying. "No ifs, ands or buts. I appreciate your candor, but as you can see, my partner and I, well, we're in a bit of a rush here. You understand?"

Reed could tell that H-man had lost it, the once-fierce hold he'd clamped on himself.

"This isn't right," the lady, *C,* was saying.

"I don't want to have this discussion," H-man told her. "We're in the middle of business here, *comprendes?* A week or so, I'll come back, we'll have a nice heart-to-heart."

But something else had entered the store, *D,* and Reed, way in the back where he couldn't be seen, put down his milk to watch.

"Don't move, motherfucker," it shouted. "No moving, okay?"

D, Reed told the bystanders in his head, was the kid from before, and now, in a scene complicated and chilling and knuckleheaded enough to be scary, the place, "the venue," contained three pistols, another source of terror to worry about, and still one pathetic bag of money to haggle over.

"Well, fuck me." H-man spoke as if he'd banged his finger in a door, twice. "Just dump all over me."

"Hold it, asshole," the kid was saying. "No funny business."

He said it "beez-ness," with too much nose, and Reed, from his corner, had found it amusing: *D,* the kid, was Chicano, right down to his taco-teeming Hollywood accent. *D* was Raul or Chico or Ernesto. *D* was thirteen, fourteen at most, his hair in a ponytail, the sleeves of his father's coat rolled to his elbows so he wouldn't be swallowed up.

"What are you doing, muchacho?"

D contrived to appear defiant, Pancho Villa without the hearty appetite.

"I'm holding you up, mister."

Reed liked the way H-man's face went light and dark, the way you could tell he was sifting and sorting, testing in an orderly fashion each of the thousand observations that might be made.

"I have a gun," he said at last.

"No shit," the kid said. "I told you to put it down."

D, Reed found it easy to think, was that thing H-man had brought with him from way back when, that presence.

Then the lady was back, unfrozen, Larry Joe about the last thing in the world to complain about.

"I know you," she was saying. "I've seen you a million times. You're Tito or Memo, something like that. You got a girlfriend named Lupe."

"Shut up, lady," he said.

She had turned to H-man, an interested party.

"He's got this tattoo," she told him. "A cross or something. On his forearm."

For another minute, they went back and forth, who was who, what what, the two of them yelling at each other, cuss words in two languages, fingers pointing, feet stomping, saying you son-of-a-bitch this and *puta-*whore this, the kid as frightened as it seemed possible to be and still not run, the lady teed off but not prepared to act in any way mortal, a lot of spit in the air, one of them sweating too much, then H-man, everything short of rubbing his eyes to concentrate, directed everybody to shut up for a second, just shut the fuck up.

This was a dilemma, *A* began. Horns of same. Rock and a you-know-what.

Reed felt the weight in his hands then, thirty-three ounces, and knew immediately that there was a gesture *B* could perform to end this. *B:* as in bushwhack. As in barbaric.

"Tito or Memo," H-man was saying, "this is a foolish thing you're about to do, believe me."

Reed could see the kid ho-hum, nod. *B*, Reed knew, was the only sentient shape in the room that hadn't spoken its piece or otherwise demonstrated a point of view about which there could be no ambiguity. *B*, Reed informed his witnesses, was sneaking up, perhaps in an industry-approved, passion-swept manner. *B*, heretofore unseen, was about to get the lowdown. The very picture of stealth, *B* was on its tiptoes.

"I'll tell you what," H-man was saying.

"What, *cabrón?*"

"Very calm, amigo, okay?"

The kid's feet were going in and out, shaking all about, a nervous shuffle Reed had no trouble imagining on the dance floor of the Aquilon.

"I have a plan," H-man was saying. "Maybe you ought to listen to it."

Again the kid nodded, and *B*—this time another picture: creepy-crawly, the shit for which science didn't yet have the slightest—calculated the distance between it and the kid at less than ten feet, no gulf at all to leap over to shout "boo."

"I'd listen if I was you," the lady said. "This is a very bad guy here, *muy malo.*"

Reed had made contact with H-man now, a wink of reassurance.

"Okay, man," the kid said. "I listen to your plan."

H-man had his gun lowered, a haute couture accessory to be

held while a decision was reached. Reed supposed the kid had looked into *A*'s birdy-beady eyes.

"First," H-man was saying, "we take a deep breath, count to sixty or thereabouts, get a handle on ourselves, okay?"

The kid seemed to think about it, his feet less happy.

"I'm for that," the lady said. "Honest, I really am."

This was the way it would go, H-man said. There would be no more untoward movements—no pistol-waving, for instance. There would only be silence like you found in church. No more swearing. No more threats, especially that. There would be civility instead. A little please-and-thank-you. A little pardon-me. Manners that grandmothers liked.

"Yeah," the lady said. "Civility."

At which point, H-man said, Memo or Tito, whatever his name was, would step over, request the money politely and receive it, being very careful the whole time not to inadvertently pull the trigger.

"I like that," the kid said. "What's 'vertently'?"

At which point, H-man continued, bad guy *número uno* and bad guy *número dos* would excuse themselves and, as was said somehow somewhere by somebody, beat a hasty retreat.

"Número dos?" the kid said.

But *B* was already there, had been there at his back for a million-billion heartbeats, its own gun now fixed tenderly against the kid's skull.

"This is *D*," Reed whispered. "As in 'dead.'"

Afterwards, for days and days until the shivering disappeared, Reed could still see himself sneaking up, a Comanche stalking a cowboy, his attention riveted on the kid's skull, possibly the site of the soul itself, a spot out of which, were there a ragged hole, might come rushing considerably more than gore, a hole through which would pour in fact everything the kid was—his true name, his favorite TV show, the jokes his mother had taught him, the first *chiquita* he'd kissed. Reed had no problem constructing that hole from the shoot-'em-ups he'd seen, the pink tissues and vital fluids it would be. Creeping up quietly, he had not been *B* any longer. He hadn't known what he was, his gun pressed to the kid's head, just what he wasn't: not *B*, not ever again. And not, it had been feared, even Alex Allan Reed.

"Reed," H-man was saying, "this is not a chapter we covered, my man."

Reed felt nothing. He had turned off inside. Completely.

"Kid," H-man was saying.

"Tito," the boy said, an admission that came out in broken pieces, like baby talk. "What's gonna happen to me, man?"

"I don't know, Tito. Honest."

Reed watched them, H-man and the lady. She hadn't moved, her mouth open as if she couldn't get enough air. The drama was absent from her eyebrows, from even her eyes themselves. H-man, by contrast, was a different story, one with an intriguing amount of movement, fingers tapping his teeth, his head shaking away ideas, his own gun knocking against his thigh. Reed didn't know what the kid, Tito, was doing, what A, B, or C was going through his mind, what his own throng of well-behaved bystanders was saying. The boy was shaking, yes, a contraption built of sticks, the ground beneath it ready to give way; and maybe, as illustrated by that snuffling noise and this gulp, he was crying, a thirteen-year-old who would do anything—crap in his drawers, wear girls' undies, pray, anything—if this stubby, unfeeling presence at the root of his head would only go away.

"H-man," Reed said.

"What is it?"

Reed struggled to clear his throat. A rock was jammed in there, a dilemma.

"It's weird," he said. "I can't put it down yet."

H-man understood. This was new territory they were into.

"I got words going through my head," Reed said. "I gotta tell you, this is very spooky."

Like what, H-man wanted to know.

"Please, mister," the kid was saying. "I didn't mean nothing."

Like "succumote," Reed said. Like "lululation." Nonsense.

Babble. It was scary, just the scariest thing ever. A nightmare.

"The kid's upset," H-man said. "He's bawling, why don't you let him go?"

It was early still, Reed thought, nothing telltale about his arm or hand to imply that he could not sustain this pose for hours. Conceivably, he could still be here in the morning, locked, rusted, words a snarl in his head like rats in a bag, H-man across from him with the woman, theirs at least two different faces of explicit horror. So this was it, Reed was thinking, gibberish. This is what his movie had been about: the beguilingly arbitrary arrangement of a few letters into a word like "murder."

"Ohhh," the kid was moaning, like a dog.

Briefly, Reed wished for a mirror by which he could study himself. Behind his eyes, he would discover a blighted land-scape of night and ice and rock, endless and unchanging. Moving across it, he believed, would come a figure, shaggy and shrunken, possibly human. Reed could hear himself creaking, tried to locate himself between the floor and the ceiling, saw where he was and where he might need to be. You were wind, it seemed. You were noise. You were not Tito, a boy, nor Reed, a man. You were ash, vermiculate matter that sped about upright and yammering. You were a reed, a stick, a bone, a column of talking air, and there was nothing at all, simply fucking nothing, to prevent you from howling and, with the right degree of pressure, all nine pounds' worth, you could hurl someone through the oppressive chitchat into the final circum-stance where nothing was heard.

"I can do this, Carl. I really can."

Later, in the car on the road to the airport, he told H-man that he was trying not to hear the kid at this point and that mostly what he was thinking was how, well, unoriginal the boy was, how banal and abject and uninspired begging was; how, at the moment, the only syllable between Tito and the world without him was "please," sobbed maybe a thousand times in those minutes, said loud and soft and in-between until, as information to be heeded, it meant nothing. Or everything.

"Reed," H-man was saying. "Let him go, okay?"

Behind him the lady was blubbering too.

"C'mon, mister," the boy said. "I ain't done nothing. I don't tell nobody, honest."

A muscle was twitching in Reed now, a message from a corner of him that a second ago hadn't existed.

"I don't feel so good," Tito said. He'd used the Spanish, *vomitar.*

The gun had already gone off, Reed thought, like the pop from a bottle of champagne. The gun had gone off, the head had snapped down then violently back, the body had taken a single clumsy step forward before folding like a tea towel. Yes, the gun had gone *powie* and the blackness had come, and time itself had unraveled—the never now, the inconceivable conceived—but the boy was still here, immaculate, his head bone connected to his neckbone: Tito had his name again and his needs and a bed to hide under when this was over.

Now the other, Reed thought. Man versus man indeed.

"You're glowing, Carl." It was true—H-man a dazzle of lights and glints and pinwheels that Reed felt somewhat tender toward.

"It's your cold, Ace. You need to lie down for a while."

Reed saw himself at the edge of sleep, someone singing a lullaby to him. Now, he thought. Right now.

"You couldn't do this, could you, Carl?"

H-man appeared to have answered this question years ago. "No, man. No way."

It was baby talk, Reed thought. No ifs, no buts.

"C'mon, mister," Tito said. "C'mon, please."

Reed took a breath, waited for the screaming to stop.

"Just give me a minute here," he said to the boy. "I need one minute, is all, okay?"